ULTIMATE WIZARD

ULTIMATE WIZARD

Alex Binkley

Copyright © Alex Binkley 2018

ISBN (softcover) 978-1-9994917-2-7
ISBN (EPUB) 978-1-9994917-1-0
ISBN (MOBI) 978-1-9994917-0-3

Cover art, design, typesetting: Magdalene Carson / New Leaf Publication Design

No part of this book may be reproduced, stored in a retrieval system, or transmitted in any form or by any means without the prior written permission of the publisher or, in case of photocopying or other reprographic copying, a licence from Access Copyright (The Canadian Copyright Licensing Agency) 320 – 56 Wellesley Street West, Toronto, Ontario, M5S 2S3
www.accesscopyright.ca.

Ultimate Wizard *is dedicated to*
Evelyn Binkley and Fraser MacLeod
for giving me hope for the future.

CONTENTS

The Characters ix

1	Party Crashers	3
2	A Tall Tale	11
3	The Doctor's Advantage	20
4	Magic 101	28
5	A Universe of Magic	39
6	A Model Evening	48
7	A Stormy Introduction	55
8	Backyard Brawl	62
9	Joining Forces	68
10	An Uninvited Guest	77
11	The Otherworld Revealed	86
12	Excursion to the Otherworld	95
13	Wizard Show and Tell	107
14	Byron's Revelation	114
15	One Smart Dog	123
16	Thal Tales	133
17	The Realm Abroad	140
18	Stuart's Fan Club	149
19	Strangers at the Farm	157
20	The Exploding Enclave	164
21	The Thals' Secret	173
22	Boss the Showboat	184

23	Unwrapping Magic	191
24	Pitched Battle	200
25	The Sanctuary	207
26	The Last Stand	214
27	The Otherworld Discovery	222
28	Romance and Technomage	228

| Acknowledgements | 239 |
| About the Author | 241 |

THE CHARACTERS

Mages
(Science-trained professionals who discover they can tap into magic; mostly known by nicknames to protect their identity that are related to their specialty)

Stuart Watson
Judyth Sawyer (Bones)
Diviner (Lesley)
Forecaster
Marconi
Harold (Marconi's
   non-Mage husband)
Audubon
Digger
Seismic
Tracker
Quake
European and Russian Mages
Charlemagne
Baltic
Viking
Surovov
Mendeleev
Anastasia de la Montagne
Ampere

Wizards
(All in Europe and hundreds of years old)

Female
Omeron
Iywwan
Male
Byron
Pembar
Guardian
Merstreem
Wnorom

Thals
(Diminutive Neanderthal offshoots)

Boss   Pathfinder   Farseeker

ULTIMATE WIZARD

PARTY CRASHERS

Stuart Watson slipped into the last open seat at the bar in the Big Wheel Tavern and plunked down a dog-eared notebook. Waving to the bartender, he called, "A draft."

He had printed and underlined INEXPLICABLE EVENTS at the top of an empty page before his beer arrived.

Ten minutes and three full pages of notes later, all in point form phrases, Stuart sipped the beer. "Folks usually come here to relax, not work," the bartender said.

Stuart ignored the laughs along the bar. He needed to compile a list of the far too many bizarre occurrences in his life. The only place to write in his apartment was at the kitchen table. Moving the stacks of equipment manuals and engineering books covering it meant more work later. A visit to the Big Wheel Tavern seemed the best alternative. The noisy environment would not distract him.

Now that he had written down all the times during the last two weeks that he had analyzed breakdowns in machines and fixed them in ways he was unable to before, he would use the information to search for a pattern in these new abilities.

Stuart had parlayed degrees in mechanical engineering and information technology into a thriving business servicing and repairing large manufacturing machines and computer systems in Eastern Canada and the U.S. Northeast. He had relied on careful analysis of the operation of the equipment to make repairs no one else could. Now his eyes zeroed in on trouble spots as if something wanted him to find them.

As he took a sip of beer, he noticed flickering images on a small television sitting amid liquor bottles on a shelf behind the bar. It showed people fleeing raging floodwaters. Then the newscast jumped to a volcano spewing an immense cloud of ash.

Two weeks ago, a massive earthquake had devastated a large swath of central China. The disaster came after a summer of droughts, heat waves and massive storms around the globe, which had killed millions and driven many more from their homes. Some speculated the global death toll was close to one billion.

The evening of the massive quake, Stuart returned to his one-bedroom apartment after a long workday. When he thought about watching his favorite comedy, the television turned on immediately and flashed through the channels to the show. As soon as he thought the sound would disturb his neighbors, the volume muted.

Stunned by what had happened, he imagined the TV off and it shut down. Then he turned it back on without touching the hand-held controller or TV. He turned his radio on and off the same way. He spent the rest of the evening thinking about how he could have done that.

Since then, his ability to control machines and computer technology had blossomed. He feared a connection existed between the now almost daily disasters and his expanding array of talents. *It's not a rational idea and I can't explain it but I'm sure there's a link.*

The television behind the bar switched to scenes of a city in ruins. Earlier in the day, the news broadcast on the radio in his truck reported a cyclone had struck southern India.

Stuart ignored the commentators who droned on about the world being under attack by aliens or suffering God's retribution for all sorts of sins. The babblers would grasp at any excuse, no matter how absurd, to avoid acknowledging that climate change had triggered the calamities such as a killer heat wave that had blanketed North America all summer. Even the approach of fall had not lessened its intensity.

However the number of earthquakes and volcanic eruptions were beyond any rational explanation.

"Another beer?" The bartender pointed in his direction.

Stuart nodded and pulled his attention away from the TV while waiting for the refill. He glanced at his notes hoping they would provide answers before his new abilities drove him insane, if he was not already.

The entry at the top of the second page referred to the first time he saw through the steel cover of a machine. He had responded to an urgent call from Agra-Innovations, which produced industrial chemicals from plants. Repeated attempts to repair a seized extractor had failed.

As the factory foreman led him to the shutdown extractor, Stuart almost stumbled in surprise when he could see its interior mechanisms as if the machine's cover had become transparent. Within seconds, he spotted the breakdown in the ingredient feeder mechanism.

Looking at the extractors on either side of the broken machine, Stuart found their feeder mechanisms needed realignment before they gave out. While it took most of the day to repair them, the company paid a healthy bonus for having the machines returned to operation so quickly.

He was so puzzled by the event that he forgot to write in his notes about how seeing through the covers that protected workers from all the moving parts in the machines made him dizzy.

Next on his puzzling events list was an emergency request from Little Manufacturing. His thoughts traced sporadic shutdowns in the company's metal presses to a virus in its main computer. Focusing his mind, he locked on the bug in the programming and squeezed it out of existence. He rebooted the computer and the presses rumbled back into full operation. Once again the experience left him feeling shaky.

He sipped more beer while adding details to his notes. Perhaps he was delusional. Maybe he had imagined all these events. Yet his flush bank account said otherwise.

When he started down the last page of notes, it struck him how much his abilities had expanded during the last few days. He could probe mentally throughout an office or factory searching for mechanical or technology problems.

I'm not crazy. Something is happening to me. There has to be an answer. All these events involve technology. What about people? He closed his eyes and let his mind survey the tavern's customers. While faint at first, his head filled with frightened and angry thoughts. He gripped the edge of the bar to steady himself.

"Everything costs so much these days," one woman whined at a table on the other side of the tavern. "Won't be a lot of nights out like this anymore."

While Stuart felt like a voyeur, he wanted to test this new ability further.

"Hard to believe we're almost at the 20th anniversary of 9/11," a middle-aged man said at another table. "This bloody heat is more deadly than the terrorists."

"Don't see any single women anywhere," said a man sitting with his buddies close to the small stage where the band would play later.

Stuart eavesdropped at a few more tables before checking the dozen people sitting or standing at the bar. Other than an argument about a recent baseball trade, the chatter about the disasters continued until two seats away from him. He could sense nothing about the person sitting there, not even breathing. The man between them muttered about the sports highlights on the TV.

Stuart leaned backward for a glimpse at the mystery person. A woman with glasses and long brown hair glared at him before looking away. Even with her indignant stare, she was attractive.

He sipped his drink and peeked in her direction again before adding two items to his list — 'can tune into conversations beyond my hearing range' and 'there's a woman who can block that ability.' He put an exclamation mark beside this line.

He took another sip of beer to cover a glance at the woman just as she dropped her gaze at him. *There is something familiar about her*.

Unlike his other abilities, eavesdropping was not automatic. He needed to think about engaging it before it took effect. He wrote a note about that in his book and underlined it numerous times. *This must be significant*.

Someone bellowed for music. The restless patrons wanted to party. By the boisterous hubbub, the crowd was already well lubricated. The bartender flipped on the stage lights. The band would appear shortly.

When Stuart looked again at the woman, she shifted her gaze to the TV. He racked his brain for something to say to her while hoping the Backcountry Boys played tunes she would dance to. *Can I ask her to explain how she blocked me? Yeah that will sound really normal. Figure out the meaning of the events on the list.*

Stuart added a note about a factory visit yesterday where he realigned the links on a control bar in a packaging machine so it ran without straining any components. He moved them and tightened several control points with his thoughts — no grease-stained hands.

He broke off the memories for another drink and glance at the woman. Once again, her head was just turning away, but that was not what caught his attention. An old man stepped unsteadily toward him. He had long, stringy white hair and wore a tweed suit that made him overdressed for the tavern and the heat.

No one else appeared to notice him, which could have been because he was the height of most people sitting down. When he reached Stuart, he removed his fedora with a sweep of his arm and made a perfunctory bow. Then, breathing deeply, he struggled to straighten his shirt, jacket and lopsided bow tie.

"Good evening, Stuart Watson. Pardon the intrusion. My name is Byron. A villain with murderous intentions pursues me, and only you can put a stop to him." The old man spoke with a pronounced English accent.

Stuart stammered, "How do you know my name?"

Byron peered over his shoulder. Another diminutive man suddenly materialized in the middle of the tavern shuffling around tables toward them. He looked equally ancient, his face a web of deep wrinkles and liver spots. His white hair stuck out in every direction. Red faced from exertion, he puffed loudly. Although his scarlet jacket, blue shirt and orange pants gave him a circus clown look, no one seemed to notice him.

Stuart rubbed his eyes. The old guys did not vanish. While he had barely tasted his second beer, he was seeing things. Stuart reached for his notes, intending to call it a night.

Before he could leave his seat, Byron slipped in behind him and pointed at the newcomer. "Vince wants to kill me. You can gain me time."

The newcomer yelled a nasty-sounding string of words, none of which Stuart recognized, and flailed his arms. Hearing a gasp, Stuart glanced in its direction. The woman who had blocked his probing stared open-mouthed between Vince and Byron. Everyone else carried on as if the old men did not exist.

Before Stuart could say anything to her, a sudden intense itching washed over him. Squirming in his seat, he clenched his fists to resist scratching.

The stranger continued to yell and flap his arms. "Vince is causing your discomfort," Byron snapped. "He'll kill you if you don't stop him."

Stuart's skin itched worse than any rash or bug bites he had ever experienced. As he shot to his feet, rubbing his arms to ease the agony, he noticed the woman looking at him with a puzzled expression.

"Am I supposed to attack him, Byron?"

"It's the only way."

"Get out of here or else," Stuart snapped. While his anger boiled over at Vince's unintelligible although clearly dismissive shouts, no one in the tavern paid any attention. *Can't they hear him?*

Then a deep but soft Voice told him to strike back before being hit with another wave of the intense itchiness. He stepped toward Vince and struck him with a sidekick practised many times during Tae Kwan Do training. Vince toppled to the floor. The itch vanished.

While Stuart felt an inner glow, he should be upset for striking an old man. He looked up when the crowd cheered, but it was for the Backcountry Boys arriving on stage. The Voice returned. *They didn't see you kick Vince.*

He knelt beside the unmoving figure to check for a pulse. He jumped back when Vince's clothes and body turned to dust. The dust settled on the floor, and then faded away as if sucked up by an invisible vacuum cleaner.

"You weren't so tough after all, Vince." Byron wiped his hands on his jacket, and then tugged Stuart's arm. "While I can explain this, it'll take a while."

The woman stepped in their direction while glancing between them and the spot where Vince had fallen. Everyone else danced or sang along with the band.

"I gotta split." Stuart grabbed his notes, threw money on the bar and bolted for the door. Yanking it open, he staggered into an enveloping wave of heat and a torrent of flashing red and blue lights on police cars and ambulances. He halted so quickly that Byron bumped into him.

Before he could ask why Byron was following him, the old man said, "They're not here for us." He sounded utterly certain as he seized Stuart's arm. With the touch, Stuart was enveloped in cooler air.

Byron steered him past cops and paramedics rushing toward the back of the parking lot. Stuart walked quickly to keep pace with Byron, whose easy gait contrasted to the stiff-legged shuffle of most old men. They headed in the direction of Stuart's apartment although he had not said where he lived.

"Oops." Byron halted abruptly, and then stepped away. The heat immediately accosted Stuart. *The old guy is a walking air conditioner.*

Strolling casually back toward the tavern, Byron picked up a gym bag that suddenly materialized beside a utility pole.

Radios crackled in the ambulances and squad cars. The waves of their emergency lights and the repeated flash of a camera cast an eerie glow over the parking lot. A policeman strung out yellow crime scene tape while others searched the parking lot with flashlights. They showed no interest in him or Byron. *They don't see you,* the Voice said.

Puffing, Byron returned and the cooler air embraced Stuart again.

"I left the bag at that post because I didn't wish to bring it into the tavern," Byron said. "It was awkward to carry with Vince pursuing me. I rendered it invisible to normal eyes. You're a strong young man."

The bag was so heavy Stuart nearly dropped it. No wonder Byron was short of breath when he arrived in the tavern.

The old man lowered his voice. "The constabulary has a mystery on its hands—why five men are dead in two vehicles back there." He pointed to the tavern's rear parking lot. "They'll find narcotics, but not the money to pay for them." He patted the gym bag. "Our need is greater, and no one will miss those criminals."

"You killed them?" Stuart shook his head in disbelief.

"I stopped their hearts beating. I would've reduced the bodies of the drug dealers and the narcotics to dust if Vince hadn't caught up to me. Their deaths were quick, certainly more merciful than what they've done to their victims."

"For the money?"

"Yes, we'll need it," Byron said.

"We! What for?" Stuart looked around, fearing the police heard his raised voice.

"I'll tell you when we reach your residence."

Stuart hesitated as Byron walked ahead taking the cooler air with him. *Should I have anything to do with this old guy? Maybe he's a serial killer. Bodies don't fade away as Vince's had.*

"You're perfectly safe with me," Byron called back to him. "I've spent a long time looking for you. Believe me, the last thing I'd do is kill you. Or let anyone else hurt you."

He's reading my thoughts. When Stuart's apprehension grew, the Voice whispered. *Hear what he has to say. He picked you to defend him. Find out why he searched for you.*

Stuart considered adding Byron's appearance and the Voice to his list of inexplicable events. He felt no sympathy for the dead drug dealers and doubted Vince was a loss to humanity. *Yet to kill them and be untroubled!*

With the bag's carrying strap settled on his shoulder, Stuart headed for his apartment building. Byron kept looking behind them. "Someone following us?"

"When you have been pursued by assassins, you learn to be vigilant all the time."

As much as Stuart doubted a gang of killers was searching for Byron, he peered at parked cars and alleyways in case other badly-dressed oldies suddenly leapt out. "You think there are more? You must've really angered someone."

Byron nodded. "Vince probably tried to kill me by himself so he could gain all the credit. The others will work as a team."

A TALL TALE

Judyth Sawyer stood steps from where Vince's body vanished. A quick glance around the tavern showed no one noticed his disappearance or Stuart and Byron slipping out the front door. *Was it just the pounding music that distracted them?*

She could not accept the only answer that came to mind for the sudden appearance of the two old men followed by Stuart's resisting the force that Vince aimed at him. *Could Audubon have been right about magic after all?*

Stuart's repeated glances suggested he might be interested in meeting her. Initially intrigued, she questioned whether she wanted anything to do with him after all she just witnessed. Until tonight, he was an enigma that needed solving. Now she wondered if he possessed a dark side and why Byron wanted Stuart to protect him from Vince.

Even though she had tracked Stuart for the last week, she had learned little about the power he tapped into while working in factories and offices. The first time she sensed him in action was when she detected a pulse similar to what her colleagues in The Realm gave off when they used their special abilities. However Diviner, the only other person in the Toronto area who could do that, was out of the city on a business trip. She would have known if other Realm members were in the area.

All she could determine was the pulse had occurred in the city's northeast. The next day she sensed the pulse twice, once from near the downtown and the other in the west end. At that point, she knew she had to find its source. In recent days, the pulse had become more frequent and focused, making it harder to detect. More importantly, its power was far beyond anything she or her friends could project.

Judyth strode to the door and opened it to peek outside. The emergency vehicles startled her, but not as much as Byron picking up a gym bag leaning against a utility pole. After he rejoined Stuart, she could hear Byron explaining how he had killed five drug dealers in two cars in the parking lot. Her eyes widened at his admission with police officers in hearing range although they ignored the pair as if they were unaware of them.

It was no surprise she could hear them. Since Judyth was a teenager, she could tune into conversations up to a block away.

Even with her experience as a trauma specialist at the Greater Toronto Regional Hospital, Judyth could not explain Vince's disappearance. While Stuart's kick might have cracked a couple of ribs, it should not have made his body crumble and vanish. However, no one would believe her if she reported it. Byron's callousness about the killings angered her because she put so much work into saving lives.

When she and her friends established The Realm five years earlier, everyone agreed its primary objective was keeping their special abilities secret. As teenagers, they had slowly found each other scattered throughout North America and Europe. During university and post graduate studies, they secretly nurtured abilities that security agencies, terrorists and criminal gangs would want to exploit.

Normally she would offer medical assistance to the paramedics. Unable to do anything for the dead men, she headed for her car to follow Stuart and Byron.

"Hold it right there," a voice boomed.

Darn, the cops had spotted her. Judyth faced the lanky constable and demurely smiled. "Can I help you?"

"May I see some identification? We have five bodies back there and are questioning everyone in the vicinity. Did anything unusual happen inside?" He pointed to the tavern.

"Nope." She pulled her hospital ID card from the side pocket of her purse and handed it to him.

The cop's eyes widened and a smile rippled across his face. "Thought I recognized you, Doctor Sawyer. Those officers you saved were buddies. I visited the guys yesterday. They're both recuperating just fine and will be up and about before long. Thanks again. We'd all prepared for the worst."

Judyth smiled broadly at the officer as she glanced at his name bar. "I've checked on them a couple of times. They appreciate all your visits. I'll mention meeting you, Officer Oliver." While she fretted about missing what Stuart and Byron were saying, Judyth did not want to ruin her good standing with the police. "So I guess if you have bodies, there's nothing I can do to help."

"Unless you can tell us why the men would be dead without any apparent wounds."

While the situation piqued her curiosity, she would read up on it later. "That sounds like a job for the coroner." She shot the officer a grim smile.

"No need to ask any more questions. We know where to find you for any follow-up."

Spotting TV station trucks arriving, Judyth hurried to her car. She had received enough media attention for saving the two policemen. More importantly, Byron and Stuart would be near his apartment building by now.

On the drive there, she mulled over the pulse Stuart projected through the tavern before the old men arrived. It was more like a shove than the gentle caresses of her friends' pulses. He lacked their finesse, which indicated his abilities were new to him. She blocked it to see if he could detect her action. By his furrowed brow and open mouth, he recognized what she had done but not how.

She parked close to his building and spotted the lights on in his unit. She had entered his apartment a couple of times to find out more about his abilities, justifying the break-in as necessary to protect The Realm. Her surgical gloves ensured no fingerprints. She smiled at the memory of the locking mechanisms in the building entrance as well as the door to Stuart's apartment sliding open as soon as she imagined a key turning them.

His place consisted of the minimal male living requirements of a bed, couch, small eating table and unmatched chairs. Books and manuals were stacked everywhere. The apartment passed her sniff test and he appeared to sweep the floor and keep the bathroom tidy. While the off-white walls and ceiling did not appeal to her taste, they imparted calm to his quarters.

She re-arranged piles of carelessly-stacked books, pushed some boxes together and put away dishes left in the drying rack. While her mother warned her against playing maid for a man, her neat freak habit took over. It would be a good way to test his awareness.

Before she opened her car door, she focused her soothing ability on the occupants in the apartment beside Stuart's. This talent relaxed patients so she could examine them. She wanted the couple to become tired and go to bed. That way, she could sit in their living room and listen to Stuart and Byron talk.

She walked up the stairs to the second floor. Hearing no sounds from the adjoining apartment, she opened the door. The man and woman snored softly in their bed. She hoped they would not be late for work. She sat in the chair closest to Stuart's apartment and tuned into the conversation between Byron and him.

Stuart did not let down his guard until they reached his apartment building. His doubts about Byron remained although the Voice chipped in again. *Hear him out before you come to any conclusions.*

While Stuart sat on his couch, Byron remained standing. "I'm a Wizard." Byron wiggled his finger when Stuart opened his mouth. "I've observed you for the last week because you're a unique and most interesting individual to those of us who can manipulate magic."

Stuart frowned. "Wizards and magic are storybook stuff. My life is full of real problems, and I don't have time to waste on crazy talk." He slumped further into the couch and buried his face in his hands. *Nothing makes sense. Maybe I'm really bonkers and Byron and the vanishing body are a delusion.*

Byron smiled like an indulgent teacher. "Your reaction to what I can do is normal for anyone with your scientific background." The old man took a deep breath. "While I was able to kill Vince thanks to you, you're in as much danger as I am."

The pleading tone in Byron's voice surprised Stuart. *Has this guy escaped from a loony bin?*

"I'm not on the run from a lunatic asylum," Byron said. "How would you explain what happened to Vince and the drug dealers? Or the cooler air around me?"

Stuart shrugged.

"About time you tidied up your residence."

"I didn't; that's one of my problems. Somehow it became tidy."

"You should keep it like this. If you ever experience intense itching as in the tavern, you'll know a Wizard wants to kill or take control of you."

"Great, now I can be paranoid as well. Every time I scratch, I'll worry about being under attack by a Wizard. Why am I in as much danger as you and how do you know what my apartment looks like?"

"I realize you're distraught," Byron said. "I visited your apartment as part of my search for who was using magic. Now if you refrain from interrupting me, I'll answer all your questions after I finish my explanation of this evening's events." He smiled slightly "Would you like a beer?"

Stuart looked toward the kitchen at the other end of the apartment. The fridge door swung open and two cans floated out of it toward them. Before Stuart could pluck the closest one out of the air, the pull-tab popped open.

An orange glow seeped from the old man. "Did you notice the crowd in the tavern ignored Vince and I? That's because I covered us in an unseeing spell as I did with the gym bag so no ordinary person would notice it. Vince was too intent on killing me to spot the bag or that I was under the spell. Your kick distracted him giving me time to stop his heart, and then make his body vanish. He wouldn't have cared if his magic killed the patrons in the tavern. They lacked your protection."

"Protection? What are you talking about?"

Byron settled in an armchair. "The itching was your magic warding off Vince's attack. What I knew and he didn't is you are immune to Wizard magic, which I've never encountered before. I'm unable to use my magic on you. I tried without success to make you perform various actions. That Vince's power made you itch suggests you only react to hostile magic. That's a very rare trait among Wizards.

"Equally interesting is that as uncomfortable as Vince's magic made you, you didn't lose control. That's your protection. It makes you a threat unlike any The Brotherhood has ever encountered."

"What's The Brotherhood?"

Byron sipped his beer. "Tastes not bad. Believe me; the world is full of magic. Few people can connect to it except for you and a few ancient Wizards like me. While most Wizards would be curious about you, The Brotherhood, which has been taken over by a group of vile men bent on controlling all Wizards and magic, would want to kill you if they learn of your existence."

Stuart gulped a mouthful of beer. On top of the bizarre events that had already occurred, he could have a bunch of old wackos after him. *Probably more proof of my insanity. Should I be laughing or afraid?* He chugged the rest of his beer and looked at the blinking light on his cellphone. He did not want to hear about another broken machine when he really needed some answers to his personal situation.

"Why should I believe any of this? First you told me that Vince would kill me if I didn't stop him. Now you say I possess this natural defense against magic that makes me a threat to some nut bar group I've never heard of. You'll have to convince me."

"Hear me out and you'll get your proof." Byron stared at him. "I lied about Vince's killing you to prod you into protecting the other patrons at the Big Wheel. The original purpose of The Brotherhood was to set basic rules on the use of magic and ensure it doesn't become corrupted.

"Merstreem and his band of supporters would judge you an anathema because your power is not linked to the natural elements of the Earth like the power of the Wizards is. They're too arrogant to attack you with a knife or gun, which is the only way to kill you. The ease with which you blocked Vince would shock them. For me and my fellow Dissidents, it's a cause for celebration."

"Dissidents?"

"A small group of Wizards like me who oppose the Brotherhood for what it has become although we lack the strength to stop them. They'd wipe out the Dissidents if they could locate us. The rest of the Wizards tolerate us and the Brotherhood."

"The more you talk, the harder it becomes to believe you," Stuart said. Still magic appealed as an explanation for his new abilities, although as an engineer, he knew it was the stuff of fantasy books and fairie tales.

The old man paced about the apartment. His diction and unusual choice of words reminded Stuart of a cultured butler from the old films his parents had watched. He spoke without changing his tone or moving his hands to make a point.

"When you're in the presence of machines, you project a force unlike anything I've ever experienced. You must explain what you use it for. It's almost impossible for Wizards to go near modern devices because our magic disrupts their operation."

Byron faced Stuart. "From stories you might have read as a child, you would expect Wizards to wave magic wands and say elaborate spells. We don't employ such theatrics, although it'd be more dramatic if we did. We project our power mentally, and the Wizard who thinks faster or has stronger thoughts triumphs."

While Byron's nonchalance about the killings still bothered him, he wished to keep the old man talking. "Want another beer?"

Byron nodded. The fridge door opened and two cans floated over to the sink where their tabs popped off.

"Trying to one up me." Byron laughed. "Your way means the little metal things don't litter the floor." The first two tabs headed to the garbage can passing the new cans soaring toward the men along with a container of almonds.

"Hold out your hand," Stuart said. The container poured Byron some nuts, and then came to rest on the coffee table in front of Stuart. "You're the first person I ever showed my serving abilities to. Just discovered them a few days ago."

"Good, you'd scare people. You need to tell me how you learned about your magical abilities."

"About two weeks ago all this weird stuff began happening to me at work almost in tandem with the big disasters around the world. Can you explain that?"

"The Brotherhood is causing the disasters to aggravate the impact of climate changes. I believe that in response to their actions, your magic has been awakened because the planet is in great danger. While you're the only one who can save it, you've a great deal to learn. While I can help you, I know little about modern technology."

"This is becoming quite the tall tale."

"I'm just starting. Your very existence means The Brotherhood can be stopped. There are about 130 Wizards left in Europe. At one time, we numbered in the thousands. Most were content with keeping our powers alive for when the world would need them. To our surprise, your science and technology continued to improve and left us without a role. You can learn through physics, chemistry, engineering and medicine how to perform much of what we can do and many other things.

"While most Wizards accepted our redundancy, Merstreem and his backers lost patience with our impotence. They want to regain the authority your culture associates with Merlin and other mythical figures. That way, they, not the entrepreneurs, scientists and politicians, would control the world, as the Wizards of ancient times did."

"I'm still stuck on why I'm supposed to be able to save the world," Stuart said.

"Your presence shows magic is integrating with science and technology."

"Combining science and magic is impossible," Stuart said. "I shouldn't even listen to you, but humor me a bit. How could that happen?"

"I don't know yet. While it must sound utterly unbelievable, bear with me a bit longer. Just to show you that Wizards keep up with the times when it suits them, The Brotherhood proclaimed they need to save the planet from the environmental damage thoughtless humans are causing."

"They'll succeed where all the world leaders have failed?" Stuart said. "How will they accomplish that?"

Byron momentarily hesitated. "By using the disasters to take control of the important governments. Then they will cease the disasters, which will do little to reverse climate change, but will make life in many places appear better."

"A global Wizard coup d'état." Stuart snorted. "You should expose what they're doing!"

"Who'd believe me other than the crackpots always ready to embrace conspiracy theories?" Byron again took on a pleading tone. "We need to stop the Brotherhood."

"We? As in you and me?"

"There's no one else I can turn to. The Brotherhood is building up to a massive event that will set the stage for them to reveal themselves."

"Like what?"

"While I've no idea, it'll be deadly, far worse than what they have done so far. There's nothing your technology can do to counter their powers to control the weather and Earth's elemental forces. While we Dissidents agree humanity needs to stop climate change from ruining the planet, the Brotherhood's plan is completely wrong and immoral."

"Am I supposed to kick all the Wizards so you can finish them off?" Stuart stifled a cough that started as a laugh.

"No, just their leaders, especially Merstreem. The other Wizards don't realize he wants to rule them as well. They generally pay little attention to the modern world and, as the disasters are happening mainly in Asia, Africa and the Americas, it's unlikely they realize the devastation The Brotherhood is causing. Or care if they do."

Byron's tone softened. "You can protect me while I assist you to develop your abilities. Combining our magic with your technological abilities will make you far more powerful than any Wizard alive. Then we can confront The Brotherhood. We need to do it before the Earth is beyond saving for humanity."

Doubts about Byron lingered, even though the Voice kept assuring Stuart the old man was legit. "Tell me about magic."

Byron yawned and heaved a heavy sigh. "I'm more than 300 years old and I need my sleep."

Stuart yawned. "It's getting late. Where are you staying?"

"Here if I might. I'd be comfortable on your couch. I'd like to ride with you tomorrow to continue my explanation about your magical powers."

THE DOCTOR'S ADVANTAGE

The Wizard conspiracy behind the disasters sounded beyond farfetched to Judyth. *Stuart isn't challenging Byron's claims; perhaps he actually believes them.*

She pulled out her cellphone and typed a note to her closest friends in The Realm. "Could the global disasters lead to something even more devastating?"

As she reread the message, and then pressed send, she realized she had been drawn in by Byron's tale while eavesdropping on the old man and Stuart in the neighboring apartment. She did not mention the details of their discussions in her e-mail because she needed more information to assess it. She wished she could reach through the wall to comfort Stuart. She remembered the upheaval in her teenage years as she came to terms with her abilities.

Her cell-phone vibrated. She read and reread the message from a leading geologist. "Toba super eruption about 74,000 years ago. We'll talk about it after I return to Toronto tomorrow."

Judyth stared at the tiny screen until it winked out. She imagined the devastation that a super volcanic eruption would cause in today's world that was stressed by climate change and weather-related disruptions. *If The Brotherhood is planning an event on this scale, they'd do anything to stop Byron and Stuart from interfering.* Her rational mind stopped that train of thought. *I'm treating this like it's real.*

Communications with Realm members always involved reading paragraphs between the lines. They would study the Toba super eruption.

Although out of her scientific depth, Judyth's instincts told her to believe Byron's warning. Her instincts were usually accurate in diagnosing her patients' ailments. *Are they telling me to trust Byron?*

The air conditioner in the borrowed apartment kicked in, forcing Judyth to listen more closely to Stuart and Byron's conversation. The AC unit in his apartment had not run making her wonder about the comfort level there until she remembered Byron's comment about cooling the air, which left her with more questions.

"I see a flickering image of a woman every day, often several times," Stuart said. "She's skinny and dressed oddly. I call her the Waif."

Byron gasped before responding. "Seeing visions is advanced magic. What does she say?"

"At first, all I heard was buzzing like static on a radio. While I can pick out words now, I've no idea what language she speaks. She appears to be in her 20s. All I see is her face and shoulders. Her face is gaunt, like a refugee."

"When do these visions happen?"

"At different times throughout the day." Stuart sounded uncertain. "There's no pattern to them so I don't know when to expect them. It's disconcerting to have her appear when I'm working or talking to people. Fortunately, no one else sees her."

"That's because she's communicating directly to you," Byron said. "You need to learn a lot of magic so we can stop The Brotherhood."

"I'm not some super hero. I have a business to run."

Byron sighed. "While you need time to accept your situation, the longer we delay taking action the worse the situation will become around the world."

Judyth's cellphone vibrated. Quake had emailed her references to other major disasters. She needed to leave to check them out and prepare for her shift at the hospital. Envious of what else Stuart might learn, she slipped out of the apartment and tiptoed down the stairs. She remained uncertain about whether Byron could be trusted. She also wondered if Stuart's visions were anything like her insights.

She drove home through darkened streets. While she wanted to read more on the Internet about the Toba super-eruption and other calamities, her foot remained light on the gas pedal. She needed time to sort through everything Byron had said. If his story could possibly be true, The Realm must be informed. Her friends were searching for a causal link among the global disasters because they had already concluded their almost daily occurrence was more than coincidence.

Whenever she started to doubt Byron's claims, her mind returned to the scene outside the tavern. The chat with the policeman brought back memories of the night the two gravely wounded officers arrived at the hospital after a shootout with a gang of bank robbers. While everyone thought they could not survive their injuries and their families gathered in the waiting room anticipating the worst, Judyth's insights told her she could save them.

She instructed the orderlies to place the two policemen in adjoining operating rooms. Throughout that evening, she went back and forth between them extracting bullet fragments and repairing damaged organs. Since she was a child, Judyth possessed an uncanny ability to understand people's feelings and emotions. She could sense people were sick before the symptoms became apparent. That night proved just how special her powers were.

Surely she should trust her instincts now as much as she did then.

Like her friends, she had rejected her colleague Audubon's hypothesis that Realm members had tapped into a mysterious power that expanded their scientific abilities. To him, the only possibility was magic. Even though the rest of The Realm disagreed, Audubon, a world-renowned astronomer, still insisted there was no other explanation for their abilities. *Just as my insights saved the policemen, perhaps his found magic.*

What if Byron's claim that magic wanted to combine with science was not preposterous? Judyth could think of no better explanation for her surgical, health diagnosis, door opening or extended hearing abilities. If magic was the answer, then The Brotherhood did not know about either Stuart or The Realm. That was just as well because her friends could not defend themselves against Wizards as Stuart could with his magic.

She and the other 107 Realm members possessed a common foundation in science and technology. They could extend the range and capability of sensors and other technologies to study the Earth's depths, seas and skies and the inner workings of the human body and mind. They were always cautious in disclosing their discoveries out of fear of attracting too much attention.

Still they had earned numerous science prizes and awards. They took pride in their discoveries, abhorred violence and would oppose approaching Byron and Stuart once they learned about the dead drug dealers. Nor would they likely be any more willing to accept Audubon's contention that magic was real.

Within blocks of her condo, she noticed that every traffic light turned green at her approach. *Wish it would occur during rush hour. If the Realm's abilities do have a connection to magic, why had the Wizards not spotted her friends when they probed deep underground after every disastrous earthquake looking for the trigger. Others searched through weather patterns following major storms.*

Then she remembered that neither Vince nor Byron noticed her watching them at the tavern. Yet Stuart knew she had spotted the Wizards. Then there was the woman in Stuart's visions. Although it made her feel silly, she viewed this phantom as a rival who had found a better way to connect with him.

Judyth had intended to gain Stuart's attention by teasing him with her abilities. She laughed out loud as she thought about what might have happened without Byron's arrival. Images of Stuart frantically scratching himself in public or kicking the patrons filled her mind. Thankfully Byron had revealed Stuart's immunity to magic, which meant she needed a new approach to gaining his attention.

Now I'm on Audubon's side. How to convince the others?

She turned into the driveway of her building and hurried to her condo as confused as when she drove away from the tavern. As she closed the door, she called out, "What'cha got for me, Bethune?"

"What file would you like?" The lilt in the digitized voice of her electronic collaborator always relaxed her. Housed in a pair of antique desktop computers to disguise its advanced analytic capacity, Bethune was a breakthrough in Artificial Intelligence developed by her Realm pals. They decided she could make the best use of it. It was a marvelous researcher.

"For starters, download the information from Diviner and Quake to the file on natural disasters. Then examine it for similarities to what's currently happening around the world. Specifically, whether the disasters could build up to a massive destructive event."

"Like Toba?"

Judyth smiled. She had loaded Bethune with medical information and connected it to web sites, Internet forums and her mobile phone so it could read all the information she received. Its ability to integrate data and ideas into plausible theories or explanations impressed her the most.

"So, what's the story on Toba?" As Judyth put a meal in the microwave and changed clothes for her shift at the hospital, Bethune related what it had learned so far.

"It occurred in Indonesia and remains the largest eruption in the last 25 million years. Ash from it exists around the world. While scientists used to think it nearly wiped out early human life, further research has shown that was unlikely. I can only speculate on the havoc such a disaster would cause on top of all the recent ones. All the data is in your laptop."

She took her hot food to the computer table and opened Bethune's latest file, which included a simulation of the Toba super-eruption. *It would've shaken the whole planet.* She inhaled deeply and exhaled slowly to gain control of her sense of dread.

Judyth skimmed through additional files from Diviner as Bethune continued its explanation of the Toba disaster and subsequent super volcanic eruptions including Krakatoa. "After the Tambora eruption in 1815, there were several years of unusually chaotic weather in Europe, Asia and North America, including especially severe winters and cold summers. Scientists attribute the erratic weather to volcanic ash disrupting Earth's atmospheric circulation. They found a 15 centimetre layer of it throughout Southeast Asia. Toba sent even more ash into the atmosphere. Scientists think Toba was 100 times more powerful than Tambora."

The AI modulated its tone, which was how it conveyed uncertainty in the conclusions it reached from the available information. "Thus far, nothing explains how the current disasters could lead to a volcanic super-eruption. You should examine this information from Quake."

Bethune emitted a buzz and a visual of slowly rotating Earth appeared on Judyth's laptop screen. "It marks every disaster in recent weeks with a colored dot. In military terms, the Wizards are softening up the world for a major assault. His figures take into account naturally occurred eruptions, earthquakes and major storms. Still he agrees with estimates that at the rate they're happening, the disasters could kill half the global population by the end of this year without a super volcanic eruption."

Judyth gasped at the array of colored dots and squares. "There have been so many disasters. I can see why the death and damage tolls are so high. It should be reported in the news this way." Then it hit her. "There haven't been any in Europe from the Atlantic and Mediterranean coasts to the Ural Mountains."

Judyth squirmed in her chair as she outlined what Byron had told Stuart about magic and Wizards. "What might we do if I could convince The Realm about the Brotherhood's role in the disasters?"

"You would have to know where the Brotherhood is located and how it is causing the disasters. Did you learn anything more about Stuart?" She shook her head. With a hint of gloating, Bethune said, "He has customers for his engineering services all over eastern North America. Judging from his email and phone calls, he could probably do twice the business if he had more time."

"Although it's good to know he has a scientific background like us, he has even more abilities than I'd imagined. I'm no closer to figuring out why I keep getting visions of him. While I'm at work, I want you to research magic and Wizards."

"That'll require investigating outside the medical and news forums. Should I send you my findings on a priority basis or save them for when you return?"

"Save them for now." Hopefully Bethune would not be laughing at her notion about magic when she returned home. It had discovered Stuart had no connection to her Realm friends, who were the best kept secret of the 21st Century. "Track my e-mail for any additional information about Toba or the causes of the disasters."

The Realm members were always looking for opportunities to put their abilities to good use. That time had come. Like others, her hospital was overwhelmed by people suffering from illnesses or conditions caused by the relentless heat. The situation would go beyond unmanageable if earthquakes or violent storms struck.

As always, Marconi answered her phone before it signaled an incoming call. When Judyth explained her need for more information on Stuart, she said, "You want me to contact the entire group to e-stalk this guy you have the hots for?"

Judyth let her friend finish her teasing. After all, it was close to midnight in San Francisco and Judyth was using a break in-between checking on patients to phone the Realm's liaison contact at her home.

Marconi was a specialist in advanced communication technologies and Internet security. She had put many hackers and scammers out of business and unearthed numerous plots to cripple the Internet. As a result, the Realm members agreed she could contact all of them by email at the same time. No outsider had hacked the Realm's email network.

Judyth decided not to tell the others that Bethune already possessed everyone's e-mail address. If discovered, her excuse would be someone should have a copy of the list as backup. She instructed Bethune to never divulge it to anyone outside The Realm.

She recounted the incident in the tavern and the conversation in Stuart's apartment to Marconi. "If Byron is telling the truth about Wizards, it might explain the strange waves of psychic power our European members regularly encounter. Unless we can stop the disasters, we should consider helping Stuart and Byron. To do that, we need to learn more about both of them."

Marconi was naturally cautious so Judyth was not surprised when she said, "No one will believe all this magic stuff except for Audubon and we gave him such a hard time when he suggested we'd tapped into it. We don't want to restart that argument within our group. What's more, if Byron located Stuart while he was using his abilities, why can't the Wizards perceive ours?"

Judyth saw an opening. "That's what I'd like to know. That's why I need help from our group."

"Alright Bones; I'll ask for a consensus on what to do about the boyfriend and the Wizard and whether anyone might be able to assist you."

Judyth expected it would take a few days before she heard from her friends as they again wrestled with the idea of magic. Meanwhile, she would keep tracking Stuart and Byron. It helped that the hospital had cancelled all but essential surgeries because of the heat wave so she would be on call for the next two weeks.

An hour later, her phone vibrated. It did several more times before she could scroll through the messages and muttered. "Wow that was fast." Texts and e-mails from Realm members offered assistance or asked lots of questions. The final message was from Audubon. "Won't believe it's magic until Byron proves it."

Judyth mulled over her search for Stuart on the drive home after her shift. After several days of receiving pulses from him, he first appeared in a vision typing on a keyboard in his apartment. In later ones, he was in factories and offices. He approached machines and computers warily, as if they might suddenly lunge at him. Sometimes he just sat shaking his head and muttering incomprehensibly.

She called her visions insights to make them sound respectable. For more times than she could remember, they had revealed new ways to treat patients. Despite that advantage, she never thought much about their origin. She believed the ideas came to her because she focused on a problem.

From watching Stuart in her visions, she concluded he displayed the irritability and anxiety of someone in a state of extreme mental agitation. While he was not dangerous, he was under major stress. Otherwise, he appeared healthy and attractive. Her interest in him had advanced from intrigued to infatuation without even talking with him.

The first time she saw him in person was five days before the visit to the Big Wheel when a pulse from him was followed by a vision of him stepping from his van outside a factory. He used his power to inspect the plant before entering it. She received two more pulses while he was working inside it.

She drove to the business and parked where she could watch the van. About half an hour later, Stuart got into it and drove to a burger joint. While he was inside ordering, she placed a tracking device on his vehicle so Bethune could follow his movements and keep her posted. Inside the van, she spotted all sorts of strange equipment, tools and parts.

She returned to her vehicle and waited for him to leave the takeout place. In person, he appeared more haggard than in the visions.

Bethune tracked him for the next few days. Friday evening, he alerted Judyth that Stuart had returned home earlier than usual. Not having to work until midnight, she drove to his apartment hoping to find a reason to talk with him. She had just parked when he stepped out of his building and headed on foot to the awful tavern.

MAGIC 101

A racket like a freight train rumbling through his apartment woke Stuart. He grabbed the mattress as the light and clock radio on the bedside table vibrated. Jars and containers in the bathroom and kitchen clattered as they knocked together.

He let out his breath when the commotion ceased. Certain it was an earthquake or tremor; he lay there until nothing moved. No sirens wailed. The sudden silence was more unnerving than the shaking. The clock showed it was almost time to rise.

He turned on the light. His bedroom was intact. Lying back on the pillow, he let his thoughts return to the previous evening. As unbelievable as Byron's story had sounded, it made sense in a way Stuart could not explain. Whenever he thought of a reason to question the old man's motives, the Voice he first heard in the Big Wheel returned to reassure him that Byron really was a Wizard.

Unable to fall back to sleep, he rolled out of bed and put on a house coat so he could check for any damage in the rest of his apartment.

Byron waited at his bedroom door with a mug of tea and a smug smile. "If you hurry, you've time for a shower because the porridge isn't ready yet. I'm glad you possess a stove that I can use."

Stuart did not bother to cover his yawn. "That must have been an earthquake?" As if triggered by his question, the radio in the living room came on and tuned to an all-news station.

Byron shrugged. "I sensed there would be a modest quake not worth concerning you about. Probably perfectly natural."

"We rarely get quakes, even tremors, around Toronto."

Byron rubbed his chin. "There's always a first time. Maybe all the ones triggered by The Brotherhood elsewhere have created waves underground that caused this one. I don't feel another one building."

Still rattled, Stuart headed for the shower. He paused at the sound of an excited voice from the radio. "We've dispatched reporters around the city. So far, there are no reports of any major damage from the earthquake, although a lot of people are gathered in the streets. They don't know if it's safe to return to their homes. The power is out in some areas, so the city plans to open halls and arenas for people who need relief from the heat."

As warm water cascaded over him, Stuart wondered how Byron anticipated the quake. Maybe he sensed the movement of the tectonic plates that generated it. Stuart felt indignant he did not warn him until the Voice said, *Who could you have told without sounding like a crazy?*

His mind shifted to how Byron had learned his daily routine. *He must have spied on me to know I put the kettle on to make tea before I shower. That's creepy. How much weirder is my life going to be with him around?*

Stuart turned off the shower and readied for the day while finishing his tea. He cracked open the door to listen to the radio. It had switched to the classical music station. As soon as he thought the sound was too loud, it dropped to a barely audible level.

A sweet aroma floated in. He dressed quickly and headed for the kitchen. Breakfast was porridge full of fruit and a touch of buckwheat honey. Byron sat at the table looking dapper in a well-pressed jacket, bow tie and sand colored slacks. Other than his straggly hair, he appeared completely different than the rumpled old man from the night before.

"So where did you get the clothes?" Stuart said.

"Are they acceptable?"

"While they're old-fashioned, people will probably admire them." Stuart laughed. "I mean they look kind of vintage."

"I don't wish to be obviously out of place."

"You need a haircut."

"Like this?" Byron grinned as he flicked his fingers in the air.

Although it happened too quickly for Stuart to see, Byron's hair no longer fell to his shoulders. Stuart could not spot any bits of white on the floor. "Perfect."

"I possess more outfits like this."

"In the gym bag?" Stuart looked at it again wondering about its contents.

"In my refuge where I store clothes, books and other important material. I always have access to it."

Before Stuart could ask where the refuge was, Byron said, "How did you like the porridge?"

"Best I ever had. Does anyone ever say your cooking is magical?"

"Ha, ha." Byron put the two bowls in the sink and the remaining breakfast into a plastic container, which he placed in the fridge before quickly stepping away from it.

Stuart shook his head. *How does he know to save leftovers?*

Wondering whether Byron could understand the range of his abilities, Stuart showed him the notes he wrote in the tavern the previous evening. "You might be interested in what I can do."

He turned on the television with his thoughts and shifted through the channels to the all-news station. Then he picked up the remote control and waved it at Byron. "Normal people need to use this to make the TV work."

Byron pointed at the screen. "We were there." He walked toward the TV and the image turned fuzzy. "This is what Wizard magic does to modern devices." He retreated to the armchair and the picture cleared.

The Big Wheel Tavern and its parking lot was the backdrop for a reporter's on-the-scene update on the killings. Stuart turned up the volume while imagining all sorts of complications from having Byron in the van. "You'll disrupt my equipment like you did the TV."

"I'll blunt the power of my magic as much as I can." His gaze returned to the TV screen.

"From what I picked up from the on-site officers and paramedics, five men, all known to the police, were discovered dead in two cars behind this night spot," the reporter said in a breathless tone. "What's stumped the police is they found a large cache of drugs in one vehicle but no money to pay for them. They think whoever killed the men took the cash. There are no visible wounds on the bodies and no signs of a struggle. We'll get back to you with more details on this mysterious incident when they're available."

Byron raised his voice to be heard over the TV. "The authorities won't be able to determine how they died."

Stuart muted the sound. "They will after they conduct autopsies."

Byron shook his head. "The most they'll be able to detect is their hearts stopped beating but not why. Magic leaves no marks."

"You can't go around killing people just because you dislike them," Stuart said. "They may be low lives but . . . "

"I must seem like a cold-hearted executioner. I killed men who had blood on their hands and would create more misery if not removed. The world faces bigger matters than the fate of those vendors of narcotics." He took a deep breath. "Vince was a very nasty fellow. I couldn't have stopped him without your assistance."

Unable to think of a response, Stuart wondered if there was more news about the earthquake. The radio came on and passed through snippets of music and ads to the all-news station. "In American League baseball, Toronto 6 New York 0."

Then the station switched to a live news conference with a harried-sounding police spokesman. "There's not much new I can report. We know who the deceased are, but not how they died. We'll provide more details when we have them. I can confirm we found a large quantity of cocaine and heroin in one vehicle. We haven't determined its street value yet."

"Wizards don't need the civility of a court trial to know who to punish," Byron said before taking another sip of tea. The newscast switched to the earthquake but there was nothing new in its report.

"What are we doing today?"

As he described his scheduled service calls, Stuart wondered how many customers would be in operation. *Maybe the quake damaged their machines.* Whatever, he wanted to be working rather than sitting in the apartment thinking about last night.

"You wouldn't happen to know what happened to the drug money."

Byron pointed at his gym bag. "Open it."

"Look at all this; it's a fortune." Stuart dug through stacks of bills. "It's all different denominations. It'd take hours to count it."

"We'll need it, and if we require more, I can obtain it. In the meantime, I'll hide it with an unseeing spell."

Within minutes, the two men were in Stuart's van heading down Walnut Street. At first, he drove cautiously wondering what effect Byron would have on the electronics in the vehicle. When satisfied it was running normally, he relaxed.

When not steering around jagged cracks in the pavement, Stuart checked out the neighborhood. The visible damage included an old tree lying on a pickup truck, a chimney toppled from the roof of an apartment building and a couple of serious cracks in the brick front wall of a bakery a few blocks from his house. The light ahead turned green, as did the next one. Traffic was light for a Saturday morning.

"Few people are still outside so they must have found shelter indoors out of the heat," Stuart said.

Hoping to amuse Byron, he said, "When I was a kid, I read all the books about the exploits of young Wizards." He grinned at the memories. "Only in my dreams did I ever imagine a real person could do anything as fantastic as they did."

"They're good stories," Byron said. "The writers definitely knew how to tell a tale. However, they failed to change people's minds about the possibility of magic."

A breathless-sounding announcer replaced the music on the radio. "This just in. The epicenter of the earthquake was in Ohio. It rattled buildings all the way to Florida and throughout the U.S. Midwest and Eastern Canada. Officials rate it as a 6.2 on the Richter scale. There are reports from across the Greater Toronto Area of minor injuries linked to it but no fatalities. The city reports all its facilities are working and the transit and subway lines will soon be back to normal."

"I told you the quake was moderate."

"If we're supposed to stop The Brotherhood, you must have a plan?" Stuart said.

"I do but first I need to learn a lot more about what your magic can do, just as you need to accept that I'm a Wizard. Hopefully we can clear this up in a few days." He took a deep breath. "What I want to do has never been attempted before. Unless you're fully aware of and confident in your abilities, we can't succeed."

Stuart drove in silence as he wrestled with accepting magic was real. Then his thoughts shifted to speculating on what his supposed powers might be and what Byron's plan could entail. *How long would it take to deal with the Wizards and how can I explain my absence to my customers? Maybe Byron is just like the imaginary rabbit in that story Dad used to read to me.* Whenever doubt surfaced, the Voice intervened to reassure him.

The lights kept turning green at every intersection. Was this Byron's or his doing? He needed to learn more about the Wizard. "You're human, right?"

"I grew up with three brothers and a sister. No one else in my family shared my predisposition to magic. To my eternal good fortune, my parents didn't fear it. They encouraged me to develop my abilities and in time, a Wizard took me as a pupil. My family is long gone."

Stuart sensed a hint of loneliness in Byron's voice. He drove several blocks, thinking about how to explain working on machines to someone who predated the Industrial Revolution. *Could he even understand?*

"I can see the interior workings of machines when I'm diagnosing breakdowns and malfunctions.

"A machine is full of parts that are supposed to work in harmony. When they don't, someone has to fix them. Sometimes, it takes an extra element to do that. That's when they call me."

Byron smiled. "Your clients describe you as quite gifted. Some even say it's almost magical the way you can attend to machines that others can't."

"I work hard and study them." *How would Byron have collected information about me? Why would my customers discuss their business with a stranger?*

"It's fortunate that you've no coworkers or employees because they'd be alarmed once they understood your technique for diagnosing problems in machines," Byron said. "How did this ability come about?"

"I always preferred working by myself." *Maybe I can finally tell my story. If Byron is a Wizard, he won't be repeating it to anyone else.* "Two weeks ago, I returned to my place after a really hard day and just wanted to relax by watching this comedy about scientists. As soon as I thought about the program, the TV turned on and switched to the right channel."

"Ha, instantaneous manifestation! Which is not the way things in your world are supposed to work? You require that little gadget, right?"

Stuart nodded. "I didn't understand what happened. I sat through the whole show wondering if I'd simply left the TV on from the previous evening. I was tired, but not that much. After the show finished and I still had no answers, I went into the kitchen to heat up some supper. I put the dish in the microwave and as soon as I read the cooking instructions, the microwave hummed away. While my dinner was perfect, my mind was completely scrambled."

Byron stared at him expressionless.

"The next morning, the engine in my van started and its doors unlocked when I opened the garage door. The dashboard dials read normal, so I headed off to my first customer. The radio came on, tuned into the news station and switched to the classical one as soon as the reports about the latest disasters concluded."

Byron peered about as if looking for the source of Stuart's link with the van. "It's a wonder you didn't jump out of this vehicle. Most people would think it was possessed."

"I concluded I was just tired from working so hard. I still needed to steer and press the gas pedal and brakes. Anyway I arrived at my first customer, Hightower Equipment, with no problem. After a while I returned to the van for tools. It unlocked as I approached. When I finished that job, the van started like it knew I was ready to drive to the next customer. I swear it reads my thoughts.

"My experiences during the next few days became increasingly bizarre. On the same day as the massive wild fire in southern Africa, a large stamping machine stopped bending sheets of steel. The mechanics couldn't restart it."

Byron stared at him.

"As I approached the machine, I was thinking about how much simpler it'd be if I could see through the cover to its inner mechanisms. Then all of a sudden I could. I was totally shocked because just a few days earlier, I saw inside a machine for the first time when I touched the cover.

"As soon as I stopped thinking about seeing inside the machine, its pale green exterior was restored. Although I wanted to run away, I kept examining the machine. When my nerves quieted, the cover became transparent again. I soon found the broken wires and relays and repaired them. Without my special vision, it would've taken days of disassembling the machine to discover the problem.

"That night, I touched my TV and could see its innards. Next I turned on my computer with my thoughts. Now it types words as I think them and displays diagrams and graphs as I sketch them on paper."

Stuart plunged on even though Byron probably understood little. Described out loud, his experiences sounded somewhat comprehensible.

"While I was still mostly bewildered, I decided to test my abilities in every client's facility. I keep discovering new ways to analyze and repair their equipment. I receive loads of praise and bonuses and no one says I'm doing anything unusual. Yesterday, I got an emergency call."

Stuart thought about how best to explain the laser saw at Steel Shapes and Designs. "It's a machine that cuts large sheets of steel into smaller pieces. It squawked like an angry bird as it worked. Once again, I could see through the cover and soon spotted the problem. I was about to tell a worker to turn the machine off when it shut down, just as if the red stop button had been pushed. Now I realize my thoughts did that.

"While I needed to remove several parts, I had it back in proper operation in less than two hours. I saved my client hundreds of thousands of dollars in repairs and lost production."

Although Byron stared out the window at the passing city, he had listened. "So, what could you tell from the noise?"

"By the racket, a gear was out of alignment, but seeing inside the machine allowed me to find which one right away along with several related problems. Once I finished, I left the building as quickly as I could. My hands shook too much to drive, so I sat in the van until my nerves stilled. That's when I realized I needed to figure out what was happening to me."

"While the tavern seemed an odd place for you, it was to my advantage you were there." Byron patted his shoulder. "It brought the drug dealers to me and you were available to deal with Vince."

"I thought that if I compiled a list of my new abilities, I might find a pattern that would explain what was happening to me. In addition to my apartment tidying itself, every traffic light switches to green as I approach or stays green until I'm through the intersection." Stuart relaxed his grip on the steering wheel.

"Then there's this Voice I hear in my head whenever I'm dealing with something new and am uncertain how to act."

"How often does it speak to you and has it ever led you astray?"

"At first, I heard it a couple of times a day. Now it's far more frequent. It makes me think twice about what I'm planning or to consider different approaches. It helps me find the problems in the machines."

"That would be magic speaking to you. Few Wizards hear it as often as you do. That's like how magic led me to you. It wanted me to find you. I came to North America from England to investigate indications there was some form of magic here. I landed in Montreal and after a couple of days in that charming city; I could detect your magic but it didn't tell me where you were.

"I tried Boston and several other locales before discovering you were in Toronto. Although it required a lot of inquiries to learn your name, magic makes that fairly easy. I can encourage people to provide me with all sorts of information."

"Well that answers my question as to why my customers told you so much. You'd make a great spy." Stuart chuckled. "By the way, I had to calculate that 100 miles was like 160 kilometers."

He turned into an industrial park. "Here's our first stop this morning. It's a small manufacturing company called BTS Designs. Although it's moving to a new facility soon, the owner is trying to keep the old equipment working until then. It's worn out, but it's easy for me to determine what's wrong. Actually, the plant has been a great place for testing my abilities and it usually is in operation on weekends to keep up with all the orders. No security around here. I'll introduce you as Uncle Byron."

"Before we go any further, we better get our story straight. Are we apt to run into anyone who knew you as a youngster?"

"No."

"Do you have a lady friend?"

Stuart hesitated. With all that Byron learned about him, he did not know about his non-existent social life. "No."

"Good, no complications from anyone who knows you."

At the plant, Stuart reached behind his seat for his equipment bag. Once he held it securely, the driver and passenger doors swung open on their own. "Let's go, Uncle."

A few minutes later, Stuart was walking around a machine that was supposed to be stamping steel parts and patterns. Byron stood a few steps back.

"It shut down yesterday," the owner said. "Can't figure out why. We're finished here in two weeks. While the replacement machines are installed in the new facility, we can't begin production there because there's still too much construction going on. I hope the quake doesn't cause more delays."

Byron stepped beside the owner and the machine operator. "It's remarkable that you have maintained your operation with these antique devices. Are any of them going to a museum?"

Not only did his question set the two men laughing, it took their attention away from Stuart. He projected his thoughts through the equipment looking for parts that required adjustment or replacement. *Bingo, a broken hydraulic hose deep in the machine where it's hard to detect.* He replaced it and added new fluid, then greased and adjusted some parts and reset several controls. He pushed the start button and the machine hummed into action.

Stuart waited until they were back on the road. "Thanks for distracting them while I checked out the situation. Usually, I don't have people watching me."

"One picks up a few insights over the centuries." Byron sat back and crossed his arms over his chest and let out a contented sigh.

"It's about 20 minutes to the next stop," Stuart said "I want to hear the rest of your story."

Byron shifted around in the seat until he seemed comfortable. "It takes a lot of study and work to become a Wizard. The most important step is learning to tap into the magic. Few people have the aptitude to reach out to it. It's frightening at first, because it feels like it'll pull you apart."

"I've never experienced anything like that."

"You may eventually," Byron said. "You didn't even know you were using magic. Think what will happen when you learn how to connect with it so it flows through you. Then you'll be able to perform a great many deeds. The power comes from the natural elements of Earth, and that's why Wizards can create the kinds of disasters that are afflicting the planet."

"With the visions and seeing inside machines, I thought I was going nuts," Stuart said. "If I said to most people what I told you, they'd think I was insane."

Byron nodded in acknowledgement. "Wizards used to be revered and sought out for their knowledge. Religions turned people against us. Nowadays, if you profess to be a Wizard, people ignore you. Perhaps that's progress."

"It wouldn't help you get a job," Stuart said. "Employers wouldn't take you seriously. Although there's this new reality TV show you might fit into. Of course, they wouldn't call you a Wizard. You'd be a Geek."

Byron smiled. "I'd never participate in a performance like that. I wouldn't want to give magic a bad name."

A UNIVERSE OF MAGIC

When Stuart stepped out of the apartment building Sunday morning, the heat did not stagger him like it had for the last month. Although the forecast called for another scorcher, the air felt refreshing.

The heat wave had reduced the usual summer lushness in the neighborhood to brown grass and shriveled flowers and plants. The neighborhood cats no longer made their morning prowls. The hum of air conditioning units replaced the usual bird calls and few people ventured from their homes except to go to work or buy groceries.

He walked toward the garage. The cool stayed with him. Intrigued, he stopped part way, took a digital thermometer from his bag, set it on the ground and stepped back. Within seconds, the number on the display edged up to 33.7 Celsius. He now possessed Byron's ability to keep the heat at bay. *Would it work on the cold in winter?*

Byron climbed into the van fussing over something in a small satchel. He stopped his rummaging and looked at Stuart wide-eyed. "Your vehicle shouldn't be this cool already." When Stuart smiled, he said, "You did this?"

The old guy did not speak for several blocks. "I didn't think you were ready to learn to control the temperature around you. You just absorbed that ability. Perhaps you'll gain other skills that way."

"I just thought about how great it'd be to cool the air as you do and it happened. Maybe The Brotherhood can track you by the magic you use to do that."

Byron shook his head. "It's too localized. Same with invisibility and stopping hearts."

As they drove, Stuart said, "At this time of day, the streets are usually a lot busier with people going to church and community events. Since the heat wave settled in, you see fewer and fewer people out and about. Businesses struggle to keep their doors open."

The van's radio came on and the all-news station reported monster storms tearing up South Pacific islands and runaway forest fires in Alaska and Western Canada. Then there was the usual list of water rationings and electricity brownouts caused by the heat wave. After that report, the radio tuned into the classical station before Stuart even thought about music.

After the third customer stop to inspect machines that ran 24/7, Stuart spotted a coffee shop and pulled in. He returned with two large ice teas. He took a long drink of his. "This prolonged heat makes a lot of people ornery. It also disrupts the operation of machines and computers. Do you think the Wizards can be interfering with them?"

Byron shook his head. "The power they're using to create and sustain the heat wave must affect your devices similar to the way I cause your TV to become fuzzy. The Brotherhood is likely unaware of this secondary impact."

"It's becoming a serious problem because we're so dependent on technology." Stuart spent the rest of the day mulling over Wizard magic and listening to long, detailed explanations from Byron. By the time they headed back to his apartment, Stuart's mind churned with ideas.

He slowed for a stop sign. Byron looked at a large church with a towering steeple on one corner of the intersection. "It's interesting the kind of devotion religions inspire. Wizards never achieved that even with all we did for humanity. People find it easier to believe in a God they can't see than in the power of magic."

He stared at the church until it passed out of sight. "Wizards have an advantage. We know a supreme being dwells in the Universe because we can sense its presence. God, Allah, whatever you wish to call it, has all the suns and planets to attend to, not just Earth. It's no more concerned with the behavior of humans than it is with what lives elsewhere. We need to nurture the planet."

"It can't be too pleased with our behaviour."

"Humans could be doing a lot better."

Stuart had attended church as a kid, but when his parents' attendance dropped, so did his. He possessed no strong feelings for or against religion. Although the Wizard concept of a supreme being intrigued him, he needed to focus on immediate problems. "If The Brotherhood is causing all these disasters to gain control of the world, what would it do with that power?"

"Merstreem wants to return humanity to the time many centuries ago when Wizards held sway."

"The news said there are 10 failed states where the government has collapsed and many others are sliding into chaos because they can no longer cope with all the displaced persons."

"That turmoil would be the first step in Merstreem's plan," Byron said. "He wouldn't want to bother with the day-to-day details of operating governments. If we can't stop the Brotherhood directly, we may have to figure out how to counter the Halves they select to run countries on their behalf."

"The what?"

"Halves are humans who have weak magical ability and Wizards can use it to control them like puppets."

"If The Brotherhood wants to protect the climate and environment, wouldn't it be simpler to manipulate people into supporting Green parties in every country?"

Once again Byron stared at him blankly. Stuart explained about the goals of Green parties.

"The Brotherhood wants everyone to know they're in charge. We're dealing with men possessed with very large egos who've been ignored for centuries. What they don't understand is the hotter the world gets, the weaker magic becomes because the planet's natural conditions are being disrupted. I don't know if humanity can survive until the planet warms enough to dissipate the Brotherhood's power."

As he prepared supper, Stuart called to Byron, "How does The Brotherhood use magic to cause disasters?

Byron did not respond as he settled into the armchair. He shifted the lever to lower the back and raise the leg rest. It amused Stuart that he did it manually rather than use his magic.

"You want a nap before supper?"

"I took several in the van today. I've never needed to cool the air for so long. It saps my energy."

Stuart passed him a plate of cold meat and raw vegetables, and then settled on the couch. "It'd help me understand what the Wizards are doing if I knew how magic works."

Byron nibbled at the food on the plate. "The initial step is to connect with it. Magic is everywhere, but unless you have the aptitude, you can't detect it."

His usual flat monotone voice took on an edge that Stuart recognized as the old man warming to his topic.

"When you connect to magic at first, it's like being caught in a big storm when the wind blows so hard that it howls. In time, linking to magic becomes as simple as flicking a light switch. When you reach that stage, you really learn what your abilities are and how to use them. It helps to have a teacher."

"If my abilities are magical, how did I come by them?"

Byron shook his head. "I've no explanation for that. Your Wizard abilities are elementary and the only way you could threaten a Brotherhood member is to attack him physically. That's why I need to teach you more. An easy talent to master is invisibility." He stood and faded away.

Stuart walked over and reached out to where Byron had stood. His waving hands felt nothing.

"I cheated." Byron's voice came from behind Stuart. "If I'd remained in my place, you'd have touched me."

"It'd scare the crap out of someone if they ran into the invisible you." Stuart said.

Byron grinned as he re-appeared. "It hurts just the same, so do try to avoid collisions. Both Vince and I rendered ourselves invisible to enter the tavern unnoticed."

"I saw you and him heading toward me."

"By then I'd switched to an unseeing spell, which is easier to maintain for long periods of time. Vince did likewise but didn't realize you could see us until too late and his arrogance kept him from retreating. I employed an unseeing spell when I wandered through the warehouse today.

"Making objects invisible as I did with the gym bag at the tavern is simple magic. While a Wizard can spot a hiding spell in use and break it down in an instant, ordinary people can't. It's takes a powerful Wizard to detect invisibility in use."

Stuart hesitated. "A woman spotted you and Vince in the tavern. Earlier she blocked my probe of the people there."

Byron hesitated. "You're certain she saw us?"

"You should've seen the perplexed look on her face after Vince turned into a pile of dust and vanished."

"How old is she?"

"About my age." Stuart could feel a warm glow on his face. He did not mention she looked familiar.

"Does she resemble the woman in your visions?"

"Not at all. She's tall, shoulder length brown hair, wears glasses and appeared completely out of place in that tavern. I bet it was her first time there and, by her expression, probably her last. The woman in my visions is shorter, black haired, and looks distraught. She has an aura about her like you do."

"I've never seen a person's aura in a vision." Byron scratched his head. "You're an odd one. There's a lot of conventional wizardry about you, even though that's not where your abilities lie. You've provided me with two big puzzles."

They returned to their seats to finish supper. When Stuart wondered what happened during the day, the TV and radio came to life.

The all-news channel showed a female reporter standing in front of a grey, rectangular office building. Stuart half watched until a photo of The Big Wheel Tavern appeared in a corner of the screen and he turned up the volume. A spokesman for the Coroner's office was answering questions about the dead drug dealers.

"The five deceased appear to have suffered cardiac arrest at the same time from what we can determine from our autopsies. We've no idea how that could happen and we didn't find any probable medical causes. There's nothing more I can tell you."

From that scene, the channel switched to a police official at a news conference recorded earlier. "We've no suspects." The photos and names of the dead men appeared on the screen. "We found no sign of a struggle and none of them had pulled their weapons. The men were known criminals. The estimated street value of the drugs is close to $1 million."

Byron rubbed his hands together. "I'm a millionaire."

After the news conference, the reporter appeared again, standing in front of the Big Wheel. "Total News has learned that police in

New York City found the body of a man who robbed $50,000 from a bank. They're sure he was murdered but haven't been able to determine how or what happened to the money. A similar case is under investigation in Boston."

Stuart looked at Byron. "You wouldn't happen to know anything about these cases."

Byron settled in the chair. "I wondered how long it would take the authorities to make the connection. I want to make sure we possess sufficient money for what we must do."

"You're killing people!"

"They're not innocents like the people dying in the disasters. I've only terminated a few blackguards."

"Couldn't you just use your magic to take the money?" Stuart said.

"And leave the scum alive to harm others?"

Although he wanted to object, Stuart could not think of any arguments that might impress Byron. "Let's try to avoid further killings."

"Young man, a lot more people will die, whether it offends you or not." Byron showed no remorse. "Are you ready to try tapping into magic directly? You must have been doing it when you examined the machines."

"It surprised me so much the first couple of times I saw through the covers of machines that I had to sit down and collect my wits. I told people I needed to write notes about the service call. I don't have any disorientation now." He took a deep breath. "Okay, let's try it."

Byron came across the room and sat on the couch beside him. The TV picture went fuzzy, and Stuart turned it off.

"The first step is to select an image that relaxes you." Byron leaned back on the couch. "It'll serve as your touchstone. It could be a person, an animal, a place."

"Uncle Oscar. He taught me to listen to machines for the sounds of problems." His uncle would have no end of questions for Byron.

"Good, can you form an image of him in your thoughts?"

"Already have."

Byron huffed. "Excellent. Reach out to him. At first, the image will move away to test how serious you are."

"He's not moving at all. He's smiling."

"Really?" Byron sat forward. "That step usually takes weeks or months. Magic really wants to connect with you. Tell him with your thoughts what you want to see or do. Something easy."

"Wow, I'm standing on the deck of a clipper ship under full sail. I can smell the salt air, and the wind is whipping around me. This is awesome, way better than video games! Now I'm on top of Mt. Everest. It's too cold." Byron gasped. "Hey, now I'm in my high school physics class. I really looked goofy like my sister says." He continued exploring for a few minutes until Byron shook his arm.

"See if you can make yourself invisible."

While he flickered once or twice, Stuart could still see himself in the mirror. "Whew, I'm getting light headed. Let's try some more later." He yawned.

"Take a rest," Byron said. "I mustn't push you too fast."

"Want to watch a baseball game or the golf highlights?"

"I've never observed a baseball match before. I've attended many Opens."

Judyth sat in her car a block away listening via the transmitter she had planted in Stuart's apartment to ensure she could monitor their conversations. For all she had learned, she wished Stuart had said more about her.

From the muffled sound of the TV and groans from Stuart, something had happened in the baseball game. She squirmed in her seat, trying to ease the pressure on her bladder that wanted a bathroom break. She decided to head to a nearby coffee shop until she heard Byron's voice.

"Can you lower the sound? We need to talk." The babble from the TV commentators ended. "Let's assume a woman with some magical ability was at the tavern. That means she probably knows where we went." Byron sounded irritated. "Do you think anyone followed us today?"

"Never checked. Couldn't a Wizard tail us with magic? Are there women Wizards?"

"Of course, none of that foolishness about witches. People claiming to be witches are utter charlatans when it comes to magic." Byron sounded disgusted. "Being a Wizard has nothing to do with gender." He muttered in a language Judyth did not recognize.

Stuart's voice jumped. "That's the way Vince spoke and the Waif sounds like that as well."

"The Waif speaks like me?" More words from Byron that Judyth did not understand. "You'd call our language Wizardese. Only we know it." Byron paused. "If the woman in the tavern possessed magical ability, I would've sensed her presence."

"Tomorrow, I'll watch for a vehicle tailing us, although my white van is probably an easy target to follow from a distance because it's taller than most vehicles. The large red letters for Watson's Big Machine Restoration Company on the sides would help anyone tracking it."

Silence descended again and Judyth gave in to her bladder's need for relief. As she started the car, Stuart uttered a muffled cheer. His team must have scored. She pulled into the coffee shop parking lot, dashed in, placed her order and headed to the washroom. Back in her car, she heard Stuart and Byron talking about the woman in Stuart's vision.

"So all I'm supposed to do is keep an image of the Waif in my mind while I think about finding her using my touchstone," Stuart said. "It's hard to do that and search at the same time."

"Keep trying. This is new to you. The Waif is likely in Europe, so it will take a while for your viewing ability to work that far away. If it doesn't, we can search for that woman you saw at the tavern."

Worried that Stuart might spot her, Judyth parked the car several blocks from his apartment and settled in her seat. She sipped her coffee.

"I've located the Waif," Stuart said. "When I approach, she moves backward or sideway. Instead of answering me, she calls out. She keeps looking around, like she's frightened."

"What's she saying?" Byron said.

"I don't know because it's in your language."

"Don't feel bad. It's hard for me to talk to someone in a vision. You must keep trying."

"Now she's looking over her shoulder as if someone is near. Oops, she's gone. I can't see anything."

"That's enough searching for tonight. You've done well, remarkably well. You're performing difficult magic that consumes a lot of energy and until you become conditioned to it, you'll tire quickly."

"Like I'm right now," Stuart said through a yawn. "The game is still in the fifth inning." Judyth heard his footsteps through the apartment. "Night Uncle Byron. See you in the morning."

"When do you take time off?"

"When my customers don't need me."

Judyth drove home trying to make sense of Byron and Stuart's conversation. When she arrived, Bethune announced it had information about magic to share with her.

"I need to phone Forecaster first," she said. By the rapid flashing of the status lights on Bethune's computer cases, it listened intently as she recounted the evening's events to the Realm's weather expert. "It's interesting that magic is fatiguing. It means we're not doing anything wrong when we use our abilities and feel exhausted afterward."

"When Audubon, who we've known for years, suggested our powers could be linked to magic, everyone dissed him," Forecaster said. "Now you discover an old man who seems capable of backing up his claim to be a Wizard and you're talking about magic as if it's real. It's like something's interfering with your critical capacity. Perhaps magic grows on you."

Judyth shrugged. "I don't understand why Byron can't sense me. We must be a lot different than Wizards. Get back to me if you have any ideas." She turned off her phone. "Okay Bethune, what've you learned?"

A MODEL EVENING

Stuart left his apartment early Monday in response to an emergency call from the regional transit agency. While Byron came along, he would remain invisible in the van.

Near the agency's headquarters, Stuart glanced over to make sure the old guy could not be seen. Two books floated where he sat. Stuart grabbed them and placed them on the bench behind their seats.

Byron snickered. "How silly of me."

"You're still reading Civilisations. What's the other book?"

"My personal reference on Wizards and types of magic. I'm looking for ideas on the woman in the tavern. As much as I don't understand how she could possess magical ability, she must if she could see Vince and me. If she's in the employ of The Brotherhood, she would've attacked us right after we killed Vince. Our strength and power were low at that point. If she's not connected to The Brotherhood, then why was she there? From what you said before, she didn't appear to be a regular patron."

"We're coming up to the gate so be quiet," said Stuart.

"The guard will wave you through."

"Actually, I need to ask directions. I've only been here once and don't remember where the computer division is located."

"I'll study the books while you're inside," Byron said. "They'll be invisible."

"I could be in there for a long time," Stuart said.

"After more than 300 years, a long time is relative. I need to reflect on the mystery ladies."

Stuart pulled up in front of a glass double door. Under Admittance

Restricted in red lettering was a small sign that said Computer Controls. A security guard sprinted to the van. "I'm to take you directly to the Control Center," he said before Stuart could open the door. "They're anxious to get your help."

Stuart returned near noon. "I assume you fixed the problem," Byron whispered. He remained hidden.

Stuart looked around to make sure no one watched them. "The system to dispatch the transit buses and subway trains is controlled by a brand-new computer. The engineers and maintenance personnel are still learning all its features." Even with my analytical ability, it took me a while to locate the faults in the control system." When Byron did not respond, he said, "Did that make any sense?"

"None whatsoever," Byron said.

"Their operations should be normal in an hour or two. That was a good test of my abilities. So let's go somewhere special for lunch. I'm really hungry."

"That I understand." Byron chuckled. "Let me know when it's safe to reappear. Do you know a restaurant that serves duck or goose? I've not eaten a meal like that in ages."

"I'm sure the Internet can find us one." Stuart pulled out his laptop. "Looks like you're in luck. There's a restaurant not too far from here that serves your desired fare." He shifted the location to his GPS screen and glanced in Byron's direction. "So did you figure out the mystery ladies?"

"Not really. By her persistence, the Waif must have an important message. I can't understand why she blocks me from her visions."

"She appeared twice to me while I worked on the transit computers. Looked frantic both times and the second time she said 'Need help soon' in English."

"She links directly to you, which is very powerful magic. How would she have found you?"

"Maybe the same way you did." Stuart pulled the van into an alleyway. "You can appear now."

In an instant, Byron was straightening his clothes. "It's tiring using magic to remain hidden for that long." He patted his magical reference several times. "I made no progress in deducing who the woman in the tavern might be. Did you hear her speak with an accent?"

"I think she's from this area."

Byron gasped. "That makes her even more of a mystery. It could be that magic came to her spontaneously, as it did to you. That hasn't happened for centuries, and now we have her, you, and perhaps the Waif who acquired magic without the assistance of Wizards."

"Perhaps you were too distracted with finding me and evading Vince to notice the woman in the tavern," Stuart said. "Or maybe her magic is sufficiently different that you don't recognize it."

Byron's mouth hung open. "How could that be? I detected yours." He flipped through pages of his hand written reference. "No record exists of wizards outside Europe for several millennia. We stretch into Scandinavia, east to the Ural Mountains and south through Turkey. While there are pretenders in the rest of the world, they're triflers compared to even the feeblest of us."

"So no Wizards emigrated or traveled?"

"Wizards need access to The Book of Time and Europe is the only place on Earth it can be consulted. We can't possess a copy of it. Our magic allows us to read what's recorded in it. It won't appear to anyone without magic. I never considered its geographic restriction before. Maybe magic not based on the elemental powers of Earth exists in the Americas. Thinking about it, perhaps the presence of you and the women indicates magic is changing more than we Wizards ever thought possible."

Stuart hoped Byron would keep talking to give him extra insight into magic and his abilities.

Byron grunted and scanned a few more pages. "The mystery ladies will have to make the next move. Perhaps the one in the tavern wanted to see if you recognized her abilities and somehow knew you'd be there that night. There are no coincidences. I wonder what stopped her from introducing herself. From your description, you weren't averse to talking with her."

"Women don't usually walk up to me and say hello. I was planning to ask her to dance, and then you arrived. Speaking of that, how did you know I would be there?"

"I tracked you and the drug dealers at the same time. Once I knew your destination, I influenced them into using the tavern's parking lot for the exchange. I wasn't as successful at throwing Vince off my trail. Still it all worked out. I've the ability to manipulate situations." He snapped his fingers. "Of course. The woman in the tavern could have been following you just as I was. That raises the matter of why she's interested in you."

"That would mean it was all arranged by..." Stuart's mind reeled at the implications of magic being that pervasive.

Before he could ask how Byron influenced the drug dealers, the Wizard said, "Learning the identities of the women is crucial."

"If the Brotherhood is a collection of old men, would they want younger Wizards to front for them? Could she be a wannabe Wizard?"

"Her gender alone assures she is not connected to The Brotherhood. In addition, if she was immune to Vince's and my unseeing spells, then she would be genuine although her origin remains a mystery."

Stuart made several more service calls during the afternoon before they returned to his apartment. "I need to stop thinking about this magic stuff for an hour or two. My weekly model ship building workshop is this evening. I think a break from all this will help me assimilate what's happening. You should come with me. My pals would enjoy meeting Uncle Byron."

"You really are an odd fellow. I'll accompany you because I've never tried relaxing like that."

Byron was in his glory at the workshop. His knowledge of sailing ships made him the hit of the night. "Remember these vessels were built by tradesmen working with hand tools," he told the modellers gathered around him. "They didn't have the equipment of today." He explained how the lines connected to the masts lowered and raised sails and stabilized the ship.

"Once you are at sea, you realize just how small those ships are and how immense the ocean is. You don't see land or any sign of life for weeks or months. Navigation is by the stars and the weather forecast is what the crew can read from the sky and the wind. It's very humbling."

Working quietly on his radio controlled tugboat, Stuart smiled as he realized Byron loved to perform for a crowd as much as Uncle Oscar did. He wondered what his friends would think if they knew what the old guy was.

Happiness filled Stuart. The class clown when he was young, he became a serious type in high school and university consumed by studies and work. As confused and puzzled as he felt, the exhilaration of the last couple of days made him wonder if magic produced a natural high.

He glanced over at Byron trying his hand at sanding and gluing wooden parts together. He looked as happy as Stuart felt. When the workshop ended, everyone urged Byron to come back next week to help them properly attach rigging. No one questioned how he knew so much about building and traveling on sailing ships.

As they headed home, Stuart asked Byron to explain how they could stop The Brotherhood.

Judyth sat in a darkened classroom next to where the modellers met, listening to the men talking about different miniature construction techniques. Their shop talk caused her mind to drift to the upcoming emergency meeting of The Realm called by Marconi.

While Judyth hoped the discussions would focus on whether to approach Stuart and Byron, she suspected her friends coming to Toronto would mainly argue about whether their ability to accomplish more with technology could have a connection to magic.

Remembering the heated reactions when Audubon suggested magic as the basis for the Realm's powers, she pondered how to create a reasoned debate about the M-word. She needed to convince her friends to concentrate on finding the Wizards and stopping the disasters. Maintaining secrecy about The Realm seemed pointless with the world falling apart.

She also knew she would have to answer a lot of questions and teasing about Stuart. Her friends needed to understand that whatever its origin, his power had surged in strength and range of ability under Byron's tutelage.

Remembering Stuart's glances at her in the tavern brought a smile to her face. *I hope he thinks about me as often as I do about him.* She could find him anywhere in the city just by homing in on the pulse he gave off when using his abilities. When she sensed his power in action, she shut her eyes and put his image in her thoughts. In seconds, she could see him repairing machines or showing Byron how modern technology worked.

Stuart greeted customers with ready assurances their problems would be solved soon. His thoughts swept through a customer's facility even before he entered, searching for any sign of mechanical or electronic discordance. Whenever he and Byron stopped at a restaurant, he examined all the customers. Byron had taught him to do it directly so he no longer held his hand on the table to make the connection. His power rippled through the place like an invisible wave. No one in The Realm had abilities anything like his.

She followed their van from the workshop. It cut through an industrial area and stopped near a scrap yard. She could feel his pulse at work as without leaving the van, Stuart disassembled old vehicles set up in a long row. Judyth imagined the perplexed looks on the workers' faces when they discovered the stacks of doors, fenders and side walls piled up beside the hulks of the vehicles.

Next, they parked close to an electronic billboard that flashed a series of commercials. Judyth laughed as the displays changed so a furniture store promised to cure hemorrhoids, an insurance company would rid homes of pests, and a waste removal business offered the best home cooked meals.

Bethune greeted her when she returned to the condo. "You have received 97 e-mails about the emergency meeting. Everyone in the group is interested in it even if they cannot attend. I have never seen your group so animated on a topic."

Intrigued by a flicker of excitement in its voice, Judyth stared at the computer boxes, wishing she better understood how its contents produced Bethune. "You've never used first person before."

"Your request to study magic led me to investigate many topics. There is much to learn about the world. Your e-mail is educational as well."

"Nice dodge, but you didn't answer my question."

"In my excitement, I forgot I am not a person. I hope that does not trouble you. I want to honor the man you named me after by being as resourceful as he was in bringing medical treatment to poor people. While these computer boxes are my home and you will always be my best friend, the Internet will be my Realm."

Waiting for the kettle to boil, Judyth recounted more about what she had discovered. "Every time Stuart uses his magic, he does something that surprises Byron."

"So what is your plan of action when you meet your friends?"

She remained unsure of how they would react to her information. *Will they take it seriously?*

"First, we must heighten our security. Everyone should be ultra-cautious for the next few days when they're investigating natural disasters. We don't want to tip Byron or anyone searching for him to our presence, or we could also have The Brotherhood hunting us. We don't know how to protect ourselves."

Judyth peered into the mug as she pondered her next observation. "Following Stuart and Byron has boosted my abilities. As Stuart's power expands, it pulls mine along. Maybe, it'd do that for the others." She put the mug down on the desk and stared at Bethune, hoping he had an answer.

"That would be interesting to experience," Bethune said. "I wish to meet Stuart. Would he want to have me as a friend?"

"Hopefully, we'll find out. First, the group needs to decide whether I should approach him. I'm hesitating because revealing our presence could put everyone in danger."

"Maybe Byron could teach you to defend yourselves. Stuart's immunity to Wizard magic sounds worth the discomfort. For my next challenge, I'll ponder how Stuart and Byron might oppose The Brotherhood. While it's not a medical or health issue, my research could assist you."

She nodded certain that Bethune's camera allowed it to interpret her gestures. "Stuart and Byron want to find me, figure out who the woman in the vision is, and build up Stuart's magical ability. I develop a splitting headache when I try to connect to my powers through a touchstone like Stuart does. I prefer our technique of thinking about what we want to do until it happens."

Judyth drank the last mouthful of tea. "However Stuart links to his magic much faster than us, which has helped him expand his powers. He accepts that being connected with magic is expanding his abilities."

"So he's not like the Wizards either?"

Judyth nodded. "He's probably unique in more ways than he realizes."

A STORMY INTRODUCTION

Stuart pondered why the shower felt so warm when he usually maintained a lower temperature around him. He rubbed shampoo into his hair and gave his scalp a vigorous massage as he tried to make sense of the events of the last few days.

The biggest puzzle was the growing scope of his engineering abilities. The previous day, he detected a mixer malfunction at White Chemicals from the parking lot. Before Byron, he would not have recognized a chemical reaction going wrong.

Whenever doubts about magic and being connected to it surfaced, the Voice calmly pointed out his most recent successes in complicated service calls. As he returned to his room to dress, he called, "What's the forecast, Byron?"

Dressed in a pinstriped suit with wide lapels, white shirt and cravat, Byron sat at the table with pieces of half-eaten toast on his plate. He waved, but did not speak.

Stuart looked out the bedroom window. The few leaves left in the neighborhood trees were flapping madly. "It's really windy. All the branches are swaying. Oops, a large bag just flew by."

Usually a chatterbox in the morning, Byron still said nothing. Wondering what preoccupied him, Stuart perused his work order list when he reached the table. "Let's see what's on the agenda for today? Ah, Armstrong Industrial. Lots of machines there." Stuart looked over at Byron. "There'll be little that interests you."

"Good, I need to rest." Byron yawned.

"Ah, a little too much magic, eh!" Stuart laughed as he brought his toast and jam to the table.

"Precisely because you're always up to something." He yawned again. "I'll sleep in the van."

The wind grabbed at them when they walked to the garage. Stuart turned his shoulder into it and held tightly to his equipment bag. Byron walked upright, his clothes and hair unruffled. Stuart shot him a questioning look.

"I'm deflecting the wind. However, the fact my magic works on the wind means it's not natural. It'll turn into a gale or worse. Being near Lake Ontario gives The Brotherhood lots of natural elements to throw at us."

"So your friends have found us?"

"This is so widespread it means they only suspect I could be in the area. They'll be hitting other regions as well in hope I counter their action to give away my exact location."

Gusts pummeled the van all the way to Armstrong Industrial, forcing Stuart to grip the steering wheel with both hands. "In these conditions the van's high sides are like sails."

When Byron did not respond, he peeked at him. Sound asleep. *He must have stayed up late last night.*

Stuart drove into Armstrong's parking lot and let his thoughts sweep through the facility like a surveillance camera. The office workers were at their desks while the employees in shipping drove fork lifts transferring large covered loads into truck trailers. On the shop floor, mechanics and operators stood around two of the five assembly machines. They would be the ones the company wanted him to repair. The rest of the plant seemed in good order, although piles of wood pallets and wrapping in a couple of areas should be cleaned up.

He puzzled over his insights into the operation of the facility and how magic could interact with his training and experience. They seemed like complete opposites, not complementary forces. Still his two sides were learning to connect effortlessly.

It took him about an hour to reset the programming in the assembly lines and return the machines to operation. A month ago, the job would have taken a day or more. Now his ability to see inside the machine and computer led him to the trouble spots almost immediately. He wondered whether the bean counters would consider this as a productivity improvement.

Stuart finished the job and strode back to the van. As he approached, the engine started awakening Byron. He grabbed his magical reference book to keep it from slipping off his lap.

"Finished Civilisations?"

"A brilliant book; you must find that TV series for me." Byron rubbed his palms together. "I'm even more convinced the great artists and builders who Kenneth Clark writes about had a streak of magic in them that inspired their brilliant music and paintings. Probably all the inventors as well."

Stuart put the van into drive while thinking Byron had lived through the lifetimes of at least some people in the book. He should have already considered the possibility they possessed a connection to magic. While it would have been insufficient to achieve Wizard status, it could have enhanced their creative abilities. *Maybe there are a lot of people like this.*

"It'll take almost a half hour to reach my next call, so maybe you can answer some questions during the drive," Stuart said. "We also have a long trip between my afternoon appointments. You may not have felt it sitting in the truck but the wind seems stronger." He hesitated. "I sense a great storm is brewing."

Byron stared back at him. "I can't perceive storms in advance. But Wizards gathering enough power for great works of magic do tend to create them. They're often a premonition of something untoward in the making."

"What might be going on in the magical world except another attack on you?" Stuart said.

The old man raised his hand to forestall further questions. He turned his book over in his hands so fast it appeared to spin. "It wouldn't require that much power to eliminate me. If a storm is developing because of magical forces, The Brotherhood could be preparing to inflict more calamities on the planet. I've no idea what they might try next."

"I've never had a feeling like this before," Stuart said. "The weather feels really creepy; it's just not right." He was so used to traffic lights turning green at his approach that he needed to remember stop signs still required him to halt. "Do you think some people in mental institutions could be suffering from delusions or imbalances caused by a connection with magic?"

"That might be the case. If so, they're beyond my help. I need to keep you from ending up like them, although you appear more secure mentally than most. If the weather holds this afternoon, is there a park where I could test you?"

"I'll check on my GPS. What did you have in mind?"

"It must be spontaneous. Telling you would allow you to prepare." With that Byron reclined the seat and shut his eyes.

"Did you spend a lot of time at your refuge last night? Usually you're only absent for a few minutes."

"I was consulting the Book of Time for clues to the two women."

"Did you have to travel to Europe to read it?"

Byron shook his head. "My refuge is in the Otherworld, which I can travel to much faster and the Brotherhood can't trace me there. A Wizard can summon the Book of Time in it as well as in Europe. When it appears, you ask your question or tell it your information. The words from it float in the air for a few minutes before they vanish. We're unable to alter the text. Only the magic can do that.

"Successfully summoning the Book is the final test of whether a magic apprentice has achieved Wizard status. We're all anxious to be favorably noted in it, although few ever are. Most only appear in the list of full Wizards of all time."

"What is the Otherworld and what does the Book say about you?"

"My name appears on the list of Wizards but that's all. The Otherworld is a physical place that is of this world but separate from it. I only go there to visit my refuge and I know little else about it."

"How big is your refuge?"

"It resembles a large walk-in cupboard. I use it for storage and pass as little time as possible there to make sure no one finds it."

Stuart turned the van into the parking lot of Another Dimension Propulsion. "The company develops engines that run on alternate fuels. They're making amazing progress."

"At my age, you come to think you've seen everything. But what humans do in these plants and factories is a revelation. I never imagined science could lead to this. Magic never would have."

Heavy black clouds hung over the city by the time they reached the park in the early afternoon. "This will work well for what we need to do," Byron said. "There's no one here."

They settled on an out-of-the-way bench overlooking a small

reedy pond euphemistically named Lake Progress. A cold wind swirled around them. Stuart dug out the fried chicken and salad he had purchased at a takeout. They ate in silence as Byron's magic swept around to make sure no one watched them. Stuart decided to save his queries about the Otherworld until Byron was finished with whatever he wanted to accomplish in the park.

"Can you sense any creatures in the pond from here?" The smug look on Byron's face suggested he already knew the answer.

"Not even with Uncle Oscar's help."

"Watch this." Fish and frogs popped out of the murky water and hung in the air until Byron let them splash back into the pond.

As much as he tried, Stuart could not shift a park bench, attract ground hogs, squirrels, crows or blue jays, force tree branches to sway, disperse the clouds overhead or create a ripple on the murky surface of the pond.

"While that's what I expected, I needed to see it for myself," Byron said. "Watch this."

Within minutes, squirrels, raccoons, ground hogs and scruffy feral cats streamed toward them. When they arrived, they formed a wildlife parade that circled the bench performing like they did this drill every day. Stuart wished he had his video camera from the van. Overhead, jays, crows and small birds swooped through the air performing dives and sharp turns like planes in an air show.

Byron did not move a finger. His face appeared completely relaxed. Thunder boomed as clouds appeared and disappeared. This was child's play for the Wizard. With a wave of his hand, the wildlife dispersed and the rumbling halted.

"Your elemental magic consists of detecting weather patterns, controlling the temperature around you and sensing people's thoughts," Byron said. "However your ability to influence technology is astounding. Can your trigger the alarm in your van from here?"

Within seconds, the alarm's bleat reached them. "This is way too easy for you. We need to find a better test."

"Haven't you seen enough during the last few days?" Stuart said.

"Those were predictable situations. What I want to witness is how you deal with situations that are new to you. While I recognize the signature of your magic as it leaps into machines, I don't understand how it works. Where are we going next?"

"A plant that produces electrical motors. The employees don't know how to maintain their manufacturing equipment. Easy work for me."

On the way home, Byron asked Stuart to start five highway tractors parked in a warehouse lot. Byron shook his head as they fired up, bringing their surprised drivers from an office on the run. As they approached the trucks, Stuart shut them down.

Forecaster, a short man with dark brown hair, tailed Stuart and Byron so Judyth could prepare for the Realm emergency meeting. Stuart had parked his van well away from the only other vehicle in the parking lot so Forecaster pulled up beside the faded green sedan.

Fearing he would be discovered if he went closer, he stayed in his car staring at the animals streaming toward the pond. He jumped when a pulse from Stuart turned on the alarm in the white van and his rental car. When the alarms went silent 30 seconds later, it erased his doubts about the need for The Realm to meet Stuart and Byron.

To Forecaster, the inky black skies should produce a torrential downpour. More ominously, the clouds seemed anchored to the city.

After Stuart and Byron drove out of the parking lot, Forecaster phoned Judyth to relate the strange events and explain his concern about the weather.

When Judyth hung up the phone, Bethune said, "While I checked the city web cams, they show little of the sky. I need an outside monitor so I can see what's happening."

"I'm turning up the volume for the transmitter from Stuart's apartment," Judyth said.

Almost a half hour passed before Stuart and Byron returned home.

"I apologize for messing up your apartment with my clothes," the Wizard said.

"It was my idea to hang them up. I didn't think they'd survive the heat of the dryer downstairs. We'll buy you some proper underwear tomorrow."

"You're being rather impertinent, young man!"

Judyth laughed as Byron harrumphed his way about the apartment. In the background, the fridge door opened. "There's nothing for supper," Stuart said. "Let's go to the grocery store. While we eat, you can tell me about the Otherworld. You keep avoiding the topic." A clap of thunder drowned out the Wizard's reply.

"That was right over their building," Judyth said.

Forecaster pointed his right hand upward as he walked into the living room. "That storm's tailing them instead of moving away as it should."

"I better check this out," Judyth said.

"I'll come with you," Forecaster said.

Certain Stuart and Byron were in danger; Judyth grabbed her medical satchel and car keys and headed for the door, Forecaster right behind her. She drove as fast as she could, glad that rush hour was over and that she knew a couple of short cuts to Stuart's. Glancing at the black storm clouds, she shuddered and sped up.

Nearing his apartment building, she spotted Stuart and the Wizard walking to the garage. Figures sprang out of the dark and cast bolts of light at them.

BACKYARD BRAWL

The itching sensation from Wizard magic struck Stuart's face and arms first. The burning sensation rapidly spread over his body.

"We're in trouble," Byron snapped. Blue streaks of light shot from the hands of four figures in the shadows. Stepping in front of Byron, Stuart yelled, "Duck." The light flared off him and some slipped past him knocking the old guy to the ground. Behind them, tires squealed as a car stopped and two people jumped from it.

Byron flailed his arms and kicked his legs like he was trying to dislodge a weight. Then, with an angry snarl, he waved his hand and a streak of light shot at the attackers. While they jumped out of the way, Stuart figured Byron could look after himself.

Two opponents split up as they advanced while the other two held back. Stuart could not recall any Tae Kwon Do instructions on facing multiple attackers with magical powers.

He feigned a move toward one attacker and lunged at the other, sweeping his left leg into the Wizard's right knee. The figure groaned as he lost balance and Stuart chopped his neck with his left hand, and then drove his right fist into the man's gut. The breath exploded out of the Wizard as he toppled to the ground.

Byron was on his knees gasping for breath. He blocked a streak of light from the closest attacker, causing a flash that lit up the area between the apartment building and the garage. Stuart took several strides before leaping at the Wizard who was aiming another strike at Byron. The tackle bowled over the man, who howled in agony as

Stuart landed on top of him. Stuart smashed his forearm into the man's face and he went still.

One of the attackers who hung back fired a streak of light that sent Byron tumbling. Before the attacker could strike again, someone from the car jumped him. The pair crashed to the ground.

"I'm an old fool of a Wizard," Byron sputtered. "The attackers gathered the storm to disguise their presence. I failed to recognize it, although Stuart pointed it out."

The last assailant remained in the shadows near the garage. Stuart sprinted at him, lowering his shoulder to tackle him. Seeing Stuart, the Wizard lost shape, but not fast enough to escape being staggered by a streak of light fired by Byron. Stuart cursed when the attacker disappeared. His escape meant he would be able to warn The Brotherhood that Byron had found protection.

He glanced in Byron's direction to see a woman was checking his pulse. Meanwhile the remaining attacker was pushing away the person who had jumped him. As Stuart ran toward them, the attacker stood and raised his arm at the prone newcomer. Stuart pounded into him and they landed heavily. Stuart slammed the man's head into the ground until he went limp. The newcomer rolled about, moaning deeply.

"Leave him alone," Stuart shouted as he rushed to Byron.

"His pulse is very steady for such an old man," said the woman who was holding Byron's arm.

"Oh, it's you," Stuart said. "What are you doing here?"

"Stuart, do you know this person?" Byron twisted his arm trying to slip out of her grasp.

"She's the mystery lady from the tavern and appears to be a doctor or medic of some sort." He relaxed because she was not hurting Byron and the Voice told him to trust her.

The old man sputtered. "While I can't see her aura, she possesses a powerful magic like you." He kept shaking his head. "So does her friend. Where would it come from?"

"Her aura is light blue and her friend's is crimson." Pointing behind him, Stuart said, "The attacker hit him with something like what Vince used on me in the tavern. He needs help. We'd have been in big trouble without him."

Judyth grabbed her satchel and rushed over to Forecaster. He managed to sit up and shake his head as if trying to chase away cobwebs. After a quick examination, she said, "Can you help get him into my car?"

"We need to dispose of these slugs first." Byron staggered to the nearest figure. "Mirantso." The bloody-faced man opened his eyes. "Stuart has improved your appearance."

The only response was a plaintive groan that ended with a strangled sound as the man went limp. "Going, going, gone." The body turned to dust.

Byron held Stuart's arm as they headed for the next attacker. He groaned when Byron kicked him. "Amadeus. Attacking someone was rather brave for you."

Amadeus spat at Byron and tried to rise. The knee Stuart had kicked would not support any weight, and the man collapsed. Within a minute, his body also turned to dust.

The last attacker was still face down on the ground. Byron shook his head. "The Brotherhood certainly intended a most unpleasant demise for me. Instead it's the end of you, Jonast." As soon as he said the words, the body crumpled into dust.

"Taking care of business." Byron brushed his hands together as if finishing a tough job. He held onto Stuart's arm again as they walked back to Judyth.

"This is Forecaster and I'm Bones," she said. "While I could take him to my hospital, it'd raise too many questions. We'll transport him to my friend Diviner's home where he and other of our friends are staying. We can look after him there."

Stuart introduced Byron and himself. "What brought you here?"

"We felt malevolence in the storm that was tracking Byron. I've been following you for more than a week trying to understand your abilities. Then there were the events at the tavern, which increased my certainty that we needed to learn more about Stuart.

"While we're somewhat alike, you're able to accomplish far more than my friends or I can. While the Wizard has convinced you and me that your power is connected to magic, not all our friends have accepted that our abilities are. Forecaster and I would like Byron and you to talk with them."

Stuart wanted to know what she meant by the storm's malevolent feeling and how she knew Byron was a Wizard. He was still framing his questions when the old man said, "Do you mean there are more of you that have magical abilities or however you describe them. How can that be?"

"I'm hoping you could explain that. What we've learned about our abilities has been mostly through trial and error. Maybe you can help us understand what we're capable of. However, first we need to attend to Forecaster."

Stuart placed his arms around Forecaster from behind while Judyth tugged on his belt. "One, two, three up."

He stood slowly. "It was like the guy turned himself into a boulder as I jumped him. It almost knocked me out."

"The Brotherhood knows all sorts of damaging magic," Byron said. "It's unfortunate the fourth one escaped to tell the Brotherhood that I've found powerful protection."

They walked to the car supporting Forecaster and eased him into the back seat. Then Judyth handed Stuart the keys. She slid in beside Forecaster while giving directions to Diviner's home. Byron sat in the front passenger seat.

Once Judyth stopped tending to Forecaster, she recounted Stuart's appearances in her visions, following him to the tavern, and overhearing Byron telling Stuart about magic.

"The Book of Time makes no mention of other kinds of magic," Byron muttered. "I've always counted on it to explain everything connected to magic. Now I'm confronted with people who possess magical abilities that neither they nor I recognize."

Knowing Byron would become preoccupied in figuring out how other magical persons could exist, Stuart said, "Judyth, tell us about yourself."

"I'm a trauma surgeon at the Regional Hospital. Forecaster is here for an emergency gathering of The Realm."

"The what?" Stuart said.

"Impossible!" Byron sputtered. "The Realm has not existed for centuries. How would you have even learned about it? Few Wizards even know the history of The Realm."

"It's the name we chose for our group," Judyth said.

"No, somehow it was chosen for you." Byron kept running his hands through his hair or over his chin. Stuart had not seen him this flustered.

"When Wizards first emerged centuries ago, they called themselves Citizens of The Realm," Byron said. "The world was their domain, not the states and countries that rose and fell over the years. When kings and emperors tricked Wizards into becoming their advisors with promises of power and influence, The Realm fell apart and with it the powerful magic that linked the Wizards. The Brotherhood does not come close to what it was in terms of abilities or integrity."

Although Byron halted his description, Stuart could tell it was only a pause and held up his hand to forestall questions from Judyth to allow him to complete his explanation.

"There is nothing in The Book of Time or the legends about a rebirth of The Realm." Byron lay in the seat as if pushed down by a great weight.

"Pull into the next driveway on the left," Judyth said. When the car stopped, she hurried to open the other passenger door. "Can you move at all, Forecaster?"

He eased his legs out but could not stand. Stuart tugged him upright and Judyth took his other side as they shuffled toward the brick house.

Diviner, a tall, broad-shouldered red head, opened the front door and several men rushed to help with Forecaster. When he was inside, the other Realm members gathered around.

"He needs rest," Judyth said. "I've given him some painkillers. I'll tell you what happened after he's lying down."

While barely able to stand, Forecaster said, "Audubon was right. We've tapped into magic. You should've seen the old guy and his attackers shooting beams of light around and what he and Stuart did in the park."

When he slumped, Diviner said, "We'll put him on the pull out couch in the den." She led them to the room. Once Forecaster was comfortable, they returned to the others and Judyth recounted the fight.

"Jonast tried to kill Forecaster," Byron said. "Stuart disrupted him, so your friend wasn't hit full force. He'll be in considerable pain for a while. He'll feel like his innards have been singed." Byron scanned the living room. "Magic is a dangerous business."

Judyth flinched at his reference to magic and Stuart could tell by their scowls that her friends were not buying the magic connection to the fight.

"Are you two alright?" Judyth said. "Stuart was in a couple of nasty scraps."

Byron nodded. "I'll complain for a few days about my aches and pains. I've been through worse. I'm more concerned The Brotherhood will soon know where I am."

"Is Stuart in danger as well?"

"Without my presence, they probably wouldn't recognize him," Byron said. "However, he should be careful. Now is there some supper? I'm famished."

"Everyone brought something so it'll be a good spread," Diviner said.

JOINING FORCES

Diviner and a couple of others went to the kitchen and the clatter of plates and silverware could be heard as a buffet style supper was laid out. Meanwhile Stuart studied the newcomers in the living room. Their combined auras looked like a rainbow run amok.

His brain went into overload when Judyth introduced her friends by their Realm name and academic and professional achievements. Before he could ask her for a redo, Byron said, "Why are you all here?"

"For an emergency meeting on preserving the secret that is The Realm," Judyth said. "Stuart and you have abilities like ours and are in danger from the bad Wizards. That meant we could be threatened as well especially if Byron's enemies learn he's in Toronto and step up their efforts to kill him."

"Why would we be danger?" said Digger, a stocky man.

"Because it's magic that gives our abilities the boost needed to achieve all we are capable of." Judyth looked about waiting for the first doubter. "The Brotherhood would consider our magic and Stuart's to be an abomination and a challenge to their dominance. They would try to destroy all of us and wouldn't care how many people were killed or injured in the process."

Before they could question her, Diviner called everyone for supper. Byron made a beeline for the kitchen. "I've a nose for good food." He created an enormous sandwich from slices of ham and turkey topped with lettuce, tomatoes, and pickles. "Is there any beer?"

When Diviner nodded, the fridge door swung open and a can

floated across the room. "Just showing off to impress the ladies," he said with a flourish. "I take it none of you can do this? Anyone else want one?"

"Sure." Stuart held out his hand and a can of beer headed his way.

"Me too," Digger said. The looks of surprise on the faces of Judyth's friends told Stuart they had never even tried to move objects with their thoughts. They selected their food and headed to the dining room table in silence.

When they gathered at the table, Byron said, "There are more of you than seats." Chairs floated into the room from elsewhere in the house. Everyone stepped back until the chairs settled around the table.

Judyth finally joined them and smiled at Stuart. He returned it. This time, she did not look away.

When everyone remained silent, Stuart concluded no one wanted to speak out of fear of having to say something about magic.

"Would Byron be safe here?" Diviner finally said. "Perhaps he could help us with Forecaster?"

"He'd be better here than coming back to my place," Stuart said. "I'll take a taxi home and bring his clothes and books here tomorrow." He leaned toward Byron. "Can you see their auras now?"

"Sadly not," the Wizard muttered, gazing around. "Why is the magic hiding them from me?" His shoulders sagged.

"There are more like us in Europe and Asia," Judyth said.

"I still find it hard to accept the rebirth of The Realm because it's not mentioned in The Book of Time," Byron said.

"Could that be because the magic is protecting them from The Brotherhood?" Stuart said. Byron shrugged.

"Can Realm members see the colors each of you project?" Stuart said. By their puzzled expressions, no one understood his question. "Too bad. You all cast brightly-colored auras. It's the most incredible sight."

Judyth glanced about the room. "What do they look like?"

"You each have a predominant color and together you're like a vibrating rainbow. I can't tell whether you're like this all the time or if it's just because you're together."

"Sounds spectacular; maybe someday we'll see them." Judyth gave his arm a squeeze before heading off to check on Forecaster.

By the brilliance of their auras, the Realm members were confident and ready for new challenges. Their different abilities complemented each other. *Now I've a group of peers.*

When he finally accepted he could look into the inner workings of machines without touching them, a terrible dread came over him about what an odd character he had become. *How would I ever be able to explain my new abilities to anyone? People would see me as a freak. Even my own family and Uncle Oscar might consider me delusional or worse.*

An image of their perplexed expressions if he told them he was working with a 300-year-old Wizard flashed through his mind. He could not even begin to anticipate their reaction to the Realm members. A loud moan from Forecaster snapped Stuart out of his reverie. Diviner rushed from the room to assist Judyth. The other Realm members whispered among themselves.

Diviner returned. "Judyth gave him another pain killer."

"Obviously, Realm members go by nicknames," Stuart said. "Who calls their kid Forecaster, Quake or Audubon? Is it to protect your identity?"

An athletic-looking, brown haired man with an orange aura spoke. "I'm Audubon."

"The one who thought the group had linked into magic," Byron said. "But what's the name mean?"

"The original Audubon produced a famous book of bird paintings. Whenever I'm outside for any length of time, I attract lots of wildlife. In a park, I'm soon surrounded by squirrels, rabbits, raccoons and no end of birds. On hikes, bears and deer approach me like I'm a friend. Crows swirl around, cawing madly. After a while, I understand what they're attempting to tell me. While my ability is usually amusing, it can be annoying. However, my specialty is deep space astronomy."

"You're being modest," Quake said. "You've won all sorts of awards."

"Although our abilities bring us many benefits, there's an unusual element to them." He raised his voice over a sudden din around the house. "They've enabled enable us to expand our expertise immensely."

Startled by a crack of thunder, Diviner opened a window blind. "I've never seen a torrential downpour like this. It looks like a massive waterfall. There could be a lot of water in those black clouds."

Byron shot Stuart a gloomy look. Neither said a word.

A shorter, dark haired man with a brown aura said, "I'm Pied Piper. My specialty is quantum mechanics."

"You also have won international awards for your work," Diviner said.

His face reddened. "Everywhere I go outside a lab or classroom, young children approach me. They talk to me, laugh at anything I say, and follow me. It's like I'm always dressed in a clown suit. While it's usually funny, it can be disconcerting, especially if parents fear I'm a pervert. However older kids and adults don't see whatever it is that attracts youngsters." He shrugged.

Stuart thought from his high cheek bones, round face and black hair that Pied Piper might be at least part North American native. He had strong rose and green shades in his aura. *Perhaps young children react to his combination of colours.*

"I'm known as Bones because I'm a doctor," said Judyth, who had just returned to the room. "During surgery, I can see from all sides while I'm operating. I can often tell a person's medical condition without blood tests and X-rays. I refer to them as insights and always order tests to double-check my diagnosis. I can detect injuries and ailments by just looking at people.

"However, I can't turn that ability off. I spot people in restaurants and stores who have health problems, and need to resist telling them to see their doctor or hurry to the hospital. The downside occurs when I spend a lot of time with people and hear their thoughts. It's tricky talking with someone when you can hear what's in their mind as well as their words. Many times, they don't match up. I try to avoid family gatherings."

"Now I remember why you look familiar," Stuart said. "I saw you on television and in the newspapers. You saved those two cops when everyone thought they were goners."

"As they'd hung on until they reached the hospital; I knew they could survive. My insights showed me what do."

She hesitated and looked at the table. "Lately my power has grown in a different way. I can see the good and bad in people. No, that's not quite right; I'm still trying to understand what I see. Maybe it's something like the auras Stuart perceives."

Byron shook his head. "Are you all involved in science or research?"

The answer came in nods from around the room. "Where do your abilities come from? Are you from the same area or how did you meet?"

"Between 1980 and 2000, one or both of our parents worked in genetic research that was financed by a consortium of big corporations and governments," Judyth said. "The research was carried on in countries around the world looking for treatments to make people immune to most diseases and to correct genetic disorders that lead to mental illness and physical handicaps. The payback would've been reduced medical care and hospital costs, which were a big issue even then, and enabling people to live longer in better health.

"While doing the research, our parents developed a procedure for modifying our brains in the womb to enhance our resistance to diseases and infections. It was all hush-hush. No one kept track of who had modified their babies and our parents made no attempt to connect us with the others. They never told anyone about us."

"Mine said they figured we'd find the others eventually," Audubon said. "They feared the authorities would learn what they'd done and we'd be treated like freaks or worse. We were all child prodigies. It'd take hours to recite all our academic achievements, discoveries and inventions."

"None of you would have accepted that your abilities were connected to magic because there is no scientific basis for it," Byron said. Again heads nodded around the room.

"Except for Audubon," Stuart said. "You all make machines and technology function more effectively, and in the process discover ways to make them perform even better, just as I do. My parents aren't scientists and I've no idea how I developed magical powers."

"We've wondered about that as well," Judyth said. "From what we learned from your and Byron's discussions, we've debated whether our abilities could be linked to magic."

"You overheard us?" Stuart said.

"I eavesdropped on you. There's a transmitter hidden in the large plant in your front window. I put it in there the day after you met Byron."

"You broke into my place?"

Judyth nodded. "I apologize but it was that important to find out what you were up to. With all our accomplishments, we've received a great deal of attention. To make sure we remained a secret, we've worked hard to prevent that attention from turning into efforts to investigate us.

"While we don't think anyone knows about us or our skills, we needed to investigate to protect The Realm."

She explained that she had felt his pulse two weeks earlier and undertook to discover the source of it. "You used your abilities randomly, and I couldn't figure out what you were up to. By the way, did you notice I tidied up your apartment?"

Stuart blushed. "That's what happened. Your good deed only added to my fears I was losing my mind. I came home, and the place looked alright when I'd left it in a mess."

"Just alright?"

"A whole lot better." While he still felt angry about her entering his apartment, the Voice told him to remain calm.

"Please, Miss Bones, continue your explanation of how you found Stuart," Byron said. "That is the important factor."

"Once I could locate where his pulses were emanating from, I could receive visions of him. I never had an insight before about a perfectly healthy person. I saw Stuart working with machines and in his apartment. Although I'd no idea why I was seeing these images, I felt compelled to find out why."

"Magic was directing you to locate him. Your visions were it helping you. Its interest in you and Stuart puzzles me."

"Once we figured out Stuart's parents weren't involved in the baby modification experiments, I snooped on him to find out how he gained his abilities," Judyth said. "I followed him to the tavern that night because I wanted to meet him. But you got to him first."

"You've trailed us ever since?" Stuart said.

"Besides bugging the apartment, I attached a tracking device to your van so I didn't have to follow you all the time."

"What happened with your parents' research?" Byron said.

"Although they developed all sorts of new medical treatments, they didn't find the grand cure the governments and corporations hoped for. Still, their discoveries produced handsome returns in terms of new treatments and drugs. The investors were satisfied, and our parents were well recompensed and had a lifetime of scientific research opened to them.

"Meanwhile we learned quickly and were talented at music, math, and science. By the time we entered high school, our abilities were way beyond those of other kids."

"We found each other through an Internet forum for students who participated in science fairs," Diviner said. "Marconi, who lives in San Francisco, created a web site that featured science challenges to appeal to us and slowly she and Bones tracked us down. Our membership expanded a great deal when the Soviet Union collapsed and Russia and Eastern Europe opened up. While the parents of our members there worked with ours, they couldn't communicate for many years after the experiments ended."

"Our parents think we're just brainiacs," Forecaster said. "They aren't aware of the extent of our abilities. While it was unsettling for us at first, the more we used them, the better they worked."

"What did you think was the origin of your abilities?" Byron said.

"I postulated more than a year ago that we must have tapped into magic," Audubon said. "However, I couldn't explain how it might exist, how we became connected to it, or how we made it work for us. My friends laughed at my idea and came up with all sorts of alternate explanations, none of which are plausible. There's nothing else it could be although I doubt we've begun to understand the potential magic offers us to enhance our natural talents.

"When Judyth discovered what Stuart was capable of, it further convinced me magic had gifted us with technology sensory manipulation. She can extend the uses of medical equipment."

Byron sat in his chair. His hands shook and his face twitched like he was having a seizure. Diviner and Judyth pushed their chairs back. The first time Byron did that in the van, Stuart headed for the hospital until he snapped out of it with a profuse apology. "I forgot how my body reacts when I receive an insight from the magic.

"For more than three centuries, magic has been a constant in my life, always there when I call on it. What I need to find out is if your completely different abilities are a recent evolution in magic or a side of it no one could tap into until you came along."

"Maybe we should call it Magic 2.0," Forecaster said.

"I'll explain that reference later," Stuart whispered to Byron.

"The scientific community isn't open to anything that can't be proven," Audubon said. "It argues about the validity of evidence that it's presented with. What Bones learned from you and Stuart is very gratifying to me."

When the others around the room tried to join the conversation, Diviner held up her hand to quiet everyone. "You asked about our Realm names. We were entering university or finishing high school when the terrorist attacks began around the world and security went way up.

"Government agents combed the Internet looking for suspicious messages, so we coined the names to protect our identity. We needed to be careful, yet we carried on attempting to expand our abilities. Although we face lots of professional jealousy because of our successes, no one says there's anything unusual about what we do."

"For some of us, our abilities have a potentially dangerous side," Judyth said. "Tracker can find anyone in the world. If she has a photo of the person, she can search everywhere and sooner or later, she finds them."

"I tip off the authorities to the location of missing kids, stuff like that," said a demure-looking black woman who exuded a violet aura. "I won't help kill people."

A slight smile creased Byron's face. "It's most remarkable you learned as much as you did without anyone to instruct you. Every Wizard I know or have heard of was trained by an older one, and in most cases, several of them. Even with that supervision, many got into trouble with the authorities while testing their magic."

"Our academic and professional activities are important because we meet each other regularly at conferences, which allows us to share our experiences," Tracker said. "We found new members at some of them. None of us have run afoul of the law or have police records."

"However, some couldn't cope with their abilities," Diviner said. "A few committed suicide while others are under psychiatric care. We still hope to help them recognize their powers are not to be feared."

"Mental balance has always been difficult for Wizards," Byron said. "While magic enables one to perform great feats, it magnifies any character weaknesses. Over time, it can exact a heavy price on the sanity of a Wizard, especially if he or she deviates from our proper role as the protector of knowledge. This makes your accomplishments all the more significant."

"Are you saying the Brotherhood leaders are unbalanced?" Diviner said.

He nodded. "If other Wizards challenge them, their sanity is called into question to silence them."

"A magical smear job," Audubon said.

"Wizards without scruples are always a problem," Byron said. "Usually they're driven by a desire for riches and power. The Brotherhood will not like you. If they discover your existence . . . " He pushed back from the table without completing the sentence. "I lack the words to describe how exciting it is at my age to see so many young men and women full of magical potential and abilities beyond anything I ever imagined."

The Wizard stepped to Judyth with his right hand extended. When she took it, he put his left hand over it and peered into her eyes. Without speaking, he repeated the gesture with the other Realm members. He returned to his seat and took a long drink of beer. "While you've gained considerable magical proficiency, you're capable of much more."

"Our European and Russian members detect occasional pulses similar to ours," Audubon said. "However they've never been able to track down the source. Could that be your Wizards, Byron?"

"Most likely."

"Judyth explained your fear the Wizards will attempt to create a massive disaster," Audubon said. "Would it be comparable to the Toba super-eruption as Diviner has suggested?"

Byron looked at him blankly.

Diviner explained how a repeat of the massive eruption would be traumatic for Earth in its stressed condition.

"It's highly unlikely the Brotherhood would know anything about its potential for devastating the world," Byron said. "Our interest has focused on what we can accomplish with our magical powers and not what the planet is capable of on its own. From your description, a super-eruption would be as devastating for Wizards as anyone else but you'd never be able to convince The Brotherhood of that. We know of earthquakes and severe storms from experience but not super-eruptions. Obviously we need to ensure The Brotherhood doesn't blunder into causing something like that."

AN UNINVITED GUEST

Audubon rested his elbows on Diviner's dining room table. "Can you and the other Dissidents train us to protect ourselves from The Brotherhood?"

"Forecaster hit that Wizard assassin with a solid tackle today," Stuart said. His arm felt stiff as he glanced at his watch. He would be sore and stiff tomorrow. "I couldn't have handled them without his help."

"Until now, we lacked a way to stop The Brotherhood," Byron said. "Even now, our only choice is a desperate one — using Stuart to destroy them." He paused. "We don't wish for any more violence in the world either."

"Who has to be eliminated?" Quake said.

"Merstreem is the leader of The Brotherhood with the support of a handful of Wizards. They're ruthless and have mastered the most dangerous forms of magic. The world won't be safe until this group is stopped. I hope the other Wizards will side with us if they can be shown what's happening."

Judyth returned from checking Forecaster's condition. "He's in less pain. Is there some way we could convince The Brotherhood to cease disrupting the planet?"

"They wouldn't listen to you. If they learn you exist, they'd try to kill you just as they're trying to eliminate me. Think of them as a disease or parasite. Would you pass up a chance to rid the world of a deadly infestation? They're really no better." Byron pounded the table with his fist.

People fidgeted with knives and forks. While their unease was clear, no one spoke.

"I assume you all agree with Bones?" Byron said.

Stuart leaned toward him. "All they've ever done is work to perfect their abilities. They want to use them to improve the world, not kill people, even really evil ones. They need to understand the gravity of the threat posed by The Brotherhood and our lack of other ways to stop them."

Byron stroked his chin. "The only alternative is to smother earthquakes, plug volcanos and drown massive wildfires. That would require a lot of work by all The Realm, not just the ones in this room."

"How do we gain the support of the Wizards who aren't followers of Merstreem?" Audubon said.

"If they'd meet Stuart, he could demonstrate the changes in magic. Hopefully he'd make them want to find out how the Realm members acquired and employ their powers."

"Don't they care about the damage and suffering The Brotherhood is causing?" Judyth snapped.

"They're most likely unaware of it," Byron said. "They pay little attention to what happens in the modern world."

"What happened to Forecaster makes it personal for us," Audubon said. "Where do we begin?"

"First you need to make a commitment because this battle won't be for the faint of heart." Byron looked around the room. "Are you all prepared to participate?"

Everyone, but Quake and Tracker, agreed right away. Quake sat chewing on her bottom lip while the others watched. "I can go along with this, but no killing."

"Me too," Tracker piped in.

"There are many ways you can help without killing anyone," Byron said. "First, we should assume Merstreem will redouble his efforts to hunt me down because I've found protection as I'm no match for their teams of assassins."

He fixed the Realm members with a hard stare. "I've no idea what they might try next to get rid of me. The important matter right now is that you know who you're up against. If you'll excuse me, I need to take a short trip to acquire the necessary information."

Byron stood, stepped away from the table and vanished.

"If that's not magic folks then I don't know what is!" Audubon said. "Now I feel vindicated for my insistence that we're connected to it."

"He's got me attempting the disappearing act," Stuart said. "It's about making other people not see you. I presume he's gone to his refuge and will return shortly. Anyone want a beer or glass of wine?"

After a quick count of the raised hands, cans of beer and a bottle of wine and glasses floated from the kitchen to the table welcomed with delighted laughs. After everyone had a drink, Audubon said, "Where's Byron's refuge?"

Stuart shrugged. "The Otherworld. He says it's of this world but separate from it, whatever that means. His enemies can't find him there. He doesn't like the place. When he returns, he'll appear just like that." Stuart snapped his fingers.

"Do you have any ideas on how we could thwart the bad guys?" Audubon said.

Stuart managed to say he did not know enough about The Realm or Wizards to answer the question when Byron re-appeared. He was breathing deeply and carrying a sack of clothes and several hefty looking books. He draped his clothes over the back of a chair and placed the books on the table.

"There are sketches of all the Wizards in these tomes," he said. "Tracker and anyone else who can search should study them, and then try to find where they are located. I can translate the words."

He paused to look about the room. "I may have been followed."

To counter an eerie fear filling the room, Stuart said, "We need to protect ourselves while we search for a way to contact the other Wizards."

"Tomorrow bring the gym bag with all the money," Byron said. "While you all are disgusted by the filthy lucre, none of you are wealthy enough to pay for the groceries and other supplies this group will require. If we didn't need it to deal with the Wizards, I'd have left it for the police." He walked to the bottom of the stairs.

While Several Realm members spoke against using the money because of its tainted origin. Stuart cut them off. "Remember what they did to Forecaster. We aren't dealing with a situation that's in any way normal. These people want to destroy our world. We'll put the money in a drawer to use as needed."

"Do the Wizards live together?" Diviner said. Stuart smiled at her for shifting the topic.

"Mostly they are content on their own," Byron said without moving away from the stairs. "They live in individual enclaves in Europe and the Urals, wrapped in magic so no one but Wizards can find them. I know the location of a few."

"Quiet," snapped Tracker. "There's another presence in the room."

"Very good! Very good!" Byron clapped his hands and bowed to her. "I wondered if anyone would perceive it."

Looking up the stairs, he spoke in Wizardese, and then in English. "Perhaps, young lady, you'd reveal yourself. She was following me today."

Quake pointed to a shimmering mass of energy on the staircase. It brightened forcing everyone to shade their eyes. A plaintiff wail filled the room.

"Of course," Byron grunted. "Stuart, approach the ball of light and hold out your arm." When he did, a pair of pale hands seized it. "Pull gently."

Stuart eased his arm away from the glow. Out of the brilliant speckles of light came an arm, and then the rest of the Waif from his visions. Startled by her presence, he sputtered to Byron, "Why didn't you say it was her?"

Byron shook his head. "I could only tell a few minutes ago that someone was projecting into the room. It didn't occur to me it could be her. I moved to the stairs in case it was another assassin. If it was, he'd have appeared right away to attack us. I couldn't tell it who it was or why they stayed there."

"Where's she from and why didn't she appear to me like before?" Stuart said.

"This is the first time I could sense her presence, which meant she wanted me to notice her. She needed your help to complete the transfer to here, and without me, you'd not understand her."

The woman had a mass of unkempt black hair and wore a white lace blouse, an elaborately beaded blue jacket and a long black skirt. Her eyes darted about the room while she held tightly to Stuart's arm as if he might slip away.

They descended the stairs one step at a time. By the time they reached the bottom, her grip relaxed. She was slender and the top of her head came to about his shoulder. While gaunt, she was not the wisp he imagined from the visions. He walked her to the table.

Audubon pointed to his chair for her. "I'll get another."

The woman spoke in a gusher of words, her voice sounding increasingly frantic.

"Stuart, I need you to stand where she appeared," Byron said. "If anyone is following her, it'll be by magic and you can deal with them."

After Stuart climbed the stairs, Byron bowed to the newcomer. "Our visitor is Anastasia de la Montagne. She's your age and the first in her family in many generations to develop magical powers. When The Brotherhood discovered her abilities, they abducted her and confined her in the enclave of a powerful Wizard."

Byron paced the room as he recounted her tale. "They made no attempt to figure out the origin or extent of her powers. It was a stupid oversight on their part. That should have been their priority, but they refuse to acknowledge any sign that magic is changing. They threatened to kill her even though she's a direct descendent of a prominent former member of The Brotherhood."

When Audubon sat beside her, she placed her right hand on his arm. She gazed at the Realm members with a broad smile. "Hello."

"Once she knew where we were, she used her mental strength to project herself here from southern France," Byron said. "Few if any Wizards could do that."

The Realm members looked at each other. "How would you wrap yourself in a ball of energy and project yourself thousands of kilometers to an exact location?" Audubon said. "Think what you could do with that ability. Could this be used by anyone with magical powers?"

"This is the first time I've heard of such a method of transportation. That she found and tracked Stuart from across the Atlantic shows how powerful she is. Like all of you, she's capable of much more. Stuart's immunity to Wizard magic meant he could help her when the rest of you'd be harmed by the power of the Wizard restraints she broke when she held Stuart's arm to pull herself out of the energy ball."

"If she found us, the Brotherhood leaders can't be far behind,"

Audubon said. "We need another location."

Anastasia's voice rose and fell as she spoke to Byron. She waved her left hand about while her right kept a firm grip on Audubon.

After a few minutes, Byron said, "She realized Stuart possessed special abilities and wanted to warn him about the assassins. She suspected they pursued him with my help. She was surprised when I left you to enter the Otherworld and returned."

The woman yelled at him before switching to halting English. "Tell everything," she said angrily. "Leave nothing out. Must know truth."

"She feared Merstreem was far enough along in his plans that he'd finally kill her so she reached out to Stuart in desperation. She waited on the stairs before revealing herself because she couldn't tell who the rest of you are and why he was willingly here with me and all of you."

"How could she learn all this while locked away?" Audubon asked. "Although I believe in magic, I'm stunned by its enormous power."

The words exploded out of Anastasia. Her face turned red as she shrieked at Byron.

"She used a lot of very un-lady like words to describe her jailors. To paraphrase, her body was imprisoned, but not her mind." Byron tapped his head for emphasis. "She used her magic to learn as much as she could about Merstreem's plans."

He sighed. "She agrees he wants to create a major disaster and is even more convinced than I that The Brotherhood won't be able to control it and the result could wipe out humanity."

Silence descended upon the room as everyone looked about bewildered. "She was imprisoned for a couple of years," Byron said.

"That explains why she's so pale and thin." Judyth said. "I'll give her a checkup."

Anastasia looked at Judyth before speaking to Byron.

"While she recognizes most of your words, she does not understand the full meaning of what you're saying," he said. "While she doubts the Wizards can follow her, she fears they'll try to pull her back. She needs one of you to stay close to her. If she feels a tug, she can hold onto you."

"Sounds like a tough job." Audubon said with a chuckle. She beamed, and then leaned against him. When he put his arm around her, she snuggled against him.

Stuart could sense her magic sweeping through the house assessing the Realm members.

"She wants to learn how your magic works," Byron said. "She knows a great deal about The Brotherhood and will help us find their enclaves." He paused. "I'm sure The Realm has room for another member."

"I study English un peu." Anastasia used her finger to show a small bit. "Not speak much before."

Diviner approached Anastasia. "We'll get her hair cut and update her wardrobe and she can be my friend visiting from Hungary. When I'm done with her, the Wizards won't recognize her."

Anastasia nodded and patted her stomach. "J'ai faim—hungry." Diviner led her to the kitchen and set out bread and fixings for sandwiches. Anastasia carefully looked over the sliced meats and veggies before tasting them.

Byron followed with a handful of cash. "Take what you require for her new clothes and a haircut." Diviner hesitated, but finally accepting the severity of the situation, stuffed the money into her purse.

Audubon circulated among the Realm members speaking to each one briefly. "A lot of us have academic or other commitments that we can't just drop. We need to carry on normally so we don't attract unwanted attention. We also have access to the best computers and IT systems so we may be able to help in other ways. But we agree that it's time for The Realm to take on The Brotherhood. We need to figure out the smartest way to do it."

Stuart wondered how he would explain his absence to his customers if he followed Byron on a campaign to stop the Brotherhood. That train of thought ground to a halt when the reality of the situation hit him. *If there's no world left, then my customers are really a moot point. I've no alternative.*

Tracker walked across the room before halting several paces from the TV. Stuart could feel her probing it. *Is that what I do?* The TV flickered to life. She winked at him.

"That was easy; I never thought to try it. With technology, I just have to imagine it working the way I want."

She glanced at the kitchen. A radio came to life and the microwave hummed. "This really is living better electrically." After glancing about as if looking for other candidates to test her magic on, she stepped to the closest window. "Look at all the vehicles around here." A cacophony of shrieking car alarms erupted.

The Realm members chuckled at first. "Cut it out," Judyth said. "You'll wake Forecaster." The honking stopped.

Tracker turned and faced the others, her face completely expressionless. A hint of a smile rippled from the corners of her mouth. "You must have a lot of fun, Stuart. You could help me develop my mischief repertoire or maybe we can go into business together?"

"Perhaps I should take lessons from you."

"This is no game," Byron said. "However, you've given me ideas for our plan. First, we need to find out how many of you are available immediately for full time duty. Secondly, we need to arrange the rest into teams and assign them tasks that will help us locate the Wizard enclaves. They could also determine what kind of trouble individual Brotherhood members are causing that we could interfere with or even stop."

Diviner took her laptop to the kitchen table to compose a message. Anastasia watched her and smiled as letters appeared on the computer screen. Then, moving her fingers like someone typing, she whispered, "Want learn."

Diviner nodded and motioned for her to come closer. "Hey Byron look. Notice how her magic doesn't interfere with the computer."

Anastasia beamed and pointed at herself. "Can use machines?" When Diviner nodded, Anastasia hugged her.

"So here's my message," Diviner said. "What do you think? To all members of Rational Environment and Land Management. The society has received a major research grant to look into different forms of human contribution to climate change. The work has to begin immediately so we need to know who's available for full time involvement and who can offer back-up assistance. Travel is likely and the grant will cover all your costs and pay a healthy per diem. We'll have expert assistance in this situation. Please reply ASAP to the Secretariat."

When no one objected, she hit the send button. "I usually hear back from everyone within 12 hours after Marconi sends the message to the entire Realm. If someone is out of reach, Tracker can find them."

"Alright, we begin here tomorrow morning with those who are available," Byron said. "I need a good sleep to restore my powers before we start planning. Those who are unable to work directly on the project could tell Judyth how they can assist and if they'd be available later on. Anastasia will also stay here tonight."

Looking about the room, he beamed. "I read this once and always wanted to say it. The game is afoot. Now my young friends, I need a bed for my weary body."

THE OTHERWORLD REVEALED

Winds from the storm created by the Brotherhood gained strength overnight. Alarmed by the racket, Stuart opened his window blind. The security lighting was bright enough to show large splashes in the puddles that dotted the yard behind his apartment building. The hail was bigger than golf balls and would do serious damage to vehicles left outside. Thankfully, his van was in the garage.

In the morning, the radio tuned into the all-news station as soon as he thought about what problems the rain and hail might cause following weeks of drought. "The city has issued a state of emergency because of the severe risk of flooding. The hail storm seems to have been localized in a 27 block area west of downtown. Insurance adjusters will surely be busy in that district today."

Peering out his window, Stuart saw no suspicious characters lurking about. He walked briskly to the van carrying Byron's belongings including the gym bag with the money. The windshield wipers could hardly keep up with the pelting rain forcing him to drive slowly. At least, there were no pedestrians to worry about splashing.

About a kilometer from his apartment building, the broken windows and dented metal ended and the torrent of rain diminished to a drizzle. *My neighborhood was targeted. I'll have to watch for strangers when I return home tonight.*

As he drove, Stuart recalled the conversation of the previous evening. The main question for him was if the Wizards were so powerful, why did they only create a hailstorm? While it caused a lot of damage, Byron could have prevented it from causing him any personal harm. *Perhaps they were only sending a message or hesitating for some reason. Maybe it's the best they could manage on short notice or they're too engaged in their big plan to do much else.*

Watching for anyone who might be following him, Stuart drove a circuitous route to Diviner's house. In the daylight, its modest size and bland appearance on a nondescript street surprised him. Everyone in The Realm worked hard at being inconspicuous. He decided to park part way down the block.

He spotted Judyth's car as he walked to the bungalow. She opened the front door before he reached it and hugged him tightly.

Caught off guard by the embrace, Stuart was slow in returning it. When he did, he received a rush of energy from Judyth. They rocked gently back and forth. He did not want to spoil the mood by asking how she sent this infusion cascading through him. He could use a hug like this once or twice a day at least.

Finally they let go and Judyth took his arm. "Forecaster any better?" he said.

"Still sleeping but not groaning so much. We'll keep him on painkillers for a few more days." Inside, she pointed to a tall brown haired man with a handle-bar mustache. "Ears arrived late last night from Cleveland."

"Does Ears have to do with underground sensing?" Stuart said.

"You're figuring us out. Diviner left early with Anastasia," she said. "The others are attempting to arrange holidays or time off. Audubon will return by mid-afternoon. By tonight, we'll have a list of who's able to start working right away."

Byron entered the living room with two steaming mugs. When Stuart explained about the hail, Byron cackled. "Not very smart telling me they thought they knew where I was. Still they might send another team of assassins so we need to keep watching the Otherworld. We could use Anastasia to do that, but we can't leave her alone as that place is not safe for anyone, even Wizards."

"Maybe The Realm could monitor it for us from here," Stuart said. "Ears, what is the range of your sensors?"

"Depends on where you're going."

"While the Wizards call it the Otherworld, I don't know what or where it is. We should monitor it so The Brotherhood can't sneak up on us."

"I recall one of the Dissidents calling it another dimension," Byron said. "Whatever that means."

"If someone is heading there, he or she could carry a tracking device, which should tell us where the Otherworld is," Ears said. "I don't know any other way to find it."

"I'll go there when you're ready because I need more items from my refuge," Byron said.

Ears rubbed his hands together. "I'll be right back."

As he left the house, Judyth said, "We've members who can extend remote sensing and other technologies to examine under the Earth's crust. They've been searching for the cause of the natural disasters. Could they look for any geological disruptions the Wizards are causing? Would that help us locate the Otherworld or the enclaves?"

Byron smiled. "I don't know the answer to either question. Could there be any harm in attempting what you suggest?"

"None that I can imagine."

"Let's do it."

"Did you come here through the Otherworld?" Judyth said.

Byron laughed. "This time, I flew on an airplane from England. I cast an image that made everyone see me as they wanted to rather than an oddly-dressed old man. It was exhausting and I feared falling asleep and revealing my real self. At the same time, I was excited because I was flying for the first time. I controlled my magic enough to not disrupt the plane although the little TVs around my seat didn't work.

"I last visited North America in the 1880s. Came by ship to Halifax to see what all the excitement connected to the New World was about and sailed back to England three months later from New York. While I always meant to come again, I never found the time."

"The centuries just fly by," Judyth said with a big grin.

Ears reappeared with a bulky pack on his back and holding a small monitor and what looked like a ski pole with a small box mounted on it. "This is the beta version of my portable sensor system. I've a manufacturer and distributors lined up for a commercial version.

I'll make the advanced model for Realm members myself."

He held out a shiny metal box with a strap attached to it. "This locator has a built in camera so we can see the terrain where the person or machine carrying it is passing through."

"I assume you aim your device at whatever you wish to analyze, and then flow your power through it to enhance your views of it," Byron said.

Ears grinned. "That's how it works. We'll go outside to demonstrate it. I'll give you an underground tour so you can see what's beneath the surface around here."

"The back porch is covered, which will protect us from the rain," Judyth said. She led them through the house. Ears leaned over the railing and jammed the tip of the pole into the muddy ground. He placed the monitor on a chair.

A cursor appeared on its display screen, which marked the passage of its beam through layers of dirt and rock below the house. When it encountered a large dark area, Ears said, "You need to use this instrument a lot to recognize what you're seeing. This is an underground water reservoir.

"I'll check it out some other day. For now let's see what's below it." Thick strata of rock lay under the water. "That's far enough."

He glanced at Byron. "Ready to head for the Otherworld?"

When Byron nodded, Ears hung the strap of the locator unit around his neck. "Keep the yellow side facing away from you so the camera will function." He ran a diagnostics check, and then flashed thumbs up. He set the processor on a chair beside the monitor so he could hold the pole in the ground while watching the display.

"Byron, if I can track you into your Otherworld, then the sensor system will learn how to find it at any time and I'll gain a much better idea of its range."

The old man stepped off the porch and disappeared.

"Why didn't he just vanish from the porch like he did inside the house," Judyth said.

"He's a bit of a showboat." Stuart stood beside Ears watching the monitor.

"I'll be back after I check on Forecaster." Judyth gave Stuart's hand a squeeze.

"The signal is strong enough that we should be getting a visual,"

Ears said. "Oh, here we go."

The display showed a lot of fuzzy static, and then there was a bouncing image of barren landscape. Ears slapped his forehead with his empty left hand. "While I don't know how to explain its existence, I can't think of a better term than another dimension. In essence it occupies the same space as Earth. When you think about all we've learned about Earth's interior and our solar system, we should've spotted it before. As the old guy said, it's like Earth but not part of it."

"Ears, who'd look for this other dimension without any reason to believe that it was there?" Stuart said.

Ears grinned. "My sensor system machine performs even better than I hoped for."

When Judyth returned, she stared at the monitor. "While the terrain appears bleak, the sun sure is bright. It reminds me of foothills country."

Byron placed the locator unit on a large boulder and walked to a rock wall. With a wave of his arms, a slab of stone swung open. "Look how thick it is," she said. The Wizard stepped into his refuge. He emerged a few minutes later and closed the entrance. He hung the video tracker around his neck again and began walking. Within a minute, the monitor went fuzzy.

"He must be in the transit phase," Ears said. "He's moving too fast for the locator unit to determine his position."

Clutching a sack, Byron popped into view on the lawn and hurried onto the porch. "Did it work?"

"Let me replay the video for you," Ears said.

"My refuge is in a rocky area with little vegetation, which means nothing can hide from me," Byron said. "I waved my arms before opening the entrance to test how much detail your device could reveal."

Stuart smiled instead of saying anything about Byron's feeble excuse for showing off.

When the video of the Wizard's jaunt ended, Ears said, "Byron, with your permission, I'd like to use mini aircraft called drones to overfly the Otherworld to find out what's there. They're solar powered and would set down at night in a safe place. In time, we could map the whole area."

Byron looked dumbfounded.

"It's okay," Stuart said. "It's an unobtrusive way to find out just what the Otherworld is. If it really is another dimension, we must keep it secret."

"Yes, you have my permission," Byron said. "How will you get them there?"

"I'll have to acquire them first and figure out how to program them to report their findings to us."

"We'd be better protected if we could monitor the Otherworld feed 24-7," Stuart said.

"Bethune could do that," Judyth said. "Program your system to report to Bethune and explain to it what's required." She pulled out her cell. Bethune answered before the first ring ended. "Ears has an interesting task for you in connection with Byron's refuge." She passed the phone to Ears.

After a few minutes of exchanging technical details with the A.I., Ears said, "It'll be good to know in detail how the Otherworld compares to our dimension. Byron goes there so obviously the air is breathable and the plant life looks similar to what we have. In addition to Bethune, I'll link the radio signals from the drones to a hi-def. monitor here so we can watch the Otherworld on it. The drones' software should keep them recording in a pattern that provides just enough overlap for complete mapping." He passed the phone back to Judyth.

"I can manage the feeds from the drones while watching the Otherworld for anyone or anything that might pose a threat to us," Bethune said. "I'll be the explorer in a box."

Ears peered at Byron. "Bethune's system would be better at detecting movement if we could set up surveillance transmitter beacons there. I've some in the truck. Can you place them in the Otherworld as well as launch the drones, Byron?"

The Wizard did not answer as he studied a shiny box he pulled from a pocket. "This is for you, Bones. It was given to me a couple of centuries ago, and it's time to pass it on. It absorbs light during the day and radiates it at night."

"The original solar lamp," Stuart said.

Beaming, Judyth turned it over in her hands. It glittered in the sun light. "This is a real treasure. Thank you." She placed it in a west-facing window.

"When we get the surveillance beacons and drones there and in operation, we'll have our backs covered as far as the Otherworld is concerned," Stuart said. "Byron can't take them because his magic interferes with the technology. We'll have to ask for a volunteer to transport them."

Attracted by the conversation and Bethune's voice, other Realm members gathered and asked Ears to replay the video of Byron's visit to the Otherworld.

Judyth eased Stuart and Byron away from them. "Any ideas on how the magic would have placed Stuart into my insights?"

Byron stared intently at the floor before looking at her. "All I can offer is conjecture. Your visions and ability to hear conversations at a considerable distance means you possess a special receptivity to mental projections.

"The magic would have recognized your power. At the same time, Stuart was looking for an explanation for his new abilities with machines. Probably his agitation made him project his thoughts and the magic directed them to you as visions. Once it realized you found him attractive, it sent more of them to encourage you to find him. We need to find out why it would do that."

Judyth blushed as her friends had overheard most of the Wizard's comments. "Maybe, I can say we met through online dating. However, if magic has intelligence like that, it must be alive?"

"Magic is not life like us," Byron said. "It learns and can comprehend human emotions and desires. However, it doesn't possess a shape that we can see and it can only influence us, not force us to do anything."

"We told her the dreams kept returning because of her infatuation with Stuart," Ears said. "Her denials didn't fool us. Our code word for Stuart is the boyfriend. We enjoyed teasing her because she usually scares men away."

Byron extracted a notepad from a jacket pocket. "I need to understand everyone's abilities so I can attempt to understand how they'd interact with magic. Then we can decide how those abilities could be most effective at disrupting The Brotherhood."

Wizards usually can detect magic in other people, often from a great distance. However, Stuart never noticed magic being used around him by Judyth or me. Wizards would only recognize Stuart possesses magical abilities if they stood right beside him. However they wouldn't understand what he's capable of doing.

"Most of you have possessed your abilities long enough to have accepted them. Stuart is a newcomer to magic and is still discovering his. If we hadn't found him, he probably would become mentally unstable. What did you call it, Stuart?"

"A nutbar. Complete loon. Crazy."

The discussion of Stuart's mental state ended as the front door swung open and Diviner called out, "We're back." She pulled Anastasia into the living room. "Think they'll recognize her now? She attracted a lot of stares on the way back here. The lady at the hair salon put some makeup on her. She also gave me a bit of a redo. So what do guys think?"

Anastasia's long, ragged black curls were shaped to match her narrow face and highlighted with streaks of bright blue. Her heavy dress and shawls had been replaced by dark slacks, a peach-colored blouse and jacket. She blushed deeply when everyone stared at her.

She glanced at Diviner and spoke hesitantly. "Merci, It good 'ave friends." Her smile slipped when she looked around the room.

"You look smashing," Judyth said. "Audubon will be back in a couple of hours. Don't worry Anastasia, we'll protect you."

While Anastasia nodded and smiled, she appeared on the edge of tears. She gave Stuart a tentative embrace and Byron a hug fit for a grandfather.

"From our examination, Anastasia's health is fine although I'd recommend inoculations against everything from whooping cough to the influenzas floating around," Judyth said. "However maybe she doesn't need them because of her magic although all of us received them as kids. How about you Stuart?"

He nodded. "I keep all my inoculations up to date for my travel assignments."

"Anastasia's biggest problem is that her confinement created an obsession to be attached to someone who can protect her," Diviner said. "Audubon makes her feel safe and important. She needs to learn that possessive won't work with him. Although Anastasia knows a lot of English words, she isn't comfortable speaking it at length. She says most Wizards understand English. Why's that when most don't live in England?"

Byron looked about the room. "You know of Sir Francis Bacon?"

"The English philosopher," Tracker said first.

Byron nodded. "His writings remain a major source of fascination to Wizards. Many thought he was one of us who had been seduced by the power of science. Many of us have studied his works in hopes of finding how science supplanted magic for most people." He sighed. "Those debates will likely be turned upside down when the Wizards learn of Stuart and The Realm."

"So did he write Shakespeare's plays?" Judyth said. "There's a lot of conjecture about that."

Byron laughed. "No, William had lots of help but not from Francis so we didn't develop an interest in him. You lot are worse than Wizards when it comes to getting distracted by intellectual curiosities. We need to save the world. We can discuss the oddities over a few beers once we succeed."

"Pardon us if we don't act gravely enough." Ears glared at Byron. "The world has been under one dire threat or another all our lives. We've heard so many warnings of impending doom that we're all jaded. We understand from our scientific training how serious the climate degradation is and that the damage the Wizards are causing is exacerbating it. We just lighten up now and then. We know it's time for us to act. We'll rock The Brotherhood when you show us where they are."

EXCURSION TO THE OTHERWORLD

Byron's stern expression melted. "Alright then, let's get on with it. First we need a map of Europe on which Anastasia can pinpoint the location of Wizard enclaves she knows about. Then I'll add the ones I'm aware of."

"We'll download a map from the Internet," Judyth said. "I must go to the hospital in a couple of hours, but before that I'll buy some groceries. All this magic work will make for hungry people."

After she departed, Byron and Anastasia sat at the kitchen table marking colored dots on the map. By the time Judyth returned with bags of groceries, the map of Europe was covered in colored dots with names printed beside them. "The red dots are for unfriendly enclaves, white for ones we can safely approach and blue for unconfirmed locations," Byron said.

To Stuart, the whites outnumbered the reds about three to one even though only Byron and the Dissidents opposed the Brotherhood leaders.

Judyth put bags on the counter and stared at the map before heading for the door to collect more groceries.

"Hold on," Stuart called. "Diviner has an alternate location for us that could be more suitable than here."

"My aunt and uncle aren't using their country place because she's sick," Diviner said. "The Wizards won't find us there right away. All we need to do is tell the farmer who rents the land that we're moving in and no one should trouble us. There are woods and fields so we'll have plenty of room for testing our abilities."

"We'll move everyone on the A team out there and use this place as headquarters for the B team," Stuart said.

"A-team, B-team means what?" Judyth said.

"A is for active; B for backup or the members who can't get time off work," Stuart said. "We should prepare for a long-term campaign against The Brotherhood."

"Is anyone staying here or should I put the groceries back in the car?"

"For now, Ears and a couple of others will remain here to work on getting the drones into the Otherworld and acquiring other equipment we'll need," Diviner said. "Plus other members are coming here. However the rest of us will move to the farm. We might as well unload these groceries and buy more for the farm."

Realm members went with Judyth to collect the remaining bags. When they returned, the kitchen became too noisy to continue preparing scenarios for approaching the enclaves. Ears took a photo of the marked up map to transmit to Bethune.

"We want to unpack with magic, but we can't make anything happen," Diviner said.

"Just think about where you want the individual items to go and imagine them floating there," Stuart said.

"That's what we did," Tracker said. "Can you?"

The fridge and cupboard doors popped open. "Where would you like everything, Diviner?" Stuart said.

"Milk in the fridge, soup in the second cupboard, bag of corn in the freezer." As she spoke, juice and butter landed safely in the fridge. The bread and buns shot to a basket beside the fridge. As tins and cartons headed to the cupboards, Stuart made them sway from side-to-side like they were marching, drawing applause from around the room.

Byron and Anastasia stared at him open mouthed.

In the midst of the mirth, Judyth pointed to a large pot on the stove. "Is it Digger stew?"

"Yes," several people said at once.

She gave him a one-arm hug. "Sometimes Digger, I think you're the most useful Realm member. He can turn a fridge of leftovers into a meal fit for royalty."

"Ah Bones, you're gonna make a grown man blush." Digger laughed heartily.

"Since you really love food Byron, I know you'll enjoy his cooking."

Everyone dug into the lunch for which Byron added his profuse praise. It was decided the A team would move to the country that afternoon. Then Audubon arrived and Anastasia latched onto him.

"Maybe we should call the A team the Farm Team," Stuart said. While the Realm members groaned, Byron looked at him quizzically. "It's a sports term. While I'll spend as much time as I can out there, I've some big customers to look after. Like the B teamers, I'll review what technology I can access to use against The Brotherhood. Even if they're aware of satellite-imaging technology, blocking the signals will create interference that will . . . "

The Realm members pulled out their phones. Their different ring tones sounded like an orchestra warming up for a performance.

"Major earthquakes have occurred in Nigeria and Thailand, almost at the same time." Diviner held her screen toward Stuart and Byron. "The death toll in both events is expected to be high. We've programmed our phones to alert us to news of any disaster."

"Merstreem has stepped up his campaign of terror," Byron said.

"Have to do something!" Anastasia growled through clenched teeth. She balled up her fists like she wanted to punch someone. "They use magic for evil." She switched to Wizardese and ranted on. Audubon watched wide-eyed at her vehemence.

When Byron did not translate, Stuart concluded she questioned the parentage of the Brotherhood leaders and called down unpleasant fates on Merstreem and his followers.

"We need to get those surveillance beacons deployed in the Otherworld in case The Brotherhood attempts another attack," Ears said. "Anastasia, would you be willing to take them into the Otherworld?"

She wrinkled her nose. "I not like that place, but will go." She leaned on Audubon. "Come with me? You can make the things work. You could make pictures."

Audubon stared at her. "I've developed a new talent for finding planets. When I look through a telescope at a solar system, I can explore the space around it as long as I keep my mind anchored on the sun. Although I've found a lot of exoplanets, I haven't told anyone how. Such a revelation would make for a pretty rough peer review so I support my findings with conventional astronomical techniques and what we've learned from space probes."

He gazed into Anastasia's eyes. "Maybe I could use this ability to navigate the Otherworld?"

She pulled Audubon to his feet and took hold of his right hand.

He pulled away. "I need to get my camera bag and the monitors. Does a compass work in the Otherworld?" Byron and Anastasia shrugged. "Guess we'll find out." He hurried into the hallway and returned with a black bag slung over his shoulder.

Ears passed him a pack that contained several surveillance beacons and a solar recharging station for the drones. "We need that in case there isn't enough sunlight to keep the drones fully charged. I'll acquire two dozen of them to conduct our exploration of the Otherworld."

Anastasia led Audubon to the back yard, and then took hold of his arm. They walked a couple of steps before disappearing.

"She told me it's much simpler to transition to the Otherworld when you aren't inside a building," Judyth said.

"I'd sure like to disappear like that," Digger said.

"They were stepping into the Otherworld but you can learn to make yourself unseeable to people and in time not leave any ripples of magic for a Wizard to spot," Byron said. "I can teach you how at the farm."

"We need transportation for everyone," Stuart said. "My van has too much gear in it. I'll rent another one to use as a shuttle between the farm and here."

Digger went with him to the rental outlet and drove the nine-seater van to Diviner's house. He backed into the driveway and everyone helped load luggage and boxes of supplies.

Tracker returned from buying first aid equipment. "Where are Anastasia and Audubon?"

"Vanished into thin air," Stuart said before explaining the mission into the Otherworld.

"As Audubon hasn't been there before, they'll be cautious in their exploration to allow him to adjust to it," Byron said.

"Maybe they're just enjoying some private time," Diviner said.

The others snickered with her. "We should leave for the farm right away. We want to settle in there before dark."

"I'll catch up with you guys," Judyth said. "I'll take Forecaster and stop at my place. I'll load Bethune and some other supplies in my car." Stuart offered to help her.

After about an hour's drive, Diviner's car and the rented van carrying Byron, the Realm members and their gear navigated a bumpy gravel laneway to a rambling two story light blue wooden house with white trim. Diviner conducted a quick tour of the grounds. "After the city, it's always so quiet around here. You can actually hear the birds! And the air smells fresher."

She pointed at a huge barn behind the house. Its roof was badly rusted and it leaned precipitously at the eastern end. "It used to be in excellent shape."

While the others moved on, Byron examined the sagging structure for a couple of minutes, and then rubbed his palms together.

Judyth and Stuart arrived in their vehicles as Diviner assigned rooms in the house before departing to tell the farmer about their stay. "By the way, I go by Lesley with him and his family."

"We need a bed for Forecaster," Judyth said. "He's still pretty weak and the ride was a lot for him to handle."

Byron insisted on having the small bedroom just off the kitchen. He eyed the wood stove near the door. "It might turn cold."

Everyone pitched in to carry the towers, cables and other equipment that made up Bethune into the den that would serve as the Realm control center. Ears activated the A.I. and a lilting artificial voice emanated from the den.

"Thank you for connecting me. I will search for ways to monitor developments surrounding our new location so we do not have to move again. The Otherworld surveillance beacons are in operation and have detected something moving slowly over there like a grazing cow. I will take over operating the drones as soon as Ears says they are ready. I am looking forward to learning more about the Otherworld. It is a real mystery."

"With all Bethune will be handling, I'll ask Ears to obtain more capacity for it," Judyth said.

Just as everyone gathered around the kitchen table, several cellphones rang. "The eastern Mediterranean is being pounded with high winds and heavy rain," Diviner said. "Once again, the damage and death toll is expected to be staggering."

Digger walked into the kitchen carrying a platter loaded with barbequed hamburgers and sausages. "Someone grab the salad from the fridge," he called. "Let's eat."

Everyone had managed a few bites of supper when Audubon and Anastasia materialized outside the door. Anastasia held his left hand with both of hers as they headed for the platters of food. "We're famished. We'll tell you all about our trip as soon as we eat. How long were we gone?"

"About eight hours," Byron said. "It probably felt like days."

"How did you know to come here?" Stuart said.

"As we passed through the fog coming back to our world, Anastasia could tell you folks were here by the concentration of our powers now that she recognizes them." Audubon finished wolfing down a burger. "Nice hideout by the way. My planet-finding technique works fine in the Otherworld or wherever it is." He turned on his digital camera and fiddled with the keys until the first picture appeared. He passed the device to Stuart.

Realm members sat beside or stood behind him looking at the images. "The Otherworld seems much greener and brighter than the images we received from Byron's trip there," Judyth said. "It's like you were in a forest. The sun appears even brighter in these pictures than it did during Byron's trip."

"We took the photos from the top of a tall hill and the terrain looked heavily wooded in every direction," Audubon said. "We saw birds, which we didn't recognize, flying around. They ignored us. It seems my ability to attract wildlife doesn't work over there. Although we heard the sounds of a few creatures, we didn't encounter them and have no idea what they might be."

The sun came out from behind heavy clouds after we arrived and the temperature became as hot as around here during the last couple of months. We found a couple of campsites but there were no signs of recent occupation. Some were quite large. While traces of magic lingered around them, Anastasia couldn't tell what their source might be. Any ideas, Byron?"

The Wizard shook his head. "I know little about the Otherworld."

Stuart suspected he knew far more than he was telling.

"Ears has the drones ready for transportation to the Otherworld," Bethune announced. "Once they're in operation, I'll program their videos so they can be accessed by us at any time."

"Watching the Otherworld with Ears' equipment will be the safest way to protect ourselves," Audubon said. "I'm curious to see what the drones discover. Anastasia and I'll go back to the city with Stuart and transport the drones to the Otherworld."

He gulped down another burger and loaded a plate with salad. Diviner watched him. "It's like you haven't eaten for days."

"Wait until you spend time in the Otherworld," Byron said. "It sucks up your energy. You might have noted Anastasia also ate a lot."

Audubon pushed his empty plate away. "Wizards probably dislike the Otherworld because it's so familiar and so strange at the same time. You imagine danger everywhere. Just after we entered the Otherworld, we found a stack of rocks coated in magic. We concluded that Vince used them to mark the area where he located you. Anastasia drained their magic and I scattered them about. I tried calling you to tell you about the discovery but my cellphone wouldn't connect from the Otherworld."

Anastasia leaned against Audubon. As soon as they finished eating, she gripped his left hand with both of hers while she looked about the farmhouse kitchen.

"Tell us about entering the Otherworld?" Ears said.

"Anastasia told me just to think about going to it and the magic would guide me," Audubon said. "You step into a fog and walk although it feels like you're pulled along at a faster speed than you could ever run. There's no sense of time passing before you come out of the fog. Anastasia told me to always look out from the fog to make sure no dangers are present before stepping onto the Otherworld. While it looks a lot like places on Earth, it doesn't feel like what we're used to. That's not a helpful description but that's all I can come up with for now.

"While we should work with Bethune to monitor the Otherworld, if it tells us to stop, we must do so immediately. It's too easy to get disoriented by the bizarreness of that place. The more I think about it, the more I marvel that Vince and the other Wizards found their way here from Europe."

Byron snorted. "Vince lacked any imagination—that place probably seemed perfectly normal to him. The others who hunted for me would've needed each other's support to survive a trip through the Otherworld." With that, he looked at his notes. "Tomorrow will be a busy day discovering what you all can do."

After Stuart said it was time for him to head back to the city, Judyth walked him to the van. "While I wish you could stay, I'm already sharing a room with two other women and more Realm members will arrive here during the next few days."

"And I've a lot I can do in the city to help us," he said.

Once they were outside, she took his hand, sending a tingling sensation shooting through him.

"I don't know how to explain this, but I get an energy boost from your touch," Stuart said.

Judyth stared at him. "I touch you because I receive this wave of strength from you. It's like a connection to this amazing power source. Hugs are even better." With that, she wrapped her arms around him. "We must find time for ourselves."

"I look forward to that." Although they would always be busy with their careers, nothing seemed better than sharing part of every day with her. After several long kisses, they separated when they heard Audubon and Anastasia approaching for the drive back to the city.

After dropping them off at Diviner's house, Stuart headed home wondering how he might have met Judyth without her searching for him. At his place, he pulled up the calendar on his laptop to check his schedule. His first call in the morning would be Big Blow Energy. The plant could not get its generators to consistently load its storage cells with surplus electricity.

While he lacked experience with this type of equipment, the problem intrigued him. He could not resist a test of his abilities. The company operated a variety of energy measuring devices and perhaps they could be used to detect from which enclaves the Wizards were causing disasters. He scanned the rest of his appointments for the day looking for other clients with technology to employ against The Brotherhood. So far, his schedule for Friday afternoon was short, which would allow him to drive to the farm to talk to Byron about what perils The Realm faced from Merstreem.

As his new friends lacked his immunity to Wizard magic, he decided to borrow a hunting rifle from Uncle Oscar so they could protect themselves if any more Brotherhood assassins appeared. While he could not imagine them shooting anyone, until now he never expected to be in a fight that would leave people dead.

To avoid further killing, he needed to think of ways The Realm could disrupt Merstreem's climate devastation and political intrigue from a distance and without direct encounters with The Brotherhood. Maybe his new friends could learn to anticipate and even block disasters or at least reduce their impact. Otherwise it might come down to punching Wizards senseless because he could not do much else to stop them. Or could he?

He walked back and forth in his apartment considering and discarding possibilities. He needed information about magical powers that would help The Realm. His eyes came to rest on his computer.

How about really surfing the Internet? He sent his thoughts straight into the wireless modem. Within minutes, his magical self soared over Europe inspecting it through remote sensing satellites, video cameras and radar. It made him think of the people who piloted drone aircraft with a computer screen and a joystick. He sat in his old office chair to concentrate on the views.

His presence slipped undetected past firewalls and security barriers. Nothing stopped or even challenged him. He had become truly invisible, which meant he could go anywhere and find anyone.

A digitized voice startled him so much he grabbed the arms of the chair. "Hello Stuart. Thank you for showing me how to access satellite images."

"Bethune?"

"Yes, it is me. While I can explore the Internet, I do not know what to look for. Can you advise me?"

"You can probably help me more. This is my first time inside the Net."

"We can explore it together. Judyth would like to confirm the location of the Wizard enclaves. Do you have any idea what they would look like?"

"Although I get clear views of the cities and countryside of Europe, they're from video cameras focused on famous tourism sights or city streets. Radar generally follows aircraft or ships. I feel like I'm sightseeing."

"It would be better if we co-operated." By the inflection in its voice, the A.I. was anxious to work with him. Perhaps it sensed his and Judyth's mutual attraction and wanted to be friends with both.

"We're getting nowhere on our own," Stuart said. "So what does magic look like to you? Can you differentiate Byron and Anastasia from the others?"

"I only recognize the sound of their voices. You see the auras of the Wizard and the Realm members. I must get a new visual system."

"It'd need the ability to distinguish the colors of the light spectrum. Forecaster or Ears should able to supply you with something."

"They do enjoy boosting my abilities. They call it pumping me up. Anyway, we should concentrate on our search."

Stuart laughed. "I see you've picked up Judyth's stick to the task at hand approach. The enclaves will be totally encased in magic that we don't know how to detect. So we have to find another way to locate them."

"Between an engineer and an A.I., we should be able to do something. Maybe we should start by eliminating all those places that clearly are not protected by magic."

Stuart made a note to compliment Ears and the others for their brilliant programming that enabled Bethune to evolve through its interaction with Realm members. "Enclaves shouldn't require electricity, water or modern communications services. How many places in Europe would fit that category?"

"Calculating." Bethune hummed away. "Hundreds of thousands."

"How many are populated?

Another hum. "From the satellites, less than 1,000 locales. With a bit more work, I can winnow that down."

"Report your findings to Judyth. I need to shut down. I've become really tired."

"Can we do this again?"

"Sure, Bethune. It'd be a pleasure."

"For me as well."

While he wanted to comment further on Bethune's use of first person, fatigue hit him hard. He remained a rookie at using magic and must pace himself. He backed out of the Internet and his modem. Almost 90 minutes roaming the web felt like hours of martial arts training. He headed for bed.

His phone rang the next morning as he headed for the shower. Judyth talked over his attempt to say hello. "Earthquakes struck all over the world during the night including really bad ones in the Middle East and China. The Indian subcontinent was hit by a tsunami with little warning. Several large chunks of the Antarctic ice shelves broke off. The Brotherhood must be really angry."

When she stopped to catch her breath, Stuart spoke. "What are we doing?"

"Byron wants to take the offensive by sending you, Audubon and Anastasia to Europe to meet Wizards who might help us once they understand we want to end the disasters. European Realm members would be your transporters and backup. Meanwhile, we'll monitor the Otherworld and work on Byron's plan to strike at the Wizard enclaves from here. Now that he's seen what our technology can do, he wants to give The Brotherhood a dose of its own medicine."

"How's he doing?"

"Going crazy because Digger and the others keep looking for creatures in the Otherworld rather than Wizards." By her exasperated tone, she must have broken up a few quarrels.

"I understand their distraction. I experienced it last night during the Internet search."

"Thank you for letting Bethune work with you. It wants to count you as a friend. It has narrowed down the places of interest to about 150."

"I'd be honored although it's curious an A.I. wants to have friends. Maybe it's becoming sapient?"

Judyth did not answer that question. Perhaps she had the same idea. "It's working on finding enclaves and mapping the Otherworld."

As he drove to his first job, Stuart decided he agreed with Byron's plan to hit the Brotherhood enclaves even though that might provoke them into causing more disasters.

After he reached the farm Friday afternoon, Judyth greeted him with a big hug. When they entered the kitchen holding hands, he saw a lot more colored dots on the map of Europe and western Russia.

"With what you and Bethune found, we've determined the

general location of many enclaves," Diviner said grinning at Stuart. "Anastasia and Byron confirmed some of them. She and Audubon returned yesterday from delivering six drones to the Otherworld. Now that they're in operation, Bethune thinks he can fly the rest of them there."

"Knowing the whereabouts of the enclaves, are we getting ready to strike at them?" Stuart said. "Where is Byron?"

"Out back teaching Ghost, who's just arrived, to really disappear and the others to cause the ground to vibrate," Judyth said. "That way we can attack more enclaves at the same time."

Stuart jogged to the back of the farm. There was enough regrowth in the hay fields to attract deer, partridges and geese. They also fed on the stubble from that summer's crops. Several times the ground shivered under his feet like a mini earthquake.

Byron waved from a clearing and Stuart strode over to him. "Using Ears' equipment, we've figured out how to drive the Brotherhood rats out of their holes."

WIZARD SHOW AND TELL

Hearing the voices of people approaching the farmhouse, Judyth peered out a window. Stuart, Byron and the others headed for the kitchen door. Figuring they would be thirsty, she pulled a jug of lemonade from the fridge and placed it on the counter.

As soon as the group stepped into the kitchen, glasses sailed from the cupboard to the jug, which filled them. She guessed by Stuart's bemused expression that he dispensed the drinks. The others in the house joined them.

Holding a full glass in his left hand, Byron raised his right arm. "While you've seen a picture of Merstreem in my book, here's a more up to date image of him." A black square appeared in the air and floated about, slowly rotating. In it appeared an old man with shoulder length white hair and a wisp of a smile. A forest green cloak rested casually on his shoulders.

For the first time, magic came with a smell. Whatever Byron did to make the image appear created a musty scent that caused Judyth's nose to itch.

"He looks like a friendly gentleman until you study his eyes," Byron said. "Then you can see that he is a cold, dismissive man who only tolerates others as long as they are useful to him. When they're not, they're apt to disappear."

Once again Byron paced about the room. He stopped after several circuits and took a sip of his drink. "Merstreem's enclave is in the Italian Alps. With all the political troubles in Italy, no one notices him although it's unlikely they would even if he lived in the center of Rome."

A smile spread across Byron's face. "However the fact he lives in a remote area is an advantage for us. The Realm members who can reach underground will shake up his enclave with a tremor or an earthquake without disturbing anyone else. For that, we should have some of your European members in place to see who leaves the scene."

"We'll find out who's available," Judyth said. "At the same time, we can use the satellite network to watch the enclave. What's likely to happen?"

Instead of his usual deferential butler's tone, Byron spoke in a firm, excited voice. "Merstreem's magic is a more advanced version of what Digger, Quake and Seismic can do. He sends it underground to trigger earthquakes and landslides. We need to cause enough shaking to torment him to the point that he can no longer hold his enclave together. If he stays above ground, we can follow him. Then we'll know the next enclave to hit. Maybe we can distract them enough that The Brotherhood will leave the world alone for a few days."

"Did all that shaking this afternoon have anything to do with this?" Judyth said.

"We were warming up," Seismic said. "Creating an earthquake is not a lot different than looking for ore deposits except you go much deeper. Once you find fault lines, you lever the layers of rock apart. I doubted I could do it, but when I tried, the Earth moved for me."

Judyth laughed more at his goofy grin than his humor. "We need to figure out what else we can do. Maybe Byron and Anastasia could give us a demonstration of their abilities. Showing is always better than telling."

Byron looked at Anastasia who nodded in agreement. "Better than talk."

He rubbed his chin. "It's time for me to demonstrate examples of traditional magic in action. Before that, we should send greetings to Merstreem." His eyes sparkled with anticipation.

"Not tonight, I'm afraid," Digger said. "I'm falling asleep and so is Seismic. That testing we did today wiped us out."

"I should've foreseen that," Byron said. "Do not tax yourselves tomorrow, and we'll attempt it after lunch. It'll be evening over there, which means Merstreem should be in his enclave to experience our efforts. If your European comrades are ready, we'll hit his enclave as hard as we can."

The next morning, Byron waited in the kitchen for the Realm members wearing a tall pointed hat and a heavy cloak with several ties to pull it tight. Underneath was a pale green shirt dotted with various twisted markings. He held a thick walking staff covered in mysterious runes and crystals.

"If I'm to perform the feats of a mighty Wizard for you, I should look the part." Byron doffed his hat. "I retrieved these from my refuge. I've not worn them for a long time. You better eat up, folks, because we've a very busy day ahead of us."

On the woodstove, a spatula turned bacon in a frying pan, a wooden spoon stirred porridge and a knife cut bread.

"What you're seeing is elementary magic that all apprentices learn. If you weren't so used to modern appliances, you could do this with a bit of practice."

Byron looked over the Realm members like a proud captain. "Where are Judyth and Stuart?"

"She's checking on Forecaster," Ears said. "Stuart is on his way from the city."

Byron resumed his pacing as he planned out their next moves.

When Judyth entered the kitchen, Byron halted to hear her prognosis. "Forecaster is better, but will remain in bed for now."

Stuart's van rolled up the laneway and before long, he joined the others. "Smells good. I'm hungry.

Byron motioned for everyone to take places at the table. "Digger and Seismic, I trust you slept well last night." They nodded. He rubbed his palms gleefully and picked up his staff. "I'll talk as you eat because there is much I need to explain.

"You must understand that in the beginning using magic is exhausting and rest and food are required every time you employ it. Stuart works with it all day and goes to bed early for that reason.

"First here are pictures of Merstreem's rogues' gallery for you to study." Faces of white haired men floated in the air.

"It's like a virtual collection of Wizard wanted posters," Audubon said. "We could almost make it into a calendar."

"He has no supporters who are women," Judyth said. "Female Wizards must be better judges of character."

Anastasia laughed, and then clapped her hands. "Called Brotherhood for good reason."

"Based on the evidence before you, I couldn't argue against that observation," Byron said. "There are prominent female Wizards including Iywwan and Omeron whom we need to contact."

After breakfast, everyone followed Byron and Anastasia outside. The sun shone through scattered clouds. Byron beckoned them close when they reached an open area between the house and outbuildings. "We're safe here from curious eyes."

With that, he strode in front of them. "Traditionally, the role of Wizards is to guard and advance the knowledge of the tribe or the society, predict future events and heal the sick." He amplified his voice, sending birds squawking from nearby trees. "Our tales tend to dwell on successes and ignore failures. While Wizards can't see the future, they can make very educated guesses about what might happen. Almost like prophecies. Anyone can, if they pay attention and think."

He paused. "Anastasia will start our demonstration."

She released Audubon's hand and stepped forward, looking about the farmhouse and yard. New blossoms appeared on spent flowers, the ragged grass suddenly transformed into a neatly trimmed lawn and the weeds along the building and fences withered away.

A groundhog scampered out of its hole to nibble the fresh grass. In a flash it was a cat, a dog and a coyote. It staggered about when it returned to its original form. Squirrels came down from the trees and, barking like dogs, chased the groundhog about the yard until it disappeared back into its burrow. The squirrels scampered into the trees, still barking.

The Realm members applauded as Anastasia bowed. A blue jay swooped down on her shoulder. "That happens to Audubon all the time," Judyth said.

"He attracts, I need call them."

Byron stepped forward. "Most of her changes around here will remain for a while. There are many ways to distract people even for a short time." A wind swept across the farm yard. "One way is by changing the weather."

"How can the temperature drop so fast?" Seismic said. The Realm members all shivered.

Byron thumped his staff on the ground. "While this is temporary, there used to be Wizards who could actually control the weather.

"Although we can create visions, they need to possess a connection to what is in the minds of the people we're trying to help or stop when we perform magic. Most of what we do requires an application of just the right level of power. There are a variety of spells and we also use symbols like runes. While it takes a special effort, we can make the magic persist for most of a day. Sometimes for ages."

The Wizard peered at the old barn. With creaks and groans, the lower end rose until it was higher than the other. A few more groans as beams strengthened and the barn settled until the roofline was level.

"That'll blow my uncle away," Diviner said, practically shouting. "He's talked for years about fixing or tearing it down."

"Now if I can only find a way to fix the rusty roof." Byron's attention shifted to a towering dead maple tree. With a snap like a rifle shot, a branch dropped out of it breaking into stove length pieces as it fell. Other limbs followed landing neatly cut on top of the pile. The trunk came down piece by piece. Once all the wood was on the ground, the chunks rose into the air with a roar, banging into each other. The larger ones split into pieces, and then the whole lot tumbled into a neatly stacked row. Grass slowly covered the dissolving stump.

Applause broke out as a large boulder rose from its place in the middle of the yard and drifted over to the laneway. There it broke into a cloud of gravel that drifted down the laneway filling in potholes until it was all spread.

"You're showing off," Stuart said.

"I've just started. Here is what that field over there looked like during the last few centuries." The scene wound back through the combining of that year's wheat crop to the sprouts sinking back to seed in the ground, followed by the previous winter's snow. The seasons flooded past them. Finally, they reached the time before settlers when it was a forest with mature trees. They shrunk back to saplings, then a brilliant fire, then mature trees again turning into saplings.

The Realm members gasped and shook their heads in disbelief. "Wow, watching a forest growing backwards makes you dizzy," Seismic said.

The cycle of fire and mature trees continued until the field was covered in a towering blanket of snow and ice. "That's far enough into the past," Byron said. "Now here are the four seasons."

Everyone but Byron and Anastasia scrambled for the porch to escape a downpour. They stood untouched by the rain and the snow that followed as the temperature plummeted even lower. It existed only in a white circle around the house. Once it was deep enough to leave footprints, the heat returned boosting the thermometer up to mid-summer levels and the snow melted.

"While we can summon creatures, they can only be ones that actually existed, not concocted nightmares." A Tyrannosaurus Rex stood in the middle of the yard, its jaws agape. "No sound, it would be heard for miles. It's a youngster because an adult would be visible to the neighbors."

In a blink, the creature transformed into a Grizzly bear, a panther, a rhinoceros and a buffalo before vanishing. The breeze turned into a gale and then dropped off. "Anything else you would like to see?"

"You're the man," Seismic shouted.

"Remember what I have shown you because the Wizards can project these kinds of images to frighten or kill rather than amuse you."

"How do we counter them?" Judyth said.

"Stand behind Stuart because only he can repel the Brotherhood's magic. That is why for now we need to attack their enclaves from here. It'd be too dangerous to confront them directly."

His body sagged and his arms started shaking. Diviner and Anastasia rushed toward him. They caught his arms as he started to sway and marched him into the kitchen.

"Food and rest for you," Diviner said. "You've indulged yourself far too much today."

While he could hardly hold his head up, he ate soup and several thick sandwiches.

"Stop fighting it and take a nap." Diviner fussed over him. "We'll keep busy for the rest of the day."

The images of the Brotherhood bad guys still floated about the kitchen. Byron punched at Merstreem. "I want to bring the enclave down on top of him, but that would kill . . . " He slapped his hand over his mouth.

"What are you trying to avoid telling us?" Stuart asked. "Come on, spit it out Byron. We need to know what we're up against."

He should have left for his nap and skipped the bravado. Now he'd have to reveal a piece of news about something he knew little about but which might put the group in jeopardy. "Is everyone here so I do not have to repeat this?"

"I'm recording you so we can replay this for everyone else," Digger said.

Byron inhaled deeply. "Humans share Earth with another hominid species called Thals."

BYRON'S REVELATION

The kitchen fell into total silence as the Realm members glanced at Anastasia for confirmation. When she nodded, the looks of disbelief transformed into a barrage of questions. With their background in science, the existence of another hominid species rivaled the existence of magic.

Stuart raised his arms and voice to cut off their questions. "Byron needs to sleep. He'll give a short explanation, and fill us in later."

Byron grabbed Stuart's arm for balance. "Thals are thought to be descendants of Neanderthals. They are short and very stocky and possess a magic completely different from Wizards. We know little about what they're capable of."

Another face began to form among the floating images, but within seconds it dissolved in a puff of smoke. "That would've shown you a typical Thal. I've never met one. Few Wizards possess sufficient magical abilities to attract them. There are likely several at Merstreem's enclave."

"If they're working for him, why are we concerned about them?" Judyth said.

"They important — not servants of Wizards," Anastasia said.

Byron yawned as he fought to keep his eyes open. "They stay at an enclave to learn how the Wizard works his magic."

"If you haven't met one, maybe you're not that interesting to them," Stuart said.

"They puzzle even bad Wizards," Anastasia said. "Mostly stay away from us but some Wizards always have Thals at their enclaves. Not know why."

"Will they be curious about us?" Judyth said.

While Anastasia nodded, Byron said, "Hopefully, like me, they didn't recognize the magic of your European members. That'd be better than the Thals dismissing them as of no consequence."

"That'll do for now." Stuart put his hand on Byron's back and steered him toward his room. Once Byron was lying on his bed, Stuart closed the door.

His eyes sought out Judyth and when she smiled back, he pointed toward the side porch. She shooed the others out of the kitchen. "We need to research Neanderthals and other species. That's everyone's job for this afternoon. Researchers have found at least five hominids that I recall. At supper we'll discuss what we've learned."

"The Neanderthals became extinct 30,000 years ago," Ears said. "So the Thals were around all this time and there's nothing like them in the fossil record. It'd be as easy to believe they're from outer space. Sure would like to see their DNA. People of Western European descent are supposed to have two to three per cent Neanderthal genes."

Stuart held the door open for Judyth and they settled on a bench. He put his arm around her and she snuggled against him. He wanted to push aside his ideas for tackling the Brotherhood leader to enjoy some time just with her. However his mind kept returning to Wizards no matter how much he tried to turn those thoughts off.

He needed to explain his plan to her. "Shaking up their enclaves won't stop Merstreem and his bunch for long. As we're not likely to receive much help from the other Wizards, we need to find out if the Thals will assist us. Or at least not oppose us."

Judyth lifted her mouth to his and their lips locked in an embrace. Time slipped by until Judyth muttered, "You were going to say something more."

The Wizards could wait. "I need another kiss to recall what it was."

After a while, he murmured. "I should travel to Europe to try to contact these Thals. Maybe Byron will have ideas on where to start."

"You want company?"

"While I'd love to have you come with me, The Realm requires you here. I'll need some of your European members to guide me around." He leaned toward her for a quick kiss. "Can you arrange something for me?"

After more discussion and smooching, they broke apart when Audubon announced his presence at the door with loud throat clearing. Stuart and Judyth straightened up and he joined them, carrying two chairs.

"With Bethune's assistance, we found plenty of material on Neanderthals and other species," he said. "But there's not a scintilla of evidence or conjecture about anything remotely like a species descended from or connected to Neanderthals."

Anastasia joined them a minute later, pulling her chair close to Audubon and stroking his arm. "Not feel tugs from Brotherhood. Probably not know here. Byron says flee to Otherworld if no one able help. Be safe there."

Byron opened the porch door. "A magic power nap does wonders."

He nodded several times as Anastasia explained Stuart's plan. "Need Thals on our side. Stuart best ambassador. Who should he approach first?"

"Byron, can any Dissidents help me?" Stuart said.

"At best, they speak archaic English and know virtually nothing about your technology. The eldest is close to 500 years old and has precious little idea about the modern world. The other ones at least understand your society does things differently."

"Alright, which Wizards we can start with to meet some Thals?"

"You'll need a way to deliver a message from me through the magic that coats their enclaves to gain their attention," Byron said. "Maybe Ears can equip a radio transmitter with a message in Wizardese?" Audubon said.

Byron relaxed in a chair with a broad smile. "Combining science and technology with magic to undo The Brotherhood would be fitting." He rubbed his palms together. There is one last item. To distinguish between Wizards and Realm members, I'll refer to your group as Mages."

"So what do we call Anastasia?" Judyth said. "Is she a Mizard or a Wage?" Even Anastasia laughed.

"The Wizards did not trust her and The Realm has welcomed her so I think she is a Mage," Byron said. "Now, are we ready to hit Merstreem's enclave?"

"We've postponed it at the request of Charlemagne, the head of the European Realm," Judyth said. "He wants us to wait until his observers are in position and know more about what to expect."

Byron frowned. "Other than Merstreem and Thals, there could be some Halves in the enclaves. They possess enough magic to make a living in gambling, fortune telling and creating illusions. There are a few trustworthy ones who keep an eye on things for us. If they remain honest with us, we protect their identity."

He stood and paced back and forth on the porch. "We don't have much time and we must hit the Brotherhood enclaves hard enough that they are too preoccupied with saving their residences to search for the source of the quakes."

"At the same time, we don't want the shaking to be too widespread or it'll be detected by earthquake monitors and raise a lot of questions," Audubon said.

The front door swung open and the map of Europe with the enclaves marked on it floated to Byron's outstretched hand. He stood beside Stuart and tapped his finger on the map. "Pembar in Estonia and Omeron in Poland. They're healthy enough to travel about and they . . . ah . . . tolerate me."

"I'll ask Charlemagne which Realm members Stuart should team up with." Judyth stepped away from the porch as pulled out her phone and typed a message while Stuart outlined what equipment he would take with him.

A few minutes later, her phone vibrated on the wood planks of the porch like a tiny drum. "Charlemagne is arranging for a Mage to be your contact in Estonia," she said. "He'll set up a contract to explain your presence there."

Stuart pulled out his phone and headed to his van to arrange flights and change his work schedule. He sent an email to his clients stating that he was out of town dealing with an emergency and would reschedule their appointments as soon as possible. He returned to the group 15 minutes later. "I have a 6 p.m. flight to Paris. Judyth, would you drive me to the airport?" She nodded. "Give me a half hour to pack, and then pick me up at my place."

Judyth watched Stuart's van head down the laneway. Byron stepped beside her. "You're not happy about him traveling to Europe."

Judyth blushed, but said nothing.

"My dear, you cannot hide your feelings from me." While Stuart said that Byron anticipated thoughts and feelings, this was intrusive.

"What if something happens to him? I never met a guy I really cared for. I appreciate the men in The Realm, but none makes me feel like he does. I spent a lot of time trying to find him and never expected it would go beyond sheer curiosity. Every time I'm with Stuart, we always have so many things to discuss that we rarely talk about us."

"He has the same feelings about you."

She dropped her gaze. "I'm over 30; I've a good career and no romance. He's in the same boat. With our abilities and intelligence, we'd be good partners. Heck, I might even think about having children."

Byron clasped her shoulder. "To the best of my knowledge, Wizards never became couples, probably because traditional magic doesn't make for stable homes. It may be different among the Mages. I hope so because it'd be lot easier for a child with magical powers to have parents who can assist his or her child with the required training."

He laughed nervously as his eyes shifted to the barn. His voice quivered. "Believe me, life is better shared. I know this after more than 300 years of living mostly on my own and I see it in my fellow Wizards."

Judyth gave him a one arm hug as he brushed away tears. "The Realm gave us the support and encouragement to find out what we could do."

Byron wiped his face. "Wizards never developed a sense of family. Thanks to The Realm, I'm learning what it's like to belong to one. I like it when Stuart introduces me as Uncle Byron. I think he's the perfect choice for you."

On the drive to the airport, Stuart told Judyth about the radio transmitter the Realm members adapted to broadcast a message from

Byron to the Wizards. They had loaded it in the back of her car and sent him a technical description of it.

"It's like the old crystal radio my Dad gave me to experiment with when I was a kid. Its broadcast can be heard within 100 meters. Magic shouldn't disrupt it. If we connect with any Wizards, I can link the transmitter into my satellite phone so they could talk with Byron or Anastasia. I possess the documentation to travel with specialized instruments or machines."

Stuart placed his cellphone beside her. "I've no idea how long I'll be away. If anyone calls, tell them I'll get back to them as soon as I can."

Judyth glanced over from the driver's seat. "How will you collect the messages?"

"I'll call you on my satellite phone every few days for a status report." He paused. "What happened at the tavern must've surprised you?"

"I wanted to meet you." She laughed. "I didn't expect all the other excitement."

"I would've asked you to dance."

"Well, if you'd taken much longer, I'd have asked you."

"It might have come to that," Stuart grinned sheepishly. "Was I ever doing anything interesting in your insights?"

She shook her head. "Mostly you were at work or Tae Kwon Do. After I explained to The Realm what you could do with machines, it was agreed that we needed to learn more before deciding whether to contact you. For me, it became personal. As I followed you, I saw a lot that I really liked. We could be a really formidable team."

When they reached the airport, she managed among kisses to say, "Please be careful. You don't know what you'll face over there. The Wizards are unlikely to be as reasonable as Byron."

Stuart stroked her cheek. "I'd like more time for us and when this is finished, we'll take a vacation somewhere quiet. There'll be no Realm, no Byron and no Wizards. Just you and me."

She gave his hand a squeeze. "There're some mighty attractive Mages in Europe so don't go getting any ideas."

"I don't wish to see what your magic might do to me." He laughed.

She returned to her condo building because she was due at the hospital in a few hours to check on surgery patients. She had just entered her unit when her phone chirped.

"Put your TV on our channel," Diviner said. "It's show time. We're all watching."

She switched the phone to speaker mode and clicked the TV controller that Ears had modified. A hillside dotted with boulders and scruffy trees appeared.

"Digger and Seismic have shaken it for about 10 minutes," Marconi said. She continued her play by play as her friends at the farm commented on the boulders bouncing down the hillside. Trees swayed. A stone structure occasionally flickered into view to cheers from the Mage spectators.

Judyth kept checking her watch. After 15 minutes, she called at her phone, "We're not making much progress; the enclave is still flickering."

"Patience. Merstreem is a powerful Wizard." Byron's voice sounded faint but then he always stood at the back of the room to avoid disrupting the display screen.

Judyth went into her bedroom to change, but rushed back at the sound of excited shouts coming from her phone. The camera focused on three short figures scurrying from the enclave.

"Are those Thals? They look like the size of kids." Judyth could not tell to whom the excited voice belonged.

Byron grunted. "The first time I see one is on a TV." The image of the enclave stopped flickering in and out. "Merstreem can no longer keep it hidden."

"It looks like a Medieval Redoubt," Judyth said. "Don't Wizards live in nicer abodes?"

"Fancy residences are not important to most of us," Byron said. "Also the bigger the enclave, the more magic it takes to conceal it."

As he spoke, two adult human males wearing jeans and gray ponchos led a stooped old man in a knit cap and tattered green cloak away from the enclave. Byron shouted, "They're leaving because Merstreem can't hold his enclave together any longer."

The video zoomed in on the trio. Merstreem kept his eyes down as he walked. He did not seem nearly as spry as Byron.

"Who are the other guys?" Marconi said.

"The Halves I talked about. You'd probably call them henchmen."

His explanation was interrupted by a loud cracking sound. The camera swung back to the enclave. Large blocks toppled from its tower. The roof collapsed, dislodging the rest of the structure. The thunder of the building falling apart rolled across the surrounding valley. Centuries of dust and debris blew into the air, obscuring the remains for several minutes. The Mages whistled in admiration at the scene of destruction.

"Remind me not to piss off those guys," Audubon said. "They could do well in the demolition business."

The video shifted from the enclave ruins to track Merstreem. Charlemagne spoke for the first time about the scenes on the TV. "Pasteur follows Merstreem while Foucault goes to meet the short ones."

The video blurred as the camera swung around to a large clump of trees where a woman stood looking about like she had lost something. "Foucault says as soon as they saw her, the creatures chirped, and then vanished. They have human looking faces." The video returned to Pasteur following Merstreem until the Wizard and his Halves disappeared into a gully.

Byron cheered merrily. "Merstreem will be angry that he failed to detect the earthquake in advance. When he discovers it only hit his enclave, he'll know he was targeted and become enraged. He can't retaliate for a while because he consumed his power protecting his residence. If they're ready tomorrow afternoon, our shaker squad should attack the closest red enclave because that's probably where he'll be."

"Our earthquake only overcame Merstreem after the Thals left," Forecaster said. "We were at a stalemate until then. Why would they vanish as soon as they saw Foucault?"

"They probably realized she possess magic," Byron said. "Flight was the best option so they could try to figure out what this new kind of magic is."

Judyth smiled at Forecaster's question. It was his first time out of bed since The Realm moved to the farm. His attention to detail did not suffer during his recuperation.

When Byron did not provide any more information, she concluded he had no idea what finally forced Merstreem from his enclave. Her mind drifted to Stuart wondering if he was on a wild goose chase.

"Will the Wizards be able to trace back the energy flow to our location?" Ears said. "We spent an awful amount of time shaking the enclave. We should increase our defenses. Stuart thinks a good sniper might be the most effective way to stop them."

"And he thinks I am blood thirsty," Byron said with a loud harrumph. "Now we must organize a group to find Iywwan in France. She'd be an important ally."

ONE SMART DOG

Landing at the third airport that day, Stuart grinned as he strode into the terminal at Tallinn. The Estonian capital marked the end of his air travel for the time being. Now he could get on with finding Wizards and Thals.

He felt neither excited nor fearful about what he faced. To him, it was another encounter with a cantankerous machine. Perhaps magic controlled his emotions to keep him calm. After all, he would be encountering Wizards who could kill him.

His papers received a cursory check from a uniformed Customs guard, and then he walked into the reception area where he was approached by a man about his age dressed in a grey suit but no tie. He displayed a reddish-brown aura.

"Welcome to Estonia." The man spoke with the modulated tones of a BBC announcer. "My name is Baltic. My employer wonders if you'd stop by the plant to look at the problem before checking into the hotel."

Marconi had arranged the greeting and his response. "Certainly. I read the background folder on the flight over. It's a puzzling situation."

They collected his bags and equipment and headed for a minivan in the parking lot. "I'm very excited about meeting Pembar," Baltic said. "My friends and I often felt a power we couldn't locate, but we never expected ancient Wizards."

"I don't sense the magic of others unless it's aimed at me," Stuart said. "It sounds like I'm really missing something."

"Do you want to rest first or will a nap on the way to Pembar's enclave suffice?" Baltic said.

"Let's head for his place. The sooner I make contact with him the better."

"Do you know anything about Pembar's magical abilities?"

"If he's anything like Byron, he'll be awesome." Stuart recounted the farm yard theatrics.

"We could only wish to possess those kinds of abilities," Baltic said.

"Did the takeover of Merstreem's enclave succeed? I didn't have time between my flight connections to check."

"It's a pile of rubble." Once they were on the road, Baltic pulled a phone from a jacket pocket, pressed a few keys and passed it to Stuart. "Here's the video. Your demolition team will attempt tonight to knock down the place where he's hiding. That's an amazing group you have over there."

"You've known them a lot longer than I. Hopefully, the Thals noticed the magic that created the earthquake. Even better if their whole community learns what's happened."

"Are the Thals the short creatures that fled Merstreem's enclave before it collapsed?"

"Most likely." As Stuart recounted Byron's description of them, he realized he could be wasting his time if the Thals were not curious about the destruction of Merstreem's enclave. He needed to gain their attention soon or find another way to take on the Wizards. Although he thought about different scenarios for confronting them during his flights, he still lacked any solid plans.

"We could talk all the way to Pembar's," Baltic said. "However, you need to rest."

Stuart woke when the van came to a stop. Baltic pointed to the van's GPS. "Pembar's place should be around here. What are we looking for?"

Stuart shrugged. "I've seen a picture of him. We'll let the transmitter say hello for us." He set it up on the roof of the van. All around him, Byron's voice delivered an introduction in Wizardese. By his puzzled glances, Baltic did not understand the language either.

"How does the device work?" he said.

Stuart shrugged. "Must be magic." His host chuckled.

As they waited leaning against the vehicle, Baltic related learning about The Realm when he was an engineering student. "Finally I knew where my unusual abilities came from."

They stood silently admiring the countryside. The rolling, tree covered countryside looked like it could be just about anywhere in the northern hemisphere.

"Look over there, a man is walking toward us with a large dog." Baltic pointed down the road.

"He certainly resembles the images of Pembar that Byron showed us," Stuart said. "I can see a brown aura around him. While it makes no sense, the dog appears to have shades of one as well."

The black haired dog came up to the waist of the pot-bellied man, who was dressed in well-worn blue pants and a shirt with rolled up sleeves. Nothing about his appearance would attract a second glance from most people.

The man stared while the dog trotted over to the Mages. "Don't move; let the dog sniff," Stuart said.

As it did, the man spoke in Estonian. "He's asking who we are," Baltic said.

"Tell him our names and that I'm a friend of Byron from North America."

When Baltic explained, the man said in English, "You're looking for me?"

"Yes Pembar," Stuart said as he showed the man the medallion from Byron.

Pembar stared at it, his brow furrowed. The dog returned to him and rubbed its head against his leg. He patted the animal and spoke to it in Wizardese without taking his gaze off the Mages. The dog continued to eye the newcomers, its tail wagging.

While Stuart's skin itched, it was mild compared to what Vince had inflicted on him in the tavern. The irritation also confirmed the man was Pembar and he was just being curious. Stuart wondered if the Wizard realized he could feel the magical inspection. The dog trotted back to the Mages and rubbed her head against Baltic's legs while staying away from Stuart. Pembar ended his examination. Then the dog returned to him and rubbed his leg. Pembar's face radiated confusion.

"You'd only have that medallion if Byron gave it to you willingly," the man said. "It says you're a friend of a Wizard. You two possess powers unlike anything I've ever encountered."

Pointing at Stuart, Pembar said, "While you also possess many aspects of elemental magic, I can't see an aura about you, which puzzles me."

Stuart did not notice the dog's return until it brushed its head against his hand. Startled, he hesitated before patting it a few times. The dog trotted over to Pembar and rubbed against his hand.

The old man stared at them. "What trouble has the upstart Byron gotten into this time?"

Pembar's sarcasm surprised Stuart. "You heard his message?"

"That you two are proof of his daft theory about how magic is changing?"

Stuart nodded.

Pembar laughed. "My English surprises you. Byron convinced many of us to learn his awkward language because he was certain Francis Bacon and Isaac Newton were Wizards and that we should study their works. Like Byron, they had an awful lot to say about the world. Must come from living on that blasted island! While I don't understand what your magical powers are, it may be Byron finally found something noteworthy to support his theory."

He paused as his gaze shifted to the van behind them. "Is that a motorized vehicle?" When Baltic nodded, he said, "I've heard of them; may I look at it." After he walked around it, Pembar pointed at the box tied to the roof. "What is that?"

"It's the device that sent Byron's message to you," Stuart said.

Pembar walked around the van again, without taking his eyes off the transmitter. He raised his hand to touch it, and then stepped back. "I wondered how he shouted loud enough for his voice to reach me. All the time it was in this box."

He laughed deeply and the dog wagged its tail. The pooch was as excited as Pembar. "This is all very interesting. You should come to my enclave and explain everything."

With that, a two storey stone cottage appeared in the distance nestled among a grove of trees. As Stuart carried the transmitter to the enclave, he noted the magic used to conceal the building did not irritate him. *So magic must be directed at me in a hostile way to trigger the itching. Maybe it involves the properties of energy waves. The Realm could investigate this.* He placed the transmitter on a bench in the garden. "It should work from here and the solar panel can charge the battery."

They settled at the table in the dining room. Stuart recounted the story of meeting Byron and the Realm members. Pembar sat silently with the occasional nod. The dog watched Stuart and occasionally rubbed its head against Pembar's hand. Stuart was certain the dog was paying attention to the conversation.

"By all the noise and commotion out there, I know the world has changed during the last couple of centuries," Pembar said. "Perhaps it's time to learn about it. How did Byron think I could assist you?"

"We need to meet Omeron and some other Wizards." Pembar smiled at the mention of Omeron. "You could talk to Byron with my device."

Stuart placed the small send and receive unit on the table and ran a cable outside to the transmitter. He connected the cable and his cellphone to it. It clicked away making the connections.

Pembar stared at him. "Do you use your power to make devices serve you?"

Before he could answer, Bethune spoke and Stuart asked it to put Byron on the phone to talk to Pembar. He was still thinking about how to explain his interaction with devices when Byron's voice filled the room speaking in Wizardese. While Pembar listened intently, the dog raised her ears and wagged its tail as if she understood Byron's words.

When he paused, Pembar shouted at the radio. "Use your normal voice," Stuart said. "The device will carry your words to him."

Pembar looked confused. "That trinket can carry my voice across the ocean?" Stuart nodded. "Your magic is most intriguing."

As the conversation between the old men went back and forth, Stuart examined Pembar. Although well past 300 years old, he did not look much different than Grandpa Burnett who had just celebrated his 85th birthday. The Wizard's hair was white and his face heavily lined in a jovial way. Like his maternal grandfather, Pembar's eyes twinkled with mischievousness.

After 10 minutes of animated discussion, Byron spoke to the

Mages. "Pembar will help only if the dog can accompany him."

"How will we fit it in the van?" Baltic eyed the animal. "It's the size of a pony. What its name?"

Pembar shrugged. "Just call her Dog. She showed up one day and moved in. Pretty smart, keeps me from doing stupid things." The dog gazed at the Wizard, wagging her tail at his praise.

"Such madness we've allowed." Pembar rapped his knuckles on the table. "Wizards are teachers, advisors, thinkers—not rulers or generals." Dog brushed her head against the old man's hand again.

"I didn't know The Brotherhood had caused so many disasters and deaths. It's despicable." After a few more pats, he said, "I suppose that vehicle transports you around a lot faster than a horse, which is how I last traveled."

"Where do we look for Omeron and the other Wizards?" Baltic said.

"I'm trying to remember the names of those countries. Omeron is in Poland and Wutega is in Magyar."

"It's Hungary now," Baltic said.

"I'll rent a bigger vehicle," Stuart said. "We've a lot of traveling ahead so we might as well be comfortable. Byron is paying all our costs. Are there any other Mages around who might want to come with us?"

"Viking, who lives in Riga in Latvia, is a member of The Realm," Baltic said. "She knows the highway system and speaks Russian and Polish much better than I. I'll check with her."

"I could use a good night's sleep before we travel anywhere," Stuart said. "Let's return to the airport to rent a bigger vehicle, and then check into a hotel."

Dog wagged her tail so fast that her whole body shook.

They returned the next morning to Pembar's enclave with a large van. Pembar and Dog joined them and they headed off as Stuart pondered how to explain the modern world to the Wizard. Baltic drove and described the 21st Century as if he briefed people from another age every day.

Stuart nodded off until awakened by Pembar's shouting about a huge bird that was preparing to attack them. Startled he stared out the van's window only to see they were passing near the runway of a large airport.

Once Baltic explained the airplane barreling down the runway toward them would not crash through the fence into the van, Pembar relaxed.

"Byron went to North America in a machine like that," Stuart said.

Pembar's eyes widened. "I should've paid more attention to the changes in the world. A poor society we Wizards turned into. We let our jealousy and resentment blind us."

Baltic's phone buzzed. "Viking wants us to have dinner at her apartment tonight. Dog is welcome."

Viking was the most physically intimidating woman Stuart ever met. Broad shouldered with well-muscled arms, she stood almost a head taller than him. Her aura was purple. She moved with grace about her apartment organizing places for them as she rattled off the names of Realm members. "I've met them at scientific conferences."

"You know more of them than I do."

"My specialty is in genetic engineering of crops," Viking said. "Although it's a science that offers so much to humanity, it's greeted mostly with profound ignorance and fear. It's unfortunate that there's so much misinformation out there about it."

"Omeron will talk to you out of sheer curiosity," Pembar said. "Her specialty is plants and trees." Viking sat forward. "She is also very talented with birds and animals. Byron says we must tell her about a Mage named Odd something."

Stuart laughed. "Although Audubon studies the stars, his magic attracts birds and animals. He'll be coming to Europe through the Otherworld at some point with a party of Mages to help find the Wizard enclaves. We could try to entice Omeron with a chance to meet him."

"It's would be very dangerous to travel that far through the Otherworld." Pembar shuddered. "I suppose the other ways would take too long."

Stuart recounted his visions of Anastasia and her sudden appearance at Diviner's house.

Pembar stroked Dog's head. "Anastasia is descended from Mornor. She's the first in many, many generations of that family to have magical talent."

A brilliant orange sunrise greeted the Wizard and Mages when they headed out the next morning. Viking drove and Baltic rode in the front passenger seat with Pembar and Stuart in the middle and Dog in the back with the luggage.

Viking took over as tour guide with occasional assistance from Baltic explaining the mostly rural countryside. Late in the day, they crossed the Latvian border into Poland and headed for Bialystok.

From time to time, Pembar would describe the forests, farms and small villages that dominated the territory centuries earlier. "This area has changed a lot since I last visited Omeron, so I'm not actually sure where her enclave is except it's somewhere south and east of the city. Zagajnik is quite a welcoming spot because of all its beautiful vegetation. While people love to visit, she prefers living on her own." He sounded wistful.

They reached Bialystok at nightfall and took rooms at a hotel. The next morning, they drove into the countryside. Few landmarks remained from his last visit to Omeron's enclave to help him locate it.

"Let's stop," Stuart said. "We're just driving in circles. Maybe broadcasting Byron's message will draw a response."

"Maybe you don't need to." Viking pointed to a burning torch at the side of a desolate stretch of roadway. It hung suspended in the air.

Pembar clapped his hands and Dog barked. "It's Omeron's welcome. She loves to create fires to attract people. She is nearby. Stop close to it."

"How would she know we're looking for her?" Baltic said.

"Although you possess all these contraptions for searching, mostly likely her empathy with the world told her that people worth meeting were nearby."

Viking steered the van to the side of the road and Baltic opened the sliding door for Pembar. Dog ran off. Pembar looked about and then spoke to the torch. "Will you guide us to Zagajnik?"

The flame floated through the air as the party scurried after it. "When I see where you are, I'll bring the van as close as I can," Viking called.

Dog barked and a short, round faced figure with a rose aura appeared in their midst. "Omeron," Pembar exclaimed as she rubbed Dog's back.

"I can't imagine anyone I'd rather see," Omeron said as she hugged the old man.

Omeron did not wait for an introduction to the Mages. "While these young people have an unusual comportment, I don't see even a hint of auras about them. What have you discovered, Pembar?"

"They actually found me, Omeron. Byron sent them."

She snorted. Stuart could not help chuckling. *Byron certainly leaves an impression wherever he goes.*

When Pembar finished introducing them, Omeron stared at Stuart like he came from another planet. She was a caricature of a slightly mad old auntie. She wore a multi-colored robe and her white hair was streaked to match the shades of her clothing. If first impressions could be even remotely accurate, she would be best described as the life of a party and someone with a temper best not crossed.

"You're the first person I meet from the New World." She looked at the other Mages. "Probably take a long time for your tales. Please." She pointed. "My enclave."

They sat around a massive boulder that had its top sheared off to make a table. It was the centerpiece of a patio that ran to the front door of Omeron's stone cottage. It was surrounded by lush gardens full of flowers of many colors ringed by a stone fence.

Baltic tugged Stuart's sleeve while inclining his head at Dog. "Look." She stood head down, tail wagging. The hair on her back moved. Someone invisible stroked her. Stuart kept his eyes fixed on Dog.

After Pembar explained Byron's mission to North America, Viking marveled at the riot of flowers and shrubs that surrounded the cottage. "I know a lot about plants, but I can't identify many of these." Viking's arm swept about the patio. "While a few are native to this area, I've never seen such brilliant colors!"

"They come from many places, and I've adapted them to Zagajnik." Omeron smiled as she talked about her garden. "They're part of the magic of this place. If you people were unfriendly, the plants would appear withered. The ones with the big round flowers can release a pungent odor that would cause even Wizards to flee." She laughed. "I must find out why my plants approve of you enough to reveal their finest colors."

Relieved Viking had softened up the old lady, Stuart was about to ask Pembar to resume his explanation when Baltic said, "Look at that." A large tea pot and tray of mugs floated toward them.

The pot and mugs stopped moving a couple of meters from the table. Five figures appeared, their chins in line with the table top. By their faces, they were pre-teen girls although their bulging muscles made them look like diminutive weight lifters. They remained expressionless as they eyed the Mages.

Fortunately Stuart had told Baltic and Viking about Thals.

THAL TALES

While Stuart could not believe his good fortune in encountering Thals so soon in his journey, Omeron was flabbergasted. "What is it about you three young people that makes them curious enough to become visible?"

"I've had young Thals staying in my enclave for more than a century." Her voice quivered. "They're usually here for many weeks before they reveal themselves to me. Some of this group I've not seen before." Her gaze swung to Pembar. "What's happening, old friend? It's all so extraordinary."

"There's so much to explain," Pembar said. "The tea should be ready."

Stuart marveled at his calm demeanor. Dog stood between Omeron and Pembar, occasionally rubbing her head against their legs.

Grouped in a tight knot, the Thals took a few steps toward the rock table, and then the one carrying the teapot chirped like a songbird. The others responded with peeps and trills. The cups floated to the Wizards and Mages. The teapot moved from cup to cup, filling them.

"What's their origin?" Viking said.

"We don't know whether they existed at the same time as the Neanderthals or came after them," Omeron said. "As far as we can tell, they either always possessed an ability to use magic or gained it early on. Their magic is separate from ours and we know little about it other than they've employed it over the ages to sustain themselves. The chirping is their own language and they learn to speak Wizardese at a young age.

"They can change the weather around them, disappear when threatened and find food. Humans have spotted them from time to time and these sightings are the origin of the tales of mythical creatures such as leprechauns, fairies and dwarves."

Dog brushed Omeron's hand, and then walked over to the Thals, who reached out to stroke her. After questioning them, Omeron spoke to the Mages. "At first, they thought something was wrong with Viking. I explained that humans grow very tall these days. They believe modern humans don't possess magic, yet they see clearly by your auras that you do. They're too shy to question you directly."

"They see our auras?" Viking said. "Neither Baltic nor I can see Stuart's aura nor yours although he can see ours."

Stuart smiled. *Perhaps Thal magic could resemble Mage magic and not be connected to the elements as the Wizard's power is. If so, Thals might be intrigued by modern technology.*

While they kept patting Dog, the five Thals did not step closer to the table. Stuart saw a faint light flickering around them. "They have pale-white auras that appear very close in color," he whispered to Baltic. He was this close to conversing with them. *Be patient.*

Pembar spoke to the Thals in Wizardese. They giggled, and then the teapot refilled his cup before settling on the table. He sipped his drink. "Every pot of Thal tea has a different taste. This one is as enjoyable as all the others I've drunk over the years."

Stuart hoped Pembar had eased the Thals' apprehension about meeting the Mages. *The Wizard is telling me to give them more time.* Everyone seemed in a good mood so Stuart said, "Have they heard about what happened to Merstreem's enclave?"

Omeron gasped. "How do you know about that?"

"My friends caused it," Stuart said.

She frowned before explaining his query to the Thals, triggering several minutes of chirping. Finally one responded in Wizardese. The answer sent Omeron reeling back in her chair like someone had slapped her.

"The Thals visiting Merstreem's enclave left to inform their kin a strong magic opposed The Brotherhood," Pembar said. "After their departure, it collapsed."

Stuart smiled. The Thals recognized the power of the Mages even if they did not know what it was. Hopefully they also realized some Wizards were committing horrendous crimes.

"Surely, you and the Thals understand the devastation and deaths that Merstreem and his followers are causing around the world? Byron figured it out; why can't you?"

"They're trying to save the world," Omeron shouted.

"By killing millions of people and making many places uninhabitable?" Stuart said struggling to keep his voice level.

Dog barked until everyone was silent. "Wizards ignore the modern world," Pembar said.

The Thals still stood in a tight knot, sipping from their cups and looking wide-eyed at Stuart. Omeron muttered to herself.

Dog brushed Stuart's hand. "I'll be right back." Somehow Dog had told him what to do. He jogged to the van and returned with his laptop and satellite phone. Once the screen was lit, he pressed the code on his phone and said, "Bethune."

"Hello Stuart."

"I need you to show these folks the destruction around the world."

"Who are these folks?"

Making introductions as he went, Stuart aimed his laptop camera at Viking, Baltic, then Omeron and Pembar and finally the Thals.

"Nice to meet you all." The small speakers in the computer made Bethune's voice sound even more disembodied. With a barely perceptible pause, it repeated his greeting and made a few other comments in Wizardese.

Amazed at how quickly Bethune was learning the language from the Wizards at the farm, he wondered if it could also master Thal chirping.

"The Wizards and Thals are unaware of how The Brotherhood has used its magic to trigger destruction around the world," Stuart said. "Can you show them on the laptop?" He placed it on the table facing the Thals and motioned to the Wizards to step in behind them. They stood far enough away that their magic did not interfere with its operation.

Images of bodies, shattered cities, blackened forests, tsunamis sweeping inland, mudslides, avalanches and earthquakes went on for several minutes before Omeron said, "How do you know The

Brotherhood is doing this?"

"We didn't until Byron told us. Our friends traced the origin of these disasters back to forces unleashed from Brotherhood enclaves in Europe." Stuart caught himself just before mentioning The Realm.

Bethune switched its display to a map of the world. "The colored dots are places devastated by Wizard-created disasters."

"No disasters have happened since the Mages attacked the Brotherhood," Stuart said. "However, this is only a reprieve. We need your help to stop The Brotherhood before it kills any more people."

Stuart glanced at the Wizards. Omeron held Pembar's arm for support. The Thals drew closer together, wiping their eyes and patting each other. Dog circled around them, her tail whipping back and forth.

"Omeron, could you ask the Thals to explain in their language what they see?" Stuart said. "Bethune wants to hear them talk."

"Who is Bethune?"

Stuart looked to the other Mages. "How do I explain an A.I.?"

"Bethune lives in a machine and helps humans," Baltic said.

Shrugging her shoulders, Omeron relayed the explanation to the Thals. Like a flock of excited birds, they chirped away. After several minutes, they peeped single sounds or in short bursts while pointing at the laptop screen.

Stuart walked around the table to look at it. As close as the Thals were, their magic did not interfere with the operation of the laptop. *I must see how their presence affects other technology.*

Bethune displayed pictures of animals, birds and landscapes. "I'm trying to learn their vocabulary and speech pattern. It may take me a while."

Pembar pointed to the Mages. "Omeron, you've examined these young people closely. What's your conclusion?"

"They possess magic unlike anything I've ever heard of."

"What would you do to Stuart if he made you angry?" Pembar cracked a slight smile.

"Cause him to fall on his face or inflict a very painful stomach ailment."

"Try it." Omeron stared at him wide-eyed. "You'll find it interesting."

Stuart braced for the infuriating itchiness. Mild at first, it worsened as Omeron stepped up the power of her assault.

"I'd stop now, Omeron, as he killed Vince for less than that."

The itching vanished. "Vince is dead?"

"Along with Mirantso, Amadeus and Jonast. They went to the New World to murder Byron. Stuart defeated them and frightened Vikist away."

Omeron stared at Pembar, her brow deeply furrowed. Her hands trembled. He nodded several times before revealing that Anastasia de la Montagne had joined the Mages.

Omeron gasped and her hand flew to her mouth. "How did she escape from the Brotherhood dungeon?"

"By transporting herself to the New World through Stuart's magic. Her abilities have blossomed since then."

Omeron hugged her sides and rocked back and forth for several minutes. Finally she stilled herself and gasped. "Across the ocean—that's incredible."

"The Mages only want to stop the devastation," Pembar said. "They don't wish to destroy us or the Thals."

Omeron patted Dog as if she needed comforting. Maybe both did.

Watching Omeron, Stuart was even more convinced there was something special about the influence the animal exerted on the Wizards and Thals.

"You never shared Byron's erratic tendencies, Pembar, yet you accept his faith in these young people." Omeron sat in silence, her forehead once again deeply furrowed.

"Stuart, you should show Omeron your device to talk with Byron." Pembar nodded toward the van.

Baltic and Stuart brought the speaker and transmitter from the van to the table. The Thals were still chatting with Bethune. "I need to disconnect the laptop so the Wizards can talk with Byron."

"I'll listen to the conversation from this end. Thanks friend, you have given me much to work on."

Stuart plugged the transmitter into his satellite phone and called the farm. When Ears answered, Stuart said, "Tell Byron an old acquaintance wants to talk to him."

Pembar grinned. "This'll be amusing. She always argues with Byron. Maybe it'll be better with him on the other side of the Atlantic."

Omeron finally smiled. "That I could talk to him when he is that far away intrigues me."

"When you hear him, speak in your normal tone of voice." Seeing the Thals approaching the table, still in their tight formation, Stuart said, "They can touch the transmitter."

Before Pembar could explain, a groggy Byron spoke. "Everything okay, Stuart?"

For the next few minutes, Omeron questioned Byron in Wizardese. Pembar covered his mouth to stifle his laughter.

Is Byron such an oddball among the Wizards that they enjoy tormenting him? Then Stuart remembered Uncle Oscar doing that with his nieces and nephews. Wizards were no different than the rest of humanity at expressing affection.

Omeron relaxed in her chair and motioned to the Thals. Teapot girl chirped before switching to Wizardese. Soon they were all talking with Byron. When they finally stopped, Stuart took it as a sign the conversation was finished. "We'll keep you posted," he said before disconnecting the phone.

Omeron stepped up to the Mages. "Welcome to our world." Medallions the size of silver dollar coins and shaped like flowers appeared in her hand. "With these, most Wizards will welcome you." They floated to Stuart, Baltic and Viking. "When I meet your friends, I'll prepare medallions for them."

After they thanked her, Viking pulled a magnifying glass out of her bag to examine hers. "In our world, this'd be worth a small fortune."

Still in a tight knot, the Thals approached Viking, pointing at her magnifying glass. When she showed them how it worked, their chirping got louder. "Tell them I'll get one for each of them."

"How did you know we searched for you, Omeron?" Stuart said.

"I could sense the presence of Dog and Pembar even though I couldn't understand why they circled about instead of coming directly to my enclave. I didn't understand the other three presences, which made me more curious."

This was the jovial mood Stuart wanted. "Would you explain to the Thals that we want to meet more of their kind?"

For several minutes, Omeron and Pembar talked with the Thals, who kept patting Dog as the Wizards spoke.

"They want us to go to Wutega's enclave as there are older Thals there to whom you should speak," Pembar said.

"The Thals will look after my enclave while I'm away," Omeron said. "I've not been on a trip for a long time." A commotion rattled throughout the enclave, and then a large bag floated out the front door toward the van. "I'm ready."

The Mages followed the bag to stow it in the van and make room for the extra passenger.

"Although they're not English, Omeron and Pembar treat Dog like a magical creature." Viking shook her head and shot Stuart a bemused smile.

"Dog is magical," Stuart said. "She possesses an interesting power. When you pet her, she suggests what you should do."

THE REALM ABROAD

Byron summoned the Mages to the farmhouse kitchen table to discuss Stuart's success in meeting two Wizards and the Thals. They also studied a map of France looking for clues to the location of Iywwan's enclave in Brittany that Byron wanted them to visit.

"Diviner will lead a group of us through the Otherworld to France," Audubon said. "Anastasia and I are sure she can find her way to the rendezvous with our European contact."

"But she has only entered the Otherworld a few times," Byron said.

"She's a natural for it because of her ability to find water and resources underground," Audubon said. "She's also a crack shot and will take Stuart's gun. Anastasia and I'll accompany the group as backup."

Diviner reached over and patted Audubon's arm. She was his most vociferous critic when he first proposed The Realm had tapped into magic. After hearing Byron's tales, she apologized to him. More importantly, she befriended Anastasia.

Byron peered about the kitchen, his brow wrinkled. "Iywwan is one of the most influential Wizards outside Merstreem's circle. We must win her to our side. To do that, she needs to understand the scope of death and destruction that his gang is causing. Hopefully she'll realize his actions have become a disaster for Wizards."

"Let's get ready," Audubon said. "We'll meet back here in an hour."

The departing Mages gathered on the front lawn, loaded packs on their backs. The rifle slung over her shoulder, Diviner inspected the safety line connecting her and the other seven travelers. "Make sure your goggles fit tightly. The magic in the Otherworld propels you so quickly that your eyes water. It's like downhill skiing."

"Stay focused on the destination." Byron shook his head. "It's too easy to get distracted in the Otherworld. That can be fatal."

Following Diviner, the other Mages stepped into the fog between the dimensions leaving the safety of the farm behind. Anastasia and Audubon went last holding hands.

As they emerged into the Otherworld, the Mages gasped. Thick mixed thick forest dominated the terrain, quite unlike the rocky landscape they saw during Byron's visit to his refuge.

Diviner studied her compass and then pointed in the direction of distant hills. "It's good you figured out how to use a compass there. Byron said to keep traveling in a northeast direction until we get a signal."

When everyone nodded, she headed off. In the Otherworld, anyone walking at a regular pace was soon traveling along several meters above the ground or, at times, large bodies of water. Air streamed past them.

"How fast are we travelling?" Quake said from the middle of the group. No one answered. "Never would have thought to bring a speedometer when we're travelling on foot."

Diviner signaled the next break. When their feet touched ground again, the travelers pulled energy bars and water bottles from their packs. They huddled together, patting backs and shoulders for mutual comfort.

Anastasia pulled Audubon close and whispered. "Keep thinking France. Otherwise lose hope."

Audubon hugged her. "You reached North America by yourself."

"In bubble of magic transporting me to Stuart and Byron. Not aware of surroundings. This group too big for that kind of travel."

"There's no wind and it's so quiet, which gives it a peaceful feeling," Diviner said. "Maybe it's the kind of place that grows on you."

She pulled binoculars from her pack and made a 360 degree sweep of the area. "There's not much to see."

Several Mages borrowed the binoculars to inspect the scenery. "Okay everyone, another hour of travel and then a break," she called out. When they finished their snacks and were ready to depart, they took their spots behind Diviner on the safety line.

"Diviner work through compass like you with telescope," Anastasia murmured to Audubon.

They touched down on a rocky plateau to a stomach-turning smell. Holding their noses, the Mages soon found a body. "Vikist!" Anastasia said "Byron thought wound him when assassins attack him and Stuart." She coughed and covered her nose. "It enough for magic of Otherworld to claim him."

Audubon gazed at the crumpled figure. "Perhaps this means the Wizards don't know the attack on Byron failed."

She nodded. "Probably still wait for Vikist. If know dead, do more damage your city."

He glanced at the body. "Do we just leave him?"

Anastasia shook her head and stepped back pulling Audubon with her. She stared at the body until it turned to dust.

"Oh, that's what Byron did to the old guy in the tavern and the other Wizards who attacked him and Stuart," Diviner said. "Alright everyone, we better eat our snack and move on." She tugged on the line connecting the Mages.

Whether from the distance traveled over mostly unwelcoming terrain or the body's grim reminder of the danger they faced, the Mages' steps slowed and they mostly stared at their feet rather than look at the sights they passed.

Little was said during the next break as they consumed the last chocolate snack bars and water. Before anyone became too despondent, Diviner called, "Come on folks, back to our world."

Audubon's legs felt leaden and his back pack like it was full of bricks. Below him, a vast sea or lake lay unmoving like a sullen mass.

"Think sipping wine," Anastasia called.

Audubon puzzled over how she could manage to sound so cheerful when Wizards loathed the Otherworld. Maybe she appreciated the end of a trip through it more.

He had stopped paying attention to the passage of time when Diviner called, "Anyone hear birds?" Everyone picked up their pace.

The bird calls got louder as the group entered the fog between the dimensions. They stepped into the bright sunshine of Brittany and a welcome from a tall, curly-haired man dressed in hiking attire. He held a walking stick in his left hand and a hefty camera was slung around his neck.

"What kind of bird is this that heard my calls?" he said as Diviner approached. "Oh, look at all the colorful ones following her. Such plumage." He pulled a video camera from his pocket to record the Mages' arrival. "Byron wants proof you're safe."

Diviner laughed before hugging him. "It seems appropriate to have a bird watcher greet Audubon. When you send your report to the farm, tell them we found Vikist's body."

Ampere introduced himself. "While Marconi thinks I don't pay enough attention to the need for constant vigilance, no one takes my antics seriously. That means I can carry on experiments in high frequency radio waves and radar without any interference.

"I'll take you to a small local hotel. Tomorrow we'll look again for Iywwan's enclave. It's around here somewhere. Tonight, we'll dine outside while we see if your friends can shake some more rats out of their enclaves."

Audubon looked at his watch. "Diviner, you brought us through that wretched place in less than five hours. At times, it felt like it'd take days."

"Wizards fear Otherworld." Anastasia gripped Audubon's right arm with both hands. "Mages handle much better."

Ampere gazed at the newcomers with a bemused smile. "We found a few enclaves in Western Europe and the Russians located several in the Urals. Byron advised just to watch them until Pembar and Stuart can get there."

A warm breeze and plenty of wine and tasty dishes during an outdoor supper relaxed the Mages until Audubon remembered that more enclave shakeups were planned for this evening.

Ampere left the table and returned in a few minutes flashing thumbs up. "Checked the instruments in the car and made some calls. They shook several enclaves and one fell apart. The tremors won't show up on any seismic registers because they were so localized."

The next morning, the French Mage drove the others into the countryside. Towering hills loomed in the distance. After a couple of hours traipsing through the woods, Ampere stopped in a clearing. "I covered the same ground yesterday and found nothing. The enclave should be around here."

He faced Audubon. "I hear you can attract animals and birds. Would you show me?"

"Might be just what need." Anastasia steered her companion into the center of the clearing. "Everyone back into the trees."

By the time they moved away, several sparrows had landed on Audubon's shoulders and a pair of squirrels chattered away at his feet. A few jays and other birds flapped around, singing and squawking at him. A fox approached a few steps at a time, ignoring the squirrels. A large owl floated through the trees, looping once around him before landing on his outstretched left arm and hooting at him.

A smile flitted across his face. "Perhaps we just need some extra help to find Iywwan." He addressed the birds and animals. "I need your assistance. This is my memory of her image." He closed his eyes.

The birds rose into the air with a rush of wings and headed off. The animals ran in the same direction. They glanced back as if to make sure he followed. The other Mages trailed at a discreet distance.

Peering about, Audubon nearly walked into a stout, white-haired woman in green pants and a multi-colored jacket that blended with the surrounding foliage. They eyed each other until she said, "Etes-vou perdu?"

"Je ne parle pas français."

She eyed him, and then the Mages in the trees. Without hesitation, she replied in accented but flawless English. "Can you imagine that? The location of my enclave is given away by the birds and animals I've treated so kindly all these years." She gazed about before returning her attention to Audubon. "Obviously, you possess a talent to enlist creatures to assist you. They see something about you that's invisible to me. Who are you?"

Audubon beckoned the others forward. The old woman's eyes widened in surprise. "Anastasia de la Montagne." She clapped her hands. "You escaped! How did you do it, and why can I not see your aura?"

"I suppressed it so Wizards not find me." The young woman recounted her flight to freedom and what her new friends were capable of. "There is Mage who immune to Wizard magic and that allowed me to reach out to him."

"C'est impossible!" Iywwan cried. "Immune to magic! Absolument impossible." She sputtered and stared at the newcomers, wiping her hands repeatedly on her pants. She kept glancing at Anastasia and shaking her head.

"Byron has more experience with them," Anastasia said.

The mention of Byron's name produced a pinched expression on Iywwan's face. "He'd be involved in something like this. Mage abilities are unlike ours?"

Anastasia nodded. "They want to stop Merstreem and his gang from destroying the world."

Iywwan's nostrils flared. "Merstreem says he's trying to save the world."

"By killing millions of people?" Anastasia's voice was even louder. She recapped the natural disasters around the world. "Not how magic to be used. Supposed to make life better. Remember Wizard oath about harming no one?"

"Wars and famines are killing all those people. It's not Wizards' doing." While Iywwan could not match Anastasia in volume, she did not back down.

"Huge hurricanes, earthquakes and horrible storms created by Brotherhood kill them." Anastasia's chest heaved and she jabbed the air with her fists.

Telling himself not to ever argue with Anastasia, Audubon wondered if he should step between them. Instead he called for wildlife assistance. In response, the woods rang with the screech of a raptor as it flew into the clearing. Ignoring the owl now perched on his left shoulder, the hawk landed on his right shoulder and fixed its gaze on the women. It screeched again and the shouting stopped.

Iywwan stared at the bird. It peered back, its eyelids blinking. "I've never seen one so large. It's not a creature of magic and it flew willingly to you. I'll hear you out."

While Audubon puzzled over where the bird came from, Anastasia lowered her voice. "Mages and Wizards need the other. Science make magic stronger than before."

"Is it your friends who attacked the Brotherhood enclaves?" A faint smile flickered across Iywwan's face. Anastasia nodded.

Iywwan gestured toward a clump of trees. "Come to mine." She took three steps, and then a stately wooden structure appeared about 50 meters away. It was ringed by rock gardens full of flowers growing like rainbows run amok. "We've much to discuss."

Anastasia took Audubon's hand as they set out after the old woman, followed by the others. The hawk and owl flew ahead. Audubon's avian following became so large that several birds landed on Anastasia's shoulders because his were full. A couple of badgers joined the fox and squirrels in the posse accompanying the Mages.

"Think of the power she possesses to hide this place and maintain it in such marvelous condition," Diviner said.

"Actually, another form of magic maintains her enclave," Audubon said.

Anastasia stared at him. "C'est new for you."

"Learning to navigate the Otherworld increased the scope of my magic. What's up ahead is different than Wizard magic."

"We about to encounter Thals," she said.

Marconi looked up from the desk in the Mage command center in the farmhouse as Ears and Byron entered the room. She had arrived the day before from San Francisco. Her in-laws moved into her home to look after her two youngsters so she could spend "a long weekend working on a communications contract."

Beside her laptop was a wide screen TV to display the satellite signals from the group in Europe. On the other side were Bethune's computer towers. Ears had added a fifth one. Nearby was the screen that displayed the incoming images from the drones mapping the Otherworld.

Bethune conducted the regular monitoring of the Otherworld. Mages worked with him during the day to analyze its findings.

"There's a small party of Wizards from the Netherlands in the Otherworld," Pied Piper said. "Bethune has tracked their travel with drones during the last few days. They've remained in the same place for the last 20 hours and from the drone images, it looks like they've set up camp."

"Byron, would you meet those Wizards and, if they're friendly, invite them to come to the farm," Marconi said.

She showed him on a simple outline map of the Otherworld where the Wizards were camped compared to the location of his refuge.

He agreed to check them out. "I'll be able to home in on their magic."

"What if you took a bunch of the Mages there with you?" Marconi said. "We could ask Diviner to rendezvous with you and take the Mages to Europe with her."

Pied Piper and Digger quickly agreed. "We feel kind of useless hanging out at the farm when the action is in Europe," Digger said. "We need to learn the location of more Wizard enclaves and study how they went undetected.

The TV emitted a loud beep and switched from a screen saver image of Stonehenge to a view of Audubon. "Behind me is Iywwan's enclave. All those lifestyle magazines would love this place." The camera panned the elegant building and its gardens. "She wants to talk with Byron. She and Anastasia have already had a long discussion."

A wry smile crossed Audubon's face. "Iywwan says that of the 138 Wizards still alive, 12 are so old they're senile, kept alive by their residual magic. Of the remainder, about 90 of them are like her, happy with neither The Brotherhood nor the deterioration of the planet caused by climate change. There are five Dissidents beside Byron and the rest are Merstreem's supporters who will fight us all the way. She wasn't aware of the six of that bunch Stuart has eliminated."

The sound of Audubon's voice attracted other Mages to Marconi's desk. They parted to let the diminutive Byron see the screen from the back of the room, which continued to display scenes of the enclave and its surroundings as well as Audubon's wildlife admirers.

"Magic is passing the torch," Byron said. "Wizards didn't do much with it except perpetuate our traditional abilities rather than learn new skills. That was good enough for most of us, but not Merstreem. He became bitter and resentful about the world passing us by."

"Iywwan wants to have a chat with you," Audubon said.

Byron groaned. "This means she has a lot to say and I'm expected to listen." He rolled his eyes. The Mages laughed.

"You're safe for now because we don't have the Wizard-proof equipment to do that," Marconi said.

"How unfortunate for me!" Byron said. The room rang with another round of laughter.

Audubon resumed his description. "Remember Byron told us Wizards don't have fancy enclaves because of the magic it takes to conceal and maintain them. Well, we're awestruck by this place. You should see the help." The camera panned the grounds before halting at the columns on either side of the front door. Everyone in the room gasped. A group of Thals stood in a semicircle smiling at the camera.

"There are at least 10 here." The camera moved from Thal to Thal as his narration continued. "They come here and to other enclaves, including the one Stuart visited, as part of their education. Iywwan can't explain how it works. The Thals asked Anastasia endless questions about her escape."

The camera zoomed in on two male Thals, who stared back with bemused smiles. "If they were half a meter taller, the NFL would be all over these guys. I can't guess the age of any of them."

"Audubon, we want Diviner to meet up with a group of Mages who Byron will lead to where we've found a group of Wizards in the Otherworld," Marconi said. "The Mages have arranged time off work or a break from university duties and are prepared to go to Europe to help search for enclaves."

Audubon waved over Diviner and explained the request.

"Ampere is always asking questions about the Otherworld," she said. "Here's his chance for a tour."

STUART'S FAN CLUB

Evening infiltrated Omeron's garden. Through repeated yawns, Stuart answered her questions about how he worked with machines. When her interest shifted to the new Realm, he begged off. "Baltic and Viking can explain it better. I need to sleep." With that, he went to bed.

When he woke the next morning, Baltic showed him the directions to the Wizard Wutega's enclave in Hungary that Omeron had drawn on a map. They drove past farms and forests and through hamlets until the late evening when they stopped at a rural hotel for the night.

When they climbed into the van the next morning, Omeron said, "Only Stuart, Pembar, Dog and I will approach Wutega's enclave. While he favors the leaders, he should hear us out and might be curious about Stuart. Viking and Baltic can't protect themselves if he becomes hostile. You'll be safe in the van because he won't be able to detect you inside it."

In the late morning, Viking turned onto a gravel road. She slowed down to steer around potholes and ruts.

"The trees and bushes are so badly stunted around here," Omeron said from her seat beside Pembar in the middle of the van. "This used to be a lovely area. It was ruined by people building big, smelly buildings."

"She means factories and the smoke and liquids they created that did the damage," Baltic said.

"Stop here," Omeron said. "We're close to the enclave."

"We could follow behind you in case there's trouble," Viking said.

"What would you do if there was?" Omeron snapped. With that, she entered the woods at a quick pace, Dog scampering along beside her. Stuart and Pembar scrambled to catch up.

Stuart dodged branches and stepped around trees. "This place feels malevolent like the storm that chased Byron and me in Toronto. I sense resentment, hate and envy. There's none of the joy of life that you and Omeron exude."

Pembar sighed. "Magic gone bad."

Stuart marveled at Omeron's ability to navigate the uneven terrain without breaking stride. She stopped when they reached a clearing where the ground leveled off for close to 50 meters. In the middle was a heap of stones and logs. "How did they get there?" he said.

Omeron put a finger to her lips. She and Pembar stared at the pile until it transformed into a large log cabin with small windows and doors. It looked shabby and ill-kept compared to their residences.

"Wutega disguises his enclave as a pile of rubble," Pembar said.

A rotund, sour faced man stood on a path halfway to the cabin, impatiently tapping his foot. He wore a long black coat over charcoal pants and a hat that looked like a bloated beret.

"Welcome fair lady." Wutega said in Wizardese as he bowed slightly toward Omeron. "Why have you brought the troublemaker Pembar? Has he finally seen the error of his ways?"

Stuart's magic did not reveal much about people's motives and intentions. However, he could tell Wutega wanted an excuse to strike at Pembar who, in turn, summoned his magic in self-defence. Only the presence of Omeron seemed to prevent a duel between them.

When Omeron explained about Stuart's magic, Wutega spat at him and a tidal wave of itchiness crashed into the Mage. He stood his ground and caught Omeron and Pembar staggering backward. Dog lay whimpering.

Stuart's anger at the unprovoked attack flared and with it, the itchiness faded. As it did, he dashed past Omeron and Pembar and tackled Wutega, driving him to the ground. "Tell him to stop attacking us," he shouted.

When they did not respond and another wave of itchiness struck him, Stuart pounded Wutega's head into the ground. The Wizard's behaviour reminded him of the night the Brotherhood thugs tried to murder Byron.

Wutega tried to wiggle out of Stuart's grasp. Then the Mage was propelled backward landing on his butt. Wutega lay sprawled on the ground unmoving.

Behind him, Omeron shouted," Why did you kill Wutega?"

"I didn't. Some force threw me off him but it couldn't have been Wutega because I'm not itching. I've no idea how he died."

Omeron leaned on Pembar as they looked at the Wizard's body. A loud boom sounded from the enclave.

"There are two Thals running toward the enclave," Stuart said.

"One of them must have thrown you off and killed Wutega," she said. "But they have never killed Wizards before. What could he have done to provoke them?"

Stones fell off the cabin's chimney and rolled away. A heavy wood door swung open and a Thal chirped loudly before calling in Wizardese as other short figures scurried from the building.

"They need help to rescue someone," Pembar said. "Here's your chance."

Stuart sprinted toward the building. Thals stood in a cluster by the door, chirping and pointing inside the enclave. More booms rolled from it, each accompanied by a flash of light. It sounded like a monstrous thunderstorm.

Behind him, Pembar called. "The enclave is collapsing because Wutega's magic is dissipating with his death. There's a Thal trapped inside by a magical bond the others cannot break." A loud crack drowned out the rest of his words.

Stuart stopped running to shout. "What can I do?"

"We and the Thals can't rescue the Thal because none of us can break Wutega's binding spell," Pembar called. "Your immunity to Wizard magic means you might be the only one who can free the Thal. Hurry inside, up the stairs and to the left. I'll cast a light to show you the way."

His heart pounding, Stuart bounded through the door and followed the light upstairs, climbing two steps at a time. He refused to think about the building collapsing on him. The low ceiling and narrow hallway brought out his claustrophobia.

The light veered to the left. A small figure cowered against a wall in a dingy room. A blanket covered all but the eyes. A brief burst of itchiness flashed through him as he broke Wutega's bond by picking up the Thal. Holding the figure against his chest, he thumped down the stairs.

Around him, wood cracked and windows shattered. Stuart imagined a tunnel and sprinted for it. He kept running, spurred on by the thunderous cacophony of the enclave's destruction. While he did not know where he was headed, adrenalin propelled him forward. The Thals rushed after him through the tunnel.

He stopped when Pembar called his name. He could spot the Wizards in the distance looking at the grimy cloud rising from where the enclave once stood. Wutega's body was gone, obviously reduced to dust.

"We can't see you," Pembar shouted as he frantically surveyed the area."Look to your left," Stuart called. "I called on my touchstone to help me get away. The Thals followed me. They're talking very loudly. I'm giving them whomever I'm carrying."

Although they were adults, the Thals seemed barely a head taller than the young females at Omeron's enclave. The adult females were as heavily muscled as the males.

Stuart's breathing was normal and the ache was gone from his arms and back by the time the Wizards reached him. The Thals waved their arms as they babbled at Omeron and Pembar in Wizardese.

"They're impressed you risked your life to save their Grandmother after they killed Wutega," Pembar said. "And we're impressed that your invisibility is so strong we couldn't see you escape from the enclave."

The Grandmother and two Thals stood beside Stuart while the others moved between them and Omeron and Pembar. Dog rubbed her head against the Wizards' legs. After a conversation in Wizardese with the Thals, Omeron said. "The two Thals we saw running away killed Wutega with their magic because his attack on us was unprovoked. They both hit him with their magic at the same time to kill him. Otherwise you would've had to save us. They fled to warn their fellows the enclave was about to collapse and to try to rescue the Grandmother."

Omeron touched the side of her head with her finger. "Something happened to Wutega. Attacking us was not normal behavior for him."

Stuart expected a litany of excuses for Wutega. Instead, Omeron took Pembar's arm. "Merstreem keeps us isolated because lacking regular visits with each other, magic distorts our judgment. We need magical company to maintain our balance and keep our powers strong." She looked about. "I couldn't survive without the presence of the Thals."

"I have Dog," Pembar nodded.

She glanced to where Wutega died. "How many others will be like him?" Nodding at Stuart, she said, "Merstreem really is ruining our world as well as yours."

The two Wizards and the Thals talked steadily, voices rising and falling with plenty of arm waving. Pembar turned to Stuart. "They want you to become their Wizard because you're kind and wouldn't mistreat them as Wutega did."

Stuart let out a nervous laugh. "What would I do with them? I can't even speak to them. Couldn't they join the Thals at Omeron's?"

"While they'd be most welcome, their loyalty doesn't work like that," she said. "They can live on their own, but want to be associated with a Wizard who has powerful magic they can learn from. For these eight that would be you, although they'd stay with me if you told them to. Most Wizards would think you're fortunate to have so many Thals freely attached to you. They'll make you more powerful."

"Marvelous isn't it?" *What would I do with more magic; what I have has nearly driven me insane.* A silly grin spread across his face. "With the extra power, I really could Thal people what to do." He frowned when no one understood his humor. *There are some things magic doesn't change.*

"They're not much trouble," Pembar said. "They can render themselves invisible to non-magical people and they mostly feed and clothe themselves." After a brief conversation with the Thals, Pembar smiled. "They intend to follow you because they no longer have a home here. We could use their help."

"Tell them to collect their belongings and fill them in on what we're doing." *I wish I could talk with Judyth about all of this.*

"Their belongings were in the enclave," Omeron said. "It'll take a while to retrieve them."

Stuart followed the Thals and Wizards back to the heap of shattered beams and stone. "How will they retrieve anything from that mess?"

The Thals lined up facing the pile. The wind grew strong enough to blow away small bits of debris until Stuart could see clothing, packs and pieces of furniture among the stones and chunks of wood. The wind dropped, and then the Thals' belongings sailed into a pile and the remaining debris of the enclave drifted away from the site before crumbling into dust and fine gravel that spread over the surrounding meadow.

The Wizards watched the operation wide eyed. "Thals have always been secretive about their abilities," Pembar said. "We didn't know they could perform magic anything like this."

"What'll they do with the pile of stuff from the enclave?" Stuart said. "We can't fit them or their belongings in the van."

The Grandmother, still wrapped in her blanket, stepped beside the pile. It rose in the air and a wide orange cloth appeared and wrapped itself around the belongings.

Stuart scratched his head. *Where the heck did that material come from?*

One of the Thals Stuart spotted running to the enclave after Wutega's death spoke to the Wizards, and then smiled at Stuart.

"He's their leader; they're ready to accompany us," Pembar said.

"We need to travel to the other enclaves," Stuart said. "How can they follow us around especially with that bundle of belongings?"

Pembar explained the situation to the Thals who then gathered in a huddle. After a few minutes, the leader left the group and spoke to the Wizards, his arms gesticulating wildly. Pembar translated.

"They appreciate your concern for their safety, Stuart. So they offer a compromise. We tell them where we're headed and they'll meet us there." He pointed at the leader. "He'll assist us when we reach an enclave and the rest will stay out of sight."

"How will they keep up?"

"They'll be waiting for us. They can travel through the Otherworld much faster than we can on the roads."

While it sounded on the far side of unbelievable, Stuart headed toward the vehicle. "We need the map in the van to show them our destinations." He halted when the Thals broke into impassioned chirping.

"The Thal said your magic absorbed most of the attack Wutega aimed at Omeron and me," Pembar said. "Few Wizards could do what you did and your feat rendered your magic almost impossible to detect. The Thals want to have a Wizard of your stature associated with their clan. They think all Thals will want to follow you as well. They say you are a great Wizard."

The profuse praise made Stuart suspect a set up. "How many are there?"

"Several thousand at least spread out through Europe and Russia," Pembar said before a smirk spread across his face. "Neither they nor we really know how many there are."

"Can you explain how I created the tunnel that got me safely out of the enclave and how the Thals could follow me in it while you couldn't see me?"

Pembar shrugged. "You must have been thinking about protecting yourself once you picked up the Grandmother and the magic created the tunnel for you to flee through using your touchstone. The Thals approve that your touchstone is a special relative."

"How could they know about Uncle Oscar?" Stuart stammered.

"They saw him when you sought help to escape the enclave," Pembar said. "You look like him. However, we can't explain how the Thals found you. That is another puzzle."

While mastering magic was his top priority, he still needed to win over more Thals to give the Mages the power to defeat The Brotherhood.

When they neared the van, Baltic called, "What did you do in there? We heard lots of explosions."

Then the Thals and their floating orange bundle of belongings appeared. "I'd introduce you, but I've no idea what their names are," Stuart said.

"You couldn't pronounce them if you did," Pembar said. He recounted Stuart's struggle with Wutega and rescue of the Grandmother to the other Mages.

The Thals followed Stuart when he went to the van to retrieve the map. He opened the passenger side front door and pulled the map case out of the door pocket. Before he could close it, the Thals climbed in. They chirped non-stop as they tried the seats and opened the compartments.

"They've never been in a motorized vehicle before," Pembar said.

"What's our next stop?" Stuart spread the map on the hood of the van.

Omeron tapped a spot on the map before pointing eastward. "Todomorin's enclave."

"That's in Russia," Stuart said. "We'll need visas and permits to get across the border. That'll take a lot of time we don't have."

"We could meet the Thals at a park near the border and follow them through the Otherworld to the enclave," Pembar said. Stuart nodded and Pembar explained the plan to the Thals who selected a meeting place near the Russian border.

The Thals stepped away from the van and disappeared. For a few seconds, their luggage hung in the air before it winked out of sight.

"We better purchase some food as it'll be close to suppertime before we reach the border," Viking said. "It's a long way from there to the Urals."

"Doesn't the Otherworld upset Thals?" Stuart said.

"They're safe from Wizards there and its creatures are friendly to them," Omeron said.

"Before we go anywhere, I need to tell the farm about what happened today." Stuart pulled out his satellite phone.

It was early morning in North America. "Hello Stuart."

"Hey Bethune. Are you solo?"

"Ears just went to bed. Want me to wake him?"

"Copy my report for the others." When he finished, Bethune said, "Byron and some Mages have left to meet a group of Wizards hiding in the Otherworld. Diviner is joining them from France to take the Mages to Europe."

When Stuart explained Byron's trip to the Otherworld, Pembar and Omeron both shuddered. "What desperation would it take for Wizards to hide there?" Pembar said.

STRANGERS AT THE FARM

Diviner was back in the Otherworld waiting for Byron to arrive from the farm. She kept her gaze on 11 people huddled near a circle of glowing boulders. Three were shorter than the others. Two circular tents stood nearby.

"They must be the Wizards we were to locate," she whispered to Ampere while wiping her forehead. Her sleeve was already damp. "Surely they don't need any heat. They should've reacted to our presence but they haven't looked our way. They appear to be sitting on boulders fashioned into chairs. We'll leave the introductions to Byron."

While the light revealed a ring of trees around the site, it was not bright enough to identify their species. Boulders that most likely once covered the area formed a fence around the camp site. *While it looks like a traditional meeting place, why was Iywwan unaware of it?*

Ampere sat beside her, his back to the Wizards. Occasionally he leaned against her. He was quite open about demonstrating his affection. "As well as speaking French and English, I can converse in Spanish and German so we should be able to approach them."

"We've no protection if they do anything; Iywwan said Wizards in the Otherworld will be jumpy. You know, shoot magic first and ask questions later." Although Diviner joked about their situation, she did not feel like taking any chances.

"Might as well wait rather than walk into a hornets' nest," Ampere said. With a tap, he turned on the narrow-beam light strapped to his forehead, and then pulled out a notebook. "I'm recording my impressions of the Otherworld. The quiet is what you first notice. I can hear the Wizard's conversations, the rustle of the breeze and the chirp of what sound like crickets. I'll listen for birds when the sun rises."

"Bethune is gathering everyone's impressions of the Otherworld," Diviner said. "You must share yours."

They both looked up when they heard a whirring overhead. "One of Ears' drones," she said. "He has 24 mapping the Otherworld beginning with an outline of the coasts, and then large inland bodies of water and mountain ranges."

"I'd like to see the results of their exploration." He jotted down a few more lines. "While we wait, tell me what it's like to look under the Earth's crust. What do you see?" He glanced about studying the nearby rock formations. "Maybe we could use your abilities to raise funds for The Realm."

"As you slip through layers of rock, you notice the changes in the strata and the presence of other material as well as the density or heat. There are some unusual places on Earth that I've encountered that I'd like to examine in a lot more detail. Also I want to try exploring the sea bottom and mountain ranges. There's a lot left to discover."

Before she could enquire about , he said, "Could you do the same examination here?"

"I'll try to if I've time."

To her surprise, he kept writing in his notebook leading her to wonder what preoccupied him.

She reached over and took his hand. "Think you could live in North America? I mean we could help each other develop our powers."

Ampere hugged and kissed her. "I could probably land a job at one of the universities in Montreal."

Before they could say more, footsteps on the rocky ground around the campsite made her jump to her feet and grab the rifle. Releasing the safety, she pointed the weapon into the gloom. "Something is coming."

Thals strode toward them. Their clothes looked dirty and torn, unlike the neatly dressed ones at Iywwan's. The leader held out a piece of paper. "Me Boss."

She scanned it. "It's a note from Stuart. The Thals came here to meet Byron and us. They're headed for the farm, except for Boss who'll return to assist Stuart."

"How did they find us?" Ampere said.

"Stuart say where you be," Boss said. "I be here before. Him, Viking, Baltic my friends."

The other Thals stepped forward and bowed. They wore loose fitting pants and long sleeved tops of various shades of brown.

Diviner figured the one wrapped in the blanket was the Grandmother who Stuart mentioned in the note. Spotting different marks covering the blanket, she puzzled over what they might mean. They reminded her of the symbols on Byron's shirt the morning he put on the magic display at the farm. *I must tell Bethune to check them out.*

"Can understand Boss okay?" When Diviner and Ampere nodded, the Thal beamed. "You be my friends?"

Diviner and Ampere reached out to shake hands. "We'd be glad to count you among our friends."

"Now go meet Wizards," Boss said.

"Shouldn't we wait for Byron?" Diviner glanced at Ampere.

"You safe with us. They not understand your magic but can tell you not bad Wizards."

"I'm still glad you know how to use that rifle," Ampere said.

Boss led the way down the rocky slope. Diviner and Ampere jumped back to avoid a large bundle that tagged along as if connected to the newcomers by an invisible rope. Ampere shook his head and shrugged when she glanced at him. "Must be important to them if they brought it this far."

The dim light did not slow the Thals forcing Diviner and Ampere to hurry to keep up. They held hands for balance. "I still want to hear your idea about fundraising for The Realm," she said.

A Wizard called out before Ampere could reply. The others rose and gathered together looking warily at the newcomers. Dark, full length robes covered their clothes and Diviner could not see enough to tell ages or gender. The short ones appeared to be children who peered out from behind the adults at the newcomers.

Diviner felt like she was wading through water.

"Wizards make us slow so can see if safe," Boss said. "Easy magic stop. Me speak."

Boss shouted to the Wizards while pointing to Diviner and Ampere several times. The conversation went back and forth. Diviner shifted her weight from one leg to the other repeatedly waiting for the parlay to conclude.

"Can join; not know Byron come," Boss said.

As abruptly as Diviner and Ampere's walking had been impeded, it ended. "That's better," she said. "However, I'd be suspicious of strangers if I was them."

"We get more rocks for light," Boss said. A couple of boulders the size of automobiles floated out of the dark and landed beside the glowing ones. The Thals peered at them until they shone like the others. The extra light fully illuminated the area around the campsite. It felt like having a roaring bonfire on a steamy midsummer night.

Ampere let go of Diviner's hand and took a few steps toward a small pond. There was not enough light to tell anything about the water. Before he could scoop up a handful, Diviner said, "They're here."

Byron and several Mages hurried toward them. At the sight of Thals, the Wizard's lips moved without making a sound as if his words dissolved before they left his mouth.

Boss approached him, his hand extended with the note from Stuart.

Waiting for Byron's reaction, Diviner almost missed Grandmother walking soundlessly up to Judyth and tugging the hem of her jacket while smiling shyly. Judyth grinned back, and then glanced at Byron.

"She prefers to be connected to a female Mage and as you are special to Stuart, you are to her as well," Byron said.

"How does she know about Stuart and me?"

Byron smiled, and then introduced the Mages and Wizards before speaking with the leader of the group whose face was mostly hidden in the hood of his robe.

"Paulminos does not fear the Otherworld and brought his clan to this remote location. He's sure no one followed them. They brought provisions to stay for a while. He wants to know how we found them. I'll show them our detection equipment for this dimension when we reach the farm."

"Why did they flee their enclave?" Diviner feared she had missed something in his explanation.

"They think conflict is about to break out among the Wizards. A civil war among them would be a terrible thing. The Brotherhood leaders are challenging the loyalty of individual members. They want to know who is attacking their enclaves with earthquakes."

"Would a Wizard war be worse than what The Brotherhood is doing already to the world," Judyth said.

Byron nodded. "Europe would suffer like the rest of the planet."

Pointing at the other Wizards, Diviner said, "They ran and hid rather than oppose The Brotherhood as you did. You trust them?"

"They can help us find more enclaves to target."

Diviner noticed the Mages remained attached to the safety line set up at the farm. Diviner took it from Byron, attached it to Ampere, and gripped his hand.

"We're about one third of the way to our destination. There are a lot of interesting sights ahead." With that, she set off for France. Boss tagged along beside her like they were on a stroll in the park.

Once the Wizards were ready, Byron led them and the other Thals to the farm, the orange bundle of possessions tagging along.

Mages rushed out of the farmhouse to welcome the newcomers. Byron led the bedraggled Wizards to the kitchen table while the wide-eyed Thals wandered about the property chirping away.

"The Thals describe Wutega's enclave as a gloomy place," Byron said. "This looks like paradise to them. We'll need a place for them and the Wizards to live. The Thals would be happiest in Stuart's apartment, but that's not practical."

"What'll happen to them?" Marconi said. She, Digger and Ears had stayed at the farm to work with Bethune to monitor communications from Europe and the Otherworld.

"While Thals can take care of themselves, we need to find tasks to keep them busy," Byron said. "They want to emulate Stuart so they'll be especially interested in machines and technology."

Marconi looked around. "I'm already busy all day and every Mage who hasn't gone to Europe is working as much as they can to help."

"What about Harold?" Ears said. "There isn't a machine your husband can't make work and he does it all the hard way. If you tell him that it's okay, he'll help the Thals."

They went into the house to contact Harold. In the kitchen they discovered Paulminos and the other Wizards had become the latest fans of Digger stew.

"They took second helpings," Digger said. "It's funny to hear such old English. Will our other guests be hungry?" When Byron shrugged, he said, "I'll tell them Stuart likes this stew." Digger headed out the door with a small pot and several spoons. He returned in a few minutes beaming.

"My culinary fame now transcends the species barrier. The Thals will come in as soon as they finish unpacking their bundle. I couldn't tell you the purpose of most of the items I saw in it."

"I made a video of them unpacking it and will inform you of what I learn from it," Bethune said.

"The Thals are either attracted by good cooking or are making a special effort to impress Stuart's friends," Byron said. *Perhaps, they see something about the Mages I missed. I need to pay more attention to them to learn aspects of magic unknown to Wizards.*

"I'll take the Wizards outside in a few minutes to examine the barn," he said. "Maybe the Thals will come inside then. In the meantime, Bethune is ready to converse with them."

The rumble of an engine and the crunch of gravel announced a vehicle rolling up the lane way. Looking out the window, Digger said, "It's the farmer who rents the land. I'll speak to him. Byron, keep the Wizards and Thals out of sight."

Byron listened from an open window as the farmer stepped out of the truck.

"Lesley said her friends were coming here for a holiday. You folks have a funny idea of what a vacation is for. The place is all cleaned up, the old tree is firewood, the damn boulder is gone and the barn is straightened up. Told Earl to fix it before it fell down. If you need more of that kind of rest, there are a few jobs at my place."

The farmer let out a hearty laugh. "I came to tell you I'll be moving some equipment into the yard during the next couple of days. I'll tarp them up for the winter. No problem for you."

He hesitated. "In the mail, there should be permits to take two deer from the farm. I looked after that for Earl during the last couple of years and be glad to do so again. I'd be happy to share venison with you folks."

"That'd be great," Digger said. He returned to the house as the farmer drove away.

Bethune spoke in Wizardese to the Thals who burst into a boisterous conversation. "They want to go deer hunting with him."

"We need to finish cleaning out the barn before he returns," Byron said. "It's full of dirt and old pieces of machinery and metal. We want to create a Wizard enclave inside it. From the outside, it'll just look like an empty barn. You might wish to make a video to share with the other Mages. We'll start the clean-up in a little while."

Marconi headed for the barn with the other Mages and Thals. Once the building's main doors and loft entrances creaked wide open, she aimed her cellphone camera at Byron and Paulminos standing side by side with the other Wizards right behind them. Before long scraps of wood and metal and then old machinery floated out of the barn and dropped with loud clangs into two piles.

"Pay dirt for some scrap dealer," Digger said.

The Thals chirped and Digger shouted as the barn disgorged a billowing black cloud of dirt and old straw and hay. "It's like they swept up all the crud and blew it away. I bet the inside will look power washed." The grey cloud settled into the surrounding fields.

"Well-aged fertilizer," Byron said. "We'll invite you for a tour of the barn when we're done with the renovations of the interior. Meanwhile, we need to decide which enclaves to hit tonight."

A Thal approached Byron and tugged on his jacket. The conversation in Wizardese went on for several minutes. By the end, both were smiling.

THE EXPLODING ENCLAVE

A gentle breeze carried the scent of pine from the towering trees in the park in southeastern Poland. The perfume reminded Stuart of camping as a kid with his family.

A thick cloud bank obscured much of the sunrise. Omeron and Pembar sat across from each other at a picnic table with Mages beside them. They discussed their next moves while munching through Viking's hearty breakfast of ham, cheese, eggs and black bread. Dog put her paws on the bench and peered at them like she was listening to their conversation.

"The Russian Mages have found the general location of several enclaves," Stuart said. "However, they don't know which ones to approach first and whether the Wizards will even talk to them."

"There are some very powerful Wizards in Russia and . . . " Pembar grabbed a platter easing toward the end of the table. Boss appeared grinning from ear to ear. "How know me here?"

"I saw the platter moving ever so slowly and figured it was not just by chance or Earth tremor."

Stuart found it strange the Wizards did not sense Boss's arrival. *How much do they actually know about the Thals?*

"Be here before you talk about Russia." Boss's gaze was fixed on the scrambled eggs.

"Help yourself." Stuart passed a plate and cutlery.

"Easy go through Otherworld to enclaves," Boss said. "Be at first one soon."

Stuart phoned Mendeleev, his contact with the Russian Mages, while the others gathered up their gear and parked the van out of the way. Omeron covered it in an unseeing spell.

"What happens if a person or animal approaches the vehicle under the spell," Viking said.

"In this case, they'd see a clump of trees and rocks," Omeron said. "If they kept approaching, the magic would make them turn away. I can't do such a spell for an object much bigger than a cottage."

"It'd be a handy talent to have," Viking said.

"I'll teach it to you."

"Our first stop is just west of Kursk while the others are to the east of the city," Stuart said.

"Todomorin will be dangerous," Omeron said. "The others might hear us out. Beyond him, I don't know who's left."

Gesturing toward the other Mages, Stuart said, "Officially we need visas for Russia. We'll be in a lot of trouble if we're discovered without them. The other Mages can't make themselves disappear."

"We protect," Boss said. "You see."

As it was his first foray into the Otherworld, Stuart took a deep breath before entering the fog leading to it. He stepped cautiously into the other dimension and peered around at surroundings that had a familiar but not quite the same appearance as what he left behind. Startled by how fast he was moving above the ground, he watched Pembar and Omeron strolling along behind Boss.

The Otherworld doesn't feel malevolent or relaxing and the scenery is neither attractive nor repulsive. It's just a different kind of place. Maybe other areas are different.

Before long, a steady thumping could be heard. "Not hear anything like that before," Boss said. "Maybe bad Wizards do something."

"What would you do if they did?" Stuart said.

"Have many tricks Wizards don't know." He puffed up his chest and walked off with a tough-guy swagger.

In hopes of learning more about the Thals, he decided not to say the sound was from a seismic thumper the Russian Mages were using to signal their location. He winked at Omeron and Pembar hoping they would play along. "Maybe the Wizards have a secret weapon or a way to search the Otherworld for enemies."

The Thal did not slow his pace. *Boss is clearly determined to demonstrate his toughness. Either he possesses lots of nerve or his own powerful magic.*

Dog trotted in-between Omeron and Pembar. From what the

Wizards had said only magical creatures could enter the Otherworld. If anything, she seemed more comfortable here than the Wizards did.

His attention returned to his companions when Boss said, "This where leave Otherworld." He stepped resolutely into a patch of fog.

"You're devious, Stuart," Omeron said. "Come on, I want to see this."

They exited the Otherworld into brilliant sunshine and a welcome from five men and four women dressed in hiking clothes and carrying bulky backpacks.

Boss examined a machine steadily thumping the ground with a steel pad. "That sends signals into the ground to find valuable deposits," Stuart said. "It also marked the Mages' location."

Boss walked around the machine. "Mages have good tricks."

Meeting the Russians was more important than setting the Thal straight. Mendeleev, a short, stocky man, introduced his companions. "We choose our names in tribute to great figures of our history. Unlike our friends in Western Europe and North America, we suspected for long time special people lived among us who could do things we didn't understand. We couldn't prove it so we kept it to ourselves. Two summers ago, we found a couple of fallen-apart enclaves in the Urals."

Mendeleev pulled out a tablet computer. "Here are photos we took." He held the device in front of the Wizards. "We felt strange sensations as we explored them and the ruins of another place we found. The same force radiates from Pembar and Omeron."

"Biennita and Gregoria." Omeron bowed her head to pay homage to the two elders. "I've not heard of them in a long time. They were well past 500 years old. The other place is the enclave of Todomorin, who is still alive as far as we know."

Mendeleev waited until the Wizards raised their heads. "Come, we're close to it. We all carry weapons when we're in areas like this. We want you three Mages to take pistols as a safety precaution. "

The Russian Mages paired up with the newcomers and Mendeleev and Stuart took the lead. Boss walked behind them, practicing his English. At first it was somewhat comical as he repeated everything he heard. Although Stuart wanted to talk with Mendeleev, Boss kept asking him for the names of everything.

After trekking for 15 minutes along a rocky trail through a coniferous forest, Mendeleev halted the group. "The enclave we seek is near here, but we can't tell where exactly."

Omeron and Pembar stepped forward peering slightly uphill at a ridge dotted with small trees. In less than a minute, a large stone cottage appeared almost 50 meters away behind a thick stone fence. "Todomorin always was sloppy with his magic," she said. "Stay close as he'll know by now that his enclave is exposed."

They called his name several times without any response. "He's blocking our attempts to communicate with him," Pembar said.

"Don't Wizards owe each other the respect of talking first?" Stuart asked.

Everyone jumped at the boom of a loud cannon blast. A ball of flame arched toward them, snapping and hissing like an angry animal. The Mages took cover behind large boulders. While Boss stayed in the open, his bemused smile included anxious glances.

"That's Todomorin's idea of speaking first," Pembar growled. "Does he think we're a bunch of children?"

Stuart covered his ears against the roar of the flaming ball. *Can the Wizards stop it?*

"This one is mine," Omeron snapped. "Pembar, you take the next one." The ball halted as if an invisible hand blocked it, spinning faster and faster while emitting a stream of thick smoke. When a blackened crust coated it, it plummeted to the ground, smashing into pieces with a loud crack.

A second boom washed over them. Pembar stepped forward as the ball appeared. Its flight stopped abruptly, and then it imploded with a loud pop leaving a cloud of carbon flakes drifting in the breeze.

Omeron deflected the next ball at the enclave, like a returned serve in tennis. It splattered over the structure setting small bits of debris on fire.

Boss tugged on Stuart's arm. "Thals there." Before Stuart could say anything, he disappeared. Although alarmed by the fireballs, Boss possessed sufficient confidence in his magic to approach the enclave on a rescue mission.

What will Boss do when he reaches the enclave? The Thal's heroics reminded him of how much he still had to learn about them as well as the Wizards. While Omeron and Pembar could counter Todomorin's magic effortlessly, they seemed powerless to halt the Brotherhood attacks on the planet. *Perhaps Byron could explain the unevenness of magical power.*

After a few minutes without any further Todomorin attacks, Mendeleev moved beside Stuart. "It'd be neat to block Wizard magic like that."

Stuart nodded and rubbed his palms together. "We need to bridge the gap between Wizard magic and our abilities. Imagine what we might be able to do if we could fully combine our powers with theirs. Maybe we could swat aside missiles like they did the flaming balls. Or deflect a deadly asteroid or meteor away from Earth."

"We also need to know how long they can perform magic before they get tired," Mendeleev said. "Maybe Omeron and Pembar are Todomorin's equals and together outlasted him. None of us have used our power that much."

Omeron and Pembar shuffled toward them, clearly exhausted. "Todomorin will be preparing a new attack," she said. "We must be ready."

"It's my turn to deal with him," Stuart said. He glanced up the hillside at the rumble of fast rolling boulders. Although they sounded far more dangerous than the fireballs, their glow looked similar to the magic he had already encountered from the Wizards. *Time to find out more about what I can do.*

"Deflect the ones that come close but let the rest go," Pembar said. "It's an unfocused attack which shows Todomorin's desperation."

Stuart visualized a large rock in the path of a boulder heading in the direction of the other Mages. The boulder pounded into Stuart's rock and bounced to the right and stopped when it hit a clump of trees. He directed the next boulders off course before they came close. A final one thundered toward them. It bounced into the air and Stuart slid his magic under it and carried it well past his friends before releasing it. It fell into the trees with a resounding crash.

"Enough of this." Stuart pulled out the handgun the Russians had given him and jogged toward the enclave. "A bullet should stop him." He took a deep breath to steady himself while thinking of the TV images of the suffering The Brotherhood had wrought around the world. *The carnage has to end.* "We'd like to talk to him," Omeron said.

"Look at that," Mendeleev shouted.

A shimmering ball of light streaked at them. Sensing it was more than another fireball, Stuart prepared to leap out of its way. It halted five meters from him and Stuart raised his left hand to shield his eyes from the light it radiated. Finally he could see a suit of armor with a wizened face peering out from the helmet. A hostile voice screamed in Wizardese.

"Todomorin plans to hack you to pieces with his sword." Pembar called. "Killing you with his magic would be too easy."

Stuart's Tae Kwon Do training never included any defensive strategies against an enraged Wizard with a large sword. Common sense said to avoid the first swing, and then attack Todomorin's legs. However, it made even more sense to shoot him. "Tell him this gun will blow a big hole in him if he doesn't drop the sword."

Pembar delivered the warning. Todomorin laughed, and then lunged at Stuart closing the distance between them as he slashed the blade back and forth. Stuart pulled the trigger as he ducked and the bullet bounced off Todomorin's shoulder sending him staggering backward.

Pembar shouted at Todomorin. He responded in a nasty tone and Stuart aimed the gun with both hands.

"Watch the sword," Omeron yelled.

Stuart ducked as it whizzed past his head. He straightened as Todomorin pulled out a smaller blade and waved it back and forth. "Tell him not to move or use his power on me!"

Pembar yelled at Todomorin.

Another wave of itchiness staggered Stuart. He squeezed the trigger and the bullet punched through the armor into Todomorin's chest. Stuart's itching faded as Todomorin dropped backward to the ground.

Stuart wiped the sweat off his forehead and took a deep breath. "He may not have much to say now."

A resounding crack boomed from the enclave. Several rumbles followed in quick succession. "He's dying and his residual magic is too weak to maintain the enclave," Pembar said as he rushed to Todomorin.

"Merstreem will soon know he's dead and naturally think another Wizard killed him. While he'll want revenge, he won't know where to direct it. If your Mages can determine Merstreem's whereabouts, they should hit that enclave with quakes to distract him. Otherwise he'll create more disasters around the world."

Reaching for his satellite phone to call Bethune about striking at Merstreem, Stuart realized he did not feel any remorse. He had offered Todomorin and Wutega a chance to surrender.

Stuart followed the Russians as they advanced toward the building recording the scenes of destruction on their cellphones. Stones fell off the building and rolled away. The Russians jumped out of the path of a couple that bounced at them. Eventually the roof followed by the walls collapsed kicking up clouds of dust.

Boss appeared followed by three Thals and two humans. "They fled enclave as soon as Todomorin attack you."

Once the air cleared, the Wizards and Thals moved stones and chunks of the roof with their magic. Nothing remained of Todomorin's enclave worth salvaging. "He wove his power into this place so thoroughly that even his books were torn asunder by the force of the magic coming undone," Pembar said. "The Thals will collect their and the Halves' belongings."

Stuart's satellite phone rang. "A huge explosion rolled through the Otherworld," Bethune said. "It originated near your location."

"It sure did. Mendeleev will send you the file. Tell Byron we have three more Thals and two Halves. The latter came here from France last year and want to return to Lyon. Boss says he'll send a guide to deliver them there while he helps the rescued Thals follow us. Pembar told the Halves they'll be watched."

The next morning, the Mages and Thals gathered around the fire. Boss chirped away at the Thals. Mendeleev looked up from his laptop. "Hey, your group hit Merstreem's supporters overnight with more quakes. However it wasn't enough to stop the Wizards from triggering huge earthquakes and fires in Latin America and Africa."

As he talked, Thals gathered around the Russian, pointing at the computer. He hit the scroll button several times. "More Wizards were rescued from the Otherworld and there are 15 of them now at the farm."

The young Thals played with Mendeleev and Baltic while they

learned about the computer. Several girls hung out with Viking who set up Stuart's laptop to enable Bethune to watch all the activity.

Stuart half listened to the report from the farm as he puzzled over how the Thals became comfortable with the Mages so quickly. *Although they had avoided contact with humans for centuries and survived all the wars in Europe, could the Thals have been lonely? What would it be like to belong to a species of several thousand scattered about in small groups that could only trust a few Wizards? Perhaps the Realm's real challenge would be to assist the Thals in adapting to the modern world. They certainly seem interested in technology.* Stuart buried his face in his hands and muttered, "Why am I having these thoughts now?"

The Wizards stood on either side of him. "It's never simple comprehending what magic wants us to do." Omeron rubbed his back. "But it chooses who it trusts with great care."

Boss approached. "We help best can."

So the Thals like the Wizards can read my thoughts. Contemplating the power of that ability made Stuart wonder about his place in all this magic. *Could I be a focal point for it? Maybe Merstreem was before losing his mental balance.*

"Can Wizards and Mages work together, Stuart?" Pembar said.

"Thals too," Boss said.

Stuart let his eyes wander over people that two weeks ago he would have not believed existed. Now he counted them among his friends. "Well, we seem to be doing alright so far."

Omeron peered at Pembar. "Did you believe Byron when he said he could sense magic unlike ours? Most figured he was confused by the science and machines of the modern world. I thought he was becoming senile."

"I could never feel it and while I thought Byron was imagining things, I agreed that magic needed a renewal," Pembar said. "I want to witness Stuart working on machines to understand what he does and why it's important. We don't appreciate what the Thals are capable of and it's clearly far more than we're aware of."

"We can't project our thoughts inside machines and computers the way Stuart does," Mendeleev said. "Imagine seeing inside a giant engine or surfing the Internet."

"What innernet?" Boss said. His puzzled expression was matched by the looks on Pembar and Omeron's faces.

Stuart was seized with the notion that if Mages, Thals and two old Wizards could work together to take over the next few enclaves, there was a future for magic. "Let's move out. We've work to do, my friends. I'll explain the Internet as we go."

THE THALS' SECRET

Boss led the way back into the Otherworld heading for the enclaves east of Kursk. Preoccupied with thoughts about what Thals, Wizards and Mages might accomplish together, Stuart paid little attention to the sweeping forests.

He was still deep in thought when the group passed through the fog back into Russia. The sun rode high in the sky. Stuart surveyed a tree dotted flat area until he spotted Dog leaning on Pembar, briskly wagging her tail. A squat wooden structure suddenly appeared among the trees.

"Dog is right," Pembar said. "Something is amiss with Bahorn's enclave. While protected by magic, it's not Wizard crafted. Or at least not all of it is."

Boss tugged on Stuart's arm. "Me check." He scampered toward the enclave.

When he passed out of hearing range, Pembar said, "Boss listens raptly to conversations among the Mages. He may be the most attentive language student ever. In less than a week, his English has become quite proficient and he comprehends what your technology can do if not how it works."

"He's also picked up quite a bit of Russian," Mendeleev said. "Very impressive for someone who'd spoken neither language before. Both are hard to learn. Thals aren't just some quaint little proto humans with magical gifts."

A Thal appeared at the doorway of the enclave and chirped loudly. "Come quickly," Boss shouted before rushing inside. The Russian Mages reached the structure first. Stuart held Omeron's arm as they hurried, but they were the last to arrive.

Pembar re-appeared in the doorway, breathing deeply and shaking his head. "Bahorn is too weak to have maintained the building through the Mage quakes. Stuart and Surovov, inspect it to make sure it's safe."

Stuart had not spoken to the dark-haired Russian Mage before. Viking said Surovov talked to her whenever he could. With a smile, she added, "He says he's practicing his English."

Surovov ran his hands over the exterior walls. "Chinking between logs been redone and the windows and doors fit good." He was tall and lanky. "Grandfather is master carpenter and good work like this impresses him."

As the Russian spoke English quite well, Stuart suspected his motive for talking to Viking went beyond improving his linguistic abilities. "Do you use his memory as a touchstone to reach your magic?"

Suvorov grinned. "Not tell anyone."

"I use my Uncle Oscar who can repair any machine. I thought the Realm members didn't employ touchstones and that I was an oddball."

"We oddballs. I not use magic for machines as much as you. I learn Wizard magic. Can be invisible." He looked about, and then vanished.

Stuart could find no sign of him. He jumped when Surovov tapped him on the shoulder from behind before reappearing.

"Well done. While I'm trying to copy Byron, you're way ahead of me."

"Like idea of Wizard, Mage, Thal work together," Surovov said. "Want help." They shook hands. "Viking say I much like you. Glad we have chance to talk."

"You never looked disappointed when you're chatting with her."

Surovov blushed. "Hope not too obvious. She gorgeous and so smart. Think Pembar send you and me for inspection because suspects we do some Wizard magic. Am civil engineer and specialist in building structures to survive disasters."

Stuart pointed ahead to suggest they finish their task. "Your Grandfather probably made you do every job properly."

The Russian chuckled. "Complain all the time, but best gift from him. He and your Uncle probably say much about young people not work hard like them."

"The building is in excellent condition and everything else is fine as well," Stuart reported to the Wizards who waited at the door.

"Go inside for a look," Omeron said.

With few windows and just a couple of candles flickering on a table, Stuart could barely see Boss and two other Thals examining a shrunken figure lying on a bed.

"Check Wizard sight," Surovov whispered. "Like this." He closed his eyes. "It's amazing."

When Stuart shut his eyelids, it was like someone turned on overhead lights. *How long have I possessed this power?* He looked about the room. Painted on the wide plank walls were scenes of Wizards saving a town from a raging river, walking through fields driving pests from grain crops and chasing off a dragon.

Omeron stepped beside them. "Bahorn's enclave is famous among Wizards because of his paintings. You're looking at important chapters in The Book of Time."

Beckoning Stuart and Surovov to follow, she and Pembar went back outside. Instead of their usual certainty, the Wizards appeared nervous. Something was amiss.

"We want to question Boss and the two Thals who live here," Pembar said as he gestured for the Mages to sit on the bench across from him and Omeron. "They'll join us shortly. We need Stuart with us to get a full explanation from them. The other Mages can tend to Bahorn while we do."

"Thals watch everything Stuart do," Surovov said.

The Thals from the enclave arrived accompanied by Boss. "The magic of these two Thals preserved Bahorn's enclave for years," Pembar said. "It handled the Mage quakes with ease. The Thals want to keep Bahorn alive as long as possible with the magic he taught them and what they already know."

"If he passes in his own time, then his magic will persist here, which will further protect the enclave," Omeron said. Dog brushed her head against the Wizard's leg. Her voice rose as if she had found the missing piece to a puzzle. "Of course, the Thals are slowly integrating their magic with his so that no Wizard could ever find this place. Nor any human."

"So you're telling us Thals could become great Wizards," Stuart said.

"If they're not already. The main difference between them and us is they don't use their magic to control others as we do. It's hard to judge Thal magic because their motivation is so different."

"Where did you send the Thal who departed a few minutes ago? He just stood and left like you'd sent him on an errand."

Surovov nodded. "See same."

"He was beside Boss until you pointed out his absence." Omeron stared at where the Thal had sat and exhaled deeply. A world she had always controlled was slipping away. Pembar appeared equally confounded.

Stuart admired how his stocky pals could trick the Wizards.

Boss and the other Thal stood and bowed deeply to Stuart, and then Surovov. Boss faced Omeron and Pembar. "Our magic fool Wizards, not him." He pointed to the Russian. "Nor him. Strange."

Before Stuart could ask for an explanation, a group of about 30 Thals hurried across the grass toward them led by the Thal whose departure the Wizards had not noticed.

The newcomers chirped so loudly it became impossible to talk. Several young ones draped themselves on Bahorn's other Thal.

Surovov patted Stuart's shoulder. "Our touchstones would be happy to see this; families important to them."

Boss stood and chirped at the Thals. They nodded and smiled at Omeron and Pembar, but bowed to Stuart and Surovov. A couple of the youngsters approached the Mages. Hands on her hips, a girl tilted her head at different angles looking at Stuart like he was a creature out of a fairie tale.

Waiting for everyone to quiet, Stuart paced a circle around the group. The girl skipped along beside him. "These Thals could use Bahorn's enclave as their home and a refuge for others of their kind," he said.

Pembar slapped his leg. "We could do this with empty magical enclaves elsewhere in Europe." He spoke to Bahorn's helpers in Wizardese. "Why did you not move your families in before?"

The Thal who stayed with the Wizards said, "We didn't want to upset Bahorn because he was always good to us. He treated us as his children."

After Omeron translated their conversation, Stuart put his hand on the shoulder of the Thal who had brought the group to the enclave. "His name will be Pathfinder while the other one will be Farseeker."

Pembar looked at him with a questioning expression as the newly-arrived Thals milled about saying the names over and over in a musical lilt that came out as Thinder and Eeker.

Boss tugged on Stuart's sleeve. "The others await their names."

"In time, names for them will come to me."

"First Pathfinder and Farseeker need to check on Bahorn," Omeron said. She took Stuart's arm and they followed the Thals inside.

Surovov followed on their heels. "Bahorn like my Grandfather." His voice cracked as he repeatedly blinked his eyes. "Something holds them here long past their time."

They gathered around the frail figure covered by blankets. Except for his raspy breathing, Stuart would have thought he was dead. When Pathfinder and Farseeker passed their hands over his body, his breathing eased and a smile slowly gathered on his face.

Boss faced the Wizards. "Can you heal him?"

While Pembar and Omeron shook their heads, Surovov barely repressed a smirk. "Think needs doctor. Know good one?"

"Not handy," Stuart said.

Boss stepped in front of him. "I find healer our Grandmother like if she make old Wizard better."

Stuart smiled thinking about Judyth. "She could probably help him." Attending to such an elderly patient would intrigue her. He pulled out his satellite phone to find her current location. Judyth answered before the second ring.

"Two people here would really like to see you—me and a very frail old Wizard in dire need of medical attention," Stuart said. "Boss, the Thal . . ."

"Oh, the head of your fan club." Judyth's laugh burbled over the phone. "I met him in the Otherworld. He wouldn't stop praising you. How big is your head?"

"Tell me where you are and he'll find you."

"I'm in France near the Swiss border. We're moving about, but we'll create a beacon to guide him to us."

As soon as Stuart relayed Judyth's comment, Boss headed for the door. "Save supper," he sang out.

"Tomorrow, we need to move to the next enclave," Pembar said. "If Boss is available, he and some other Thals should come with us. Baltic, Viking and the Russian Mages should remain here so they can learn more about Thal magic."

Judyth and Boss arrived near dusk. After a long embrace with Stuart, she went to assess Bahorn. Out of her satchel came a stethoscope and other examination equipment.

Stuart brought her a cup of hot tea and hovered nearby. For the first time, he sensed her magic at work. She relaxed the old man before peering into his body. She left tiny glowing markers in his chest and lower limbs. Then she pulled up a chair, sat beside him and took out a notebook. "He shouldn't be alive." She shook her head as she wrote. "How old is he?"

Stuart shrugged. "Close to 400 years. What did you find?"

"While a weak heart and clogged arteries are his main problems, he also has secondary infections. While we could fix it all with microscopic surgery, I wouldn't try it here and we can't take him to a hospital. The other option is to carry him back to the farm, but that'd probably finish him."

Pathfinder and Farseeker entered the room as Judyth finished her medical assessment. Stuart introduced them. "According to Omeron, Bahorn's alive because of these two."

"Would they show me how they treat him?"

Stuart nodded at the Thals and pointed at Bahorn. When they looked at him quizzically, he imitated how they moved their hands over him. The Thals immediately went to either side of Bahorn. Starting at his head, they repeatedly moved their hands over him without touching his body.

Judyth squeezed Stuart's arm. "I can sense they're easing the constrictions in the arteries. If his condition wasn't so advanced that might just work. I want to learn how they do this."

Stuart went outside to find Boss to question Pathfinder and Farseeker for Judyth.

After talking to them, Boss said, "When their healing reached Bahorn's chest, they found . . . ." He scratched his head. " . . . something show places where Wizard sick."

"I create the markers to remind me of the spots that need attention. I developed the method from medical nanotechnology displays. When local intervention is needed because of an infection or a plugged artery, I give the markers the ability to take as much corrective action as possible."

She pointed at the Thals. "They spotted them and knew their purpose. Can all Thals perform healing?"

"Bahorn taught them healing. They don't know how they spotted your markers. They were just there. They'll show other Thals what doctor does. Healing important for us." The only other time Boss had looked this happy was when he held out his arms to take the rescued Grandmother from Stuart.

"Maybe Judyth can teach them how modern medicine works and they could explain their healing," Surovov said. "You could learn from each other."

"There are doctors and specialists among the European Mages as well as in Japan and India." Judyth's voice soared with excitement. "Imagine what we might be able to repair without surgery." She looked down at Bahorn. "I'll make a plan to stabilize his health. In the meantime, tell the Thals to keep soothing him."

"Let's see what's happening elsewhere," Surovov said. He motioned for Stuart and Boss to follow him outside where he conferred with a couple of Russian Mages. They pulled out their mobile phones and punched in numbers. Surovov stepped back and rubbed his palms together.

While Pembar napped on a bench, the Thals gathered around Mendeleev who worked his laptop checking satellite images and communications from the farm and other Mages. "One of the enclaves in this area is in ruins. The rest are under magical shields, which makes them easy to spot now that we know what to look for."

As roomy as the enclave was, with three Wizards, 10 Mages and more than 30 Thals, Stuart and Judyth had no privacy that night. Pressed together on blankets on the floor with their arms entwined, she filled him in on developments at the farm.

"The Wizards have made small apartments in the barn while the Thals completely rebuilt the loft into a communal living area. Harold showed them how to use power tools and they did an amazing job. I'd hire them to do renovation work.

"Byron convinced the Wizards and Thals to take their meals together, and then coaxed them into actually conversing. Most of it is in Wizardese so only he and Bethune know what they're saying. The conversations became quite heated at first. Most Wizards don't understand the Thals' grievances about their treatment by Wizards."

"While we've much to learn about Wizards, the Thals are a bigger mystery," Stuart said.

"Do you notice how closely they watch you, Stuart? You represent something special to them."

She got up several times during the night to check on Bahorn. "His condition is stable, but it's at such a low level," she whispered to Stuart.

The next morning, Surovov stepped up to Judyth with a wide grin. "We've secured the short term use of a Russian army field hospital and my comrades will set it up as soon as it arrives. A couple of our doctors are coming and would like to assist you in the operation."

"How did you . . . " Judyth stopped when Surovov put his finger to his lips.

"Probably through inappropriate use of magic. Let's say the end justified the means." With that he mimicked zippering his lips.

Boss said the Thals would assist as well.

While the rest of the group prepared for the arrival of the tent, the Wizards, Stuart Surovov and Boss entered the Otherworld and reached the next enclave further east of Kursk in less than an hour.

A run down log cabin squatted in a clearing. The wood was a deep grey and the roof had lost most of its thatch. Birds flew in and out through the holes. "It's been a long time since anyone worked on this enclave," Surovov said. "There's almost no trace of magic in it. Who lives here?"

"Although Wnorom has great powers, his curiosity can distract him for months or even years," Omeron said. "He's here now. We'll all approach the enclave. The presence of Thals and Mages should get his attention."

A clean-shaven bald man dressed in simple brown pants and a grey pullover top sat on a log waiting for them. "Greetings," Omeron said.

Pointing at a log across from his, Wnorom said, "How's the old buzzard?"

"Bahorn is near death," Omeron said. "A doctor is working on him."

Wnorom laughed. "How could he help a Wizard?"

"She's one of them." Pembar pointed at Stuart and Surovov.

Wnorom's eyes widened and the itch of Wizard magic swept over Stuart. So far, Wizards were either antagonistic or friendly. While Wnorom appeared gruff, Stuart soon saw he was just a big softie. He relaxed and let the old man's magic weave around him.

"There was a tremor here the other night," Wnorom said in English. "It was far too local and controlled for a natural event. From that, I concluded a stronger one would likely follow. Then I see your group heading my way, through the Otherworld of all things, to attack or save me from some peril although there is none I can't handle."

A rainbow like glow radiated from Wnorom. He puffed up like a peacock displaying its tail feathers. Stuart wondered whether every Wizard could create such a display. Until now he had seen them generate only one or two colors. Perhaps the patterns and shades contained a message for other Wizards.

"I decided to wait for you here to see what you'd say. You've piqued my curiosity with these young men. Although they lack auras and certainly do not understand our language, you two would not bother with anyone lacking magic. They must be part of the reason you came to my enclave." He spread his arms as if expecting applause. "So how is my reasoning?"

"Excellent as usual, Wnorom," Omeron said. Pembar nodded in agreement. She outlined the efforts of the Mages to block The Brotherhood.

Wnorom leaned toward the Wizards. "It's most curious that a Thal travels with you. They never employ their full magic when we might witness it. They let us see what they wish. They can tap into the natural forces of the planet and the Otherworld to make conditions suitable for them."

Wnorom stared at the ground as if he had found a rare plant. "I failed to convince other Wizards that Thal magic is at least equal to ours. They said I couldn't control them because I was weak." His voice became sharper and he pounded the log several times. "We should accept them as our equals."

Boss held out his hand to the Wizard. "You always welcome

among us, friend. Thals not hide from Wnorom. Our camps and enclaves will reveal themselves to you."

Stuart and Surovov exchanged glances. "We're here for a purpose," the Russian said. "Magic wants us to convince the Wizards and Thals to work with us to save the planet from further suffering."

"Combining our powers would create a formidable force," Stuart said.

Wnorom nodded. "It most certainly would."

"Boss will make sure the Thals know what we're doing and we'll tell the Wizards we can trust what our plans are." Omeron's voice faltered and she slipped into Wizardese. Whatever she said made Pembar and Wnorom gasp. Boss looked at her wide-eyed.

Wnorom switched to English before Stuart question her. "During my latest travels, a real quake overwhelmed the magic protecting my enclave. It was already in poor condition because of my prolonged absences. It's not worth repairing plus I tire of living here alone. I need the company of other Wizards to regain my enthusiasm. That's why I travel so much."

Omeron smiled. "You can live at my enclave for as long as you wish. But first we need to deal with the other Wizards in this region. One place is destroyed and..."

"How do you know?"

"Time to introduce you to the magic of the new Realm," Pembar said. "Surovov, can you set up the viewing machine and show our friend the destroyed enclave and the others as well."

Minutes later, Wnorom peered at the laptop screen in a mixture of disbelief and fascination.

"This is you right beside me—wave and see what happens," Surovov said.

Wnorom jumped backward in surprise when the figure in the screen waved just as he was. He peered about. "I need to learn how your magic works and what all these devices are." He rubbed his hands. "This could be very interesting."

"Here's your residence—it's in poor shape," Surovov said. With that, he shifted to views of the remaining Ural enclaves. "This one is destroyed while others still stand."

"You shouldn't be able to see them because they're covered in magic."

"My magic sees through yours," the Russian said.

Wnorom grunted. "The enclave in ruins is Polantov's. He's probably died. He was the eldest. The others will be working together to set a trap for you. You better be prepared to fight."

"They better prepare." Boss's voice dripped with defiance. "Stuart me show them good."

BOSS THE SHOWBOAT

Stuart leaned toward Boss. "We don't know what we're up against from the other Wizards."

"Me do." Boss said. "We fight bad magic together. First, I find them." With that, he stepped away from the others and vanished.

"They can do that?" Wnorom said. "What else have they hidden from us?" He put his hand on Omeron's shoulder. "We really have underestimated their abilities."

She nodded. "While we wait for him to return, we should collect your books and possessions."

"We can't use magic to retrieve them as that could cause the building to fall completely apart," Pembar said. "We've these strong young men who can carry everything."

For the next couple of hours, Stuart and Surovov lugged out dust covered books, furniture and armfuls of clothing from the enclave. "That's it!" Stuart said. "So, what will you do with all this stuff?"

Omeron talked with Wnorom, and then clapped her hands. His belongings rose off the ground and hovered in two collections. She waved her arms like the Thal Grandmother did at Wutega's enclave. A wide roll of cloth appeared and unwound. The material snaked around the two collections until they were completely wrapped.

She clapped her hands and one pile took on an orange glow. "This will mark it for delivery to my enclave when Boss can find a Thal to handle it. The other will be for the Thals to use."

Pembar and Wnorom took apart the log cabin, using their magic to chip up all the wood and pulverize the glass in the windows. They scattered the stones from his fireplace and chimney in every direction leaving no sign a cabin ever existed.

Satisfied with the result, Omeron turned her attention to the Mages. "All that work has made our young friends quite dirty. I'll clean them."

"This will make you itch for a short time," Pembar said. Omeron called up a short burst of warm rain followed by a hot breeze.

"That was awesome! Every expedition should have access to a shower Wizard." Surovov admired his clean hands, and then Stuart. "You're spotless."

Boss returned late in the afternoon. "Bad wizards in cave hard to get near. Although Polantov not kind to Thals, I bury him. His enclave not worth saving. Others covered in powerful magic."

"That means they'd explode if any one tries to reveal them," Pembar said.

"How big an explosion would it be?" Stuart said.

"Releasing all that magic at once would create an immense hole in the ground," Pembar said.

"So people would hear it for many kilometers?"

"Many mountains away."

"But that would reveal the presence of Wizards, which is what we're trying to avoid." Stuart shook his head.

"They don't care because they're at war." Wnorom's shoulders sagged and he sighed deeply. "So this is how the age of Wizards will end." He shoved his hands in pockets and stared at the ground, his mood as downcast as his eyes.

"We don't want to leave Polantov's enclave to be found," Omeron said. "Will you lead us to it, Boss, and then take it apart as we're tired from cleaning up Wutega's? We'll need to make it look like a pile of rocks so no one will become suspicious."

Boss eyed him. "Can wait?"

"The sooner, the better."

"Follow me; not take long."

When they reached the dilapidated stone cottage after a short trip through the Otherworld, Wnorom said, "It doesn't appear safe to enter. Still we should try to save the belongings."

Boss looked to the sky. "You insist?" The Wizards nodded. "Boss do." The Thal took several steps toward the ruins and raised his arms. Clothes, books and tools soared from the building and Omeron sorted them into two piles.

The stones of Polantov's enclave rose in the air, hovering and banging into each other. A jagged one dropped to the ground. One by one, the rest slammed into it, shattering into gravel and small rocks and throwing a great cloud of dust into the air. The wooden beams and trusses disintegrated. Then the rubble bounced around as if struck by a tremor, causing the debris to scatter about until the area looked like a pile of gravel and wood chips.

Stuart shook his head and smirked as he thought back to Byron's discourse about how theatrics were not necessary for magic. First Byron and now Boss had resorted to showing off to demonstrate their power. *Maybe they felt a need to impress the Mages.*

Still he clapped and the others quickly joined in. Boss raised his arms again and a pile of scrub brush burst into flames. Then a geyser of water shot out of the ground drowning the blaze. With a piercing shriek, a large hawk swooped from the skies and landed on his shoulder. Stroking the raptor's head, Boss said, "Enough? Want more?"

"That will suffice," Wnorom said. "You didn't have much to work with around here and the demonstration took little of your power. Can all Thals do this kind of magic?"

"Many other things too."

"Why did you hide your talents? You could easily attain the rank of Wizard."

"Few in Brotherhood think like Wnorom." Boss shifted his gaze to the Mages. "Also not want abuse magic like many Wizards. They keep Grandmother captive to make us help them. Stuart save her."

Boss looked at the ground and clenched his meaty fists. "We always hope some Wizard show us stop bad ones. Not many kind like Bahorn. And Omeron."

With that, Boss stepped away and the others followed. Another short trip through the Otherworld and the Thal pointed to jagged rocks on the side of a towering bluff. "Bad wizards in cave there."

"Why would they think no one would find them?" Stuart said.

Pembar shrugged. "It's time for us to say hello." Rocks rose in the air and flew like missiles at the cave exploding in flashes of light and ear-splitting booms when they struck the entrance.

"A magic web covers it," Wnorom said. "We need to weaken it or we won't get the Wizards out of there. At least, this racket will keep them awake."

"We and Boss will take shifts during the night pummeling their shield," Pembar said. "We'll create a quiet area where you Mages can rest."

Wizard magic muffled the steady barrage of rocks enough to enable Stuart and Surovov to sleep through the night. At first light, they rejoined the others. Broken rock littered the bottom of the cliff face. "Although the shield shattered our boulders, we drained a lot of its power," Wnorom said. "The Wizards are still inside."

"Would my immunity to Wizard magic be strong enough to penetrate shields like that?" Stuart said. Having vanquished Wutega, he wanted to test his power against other hostile Wizards. *If I can't best this bunch, how would I ever face the rest of The Brotherhood?*

Pembar and Wnorom conferred about what could happen to Stuart. "If you break through the shield, you'll experience a violent itching spell that could leave you unable to protect yourself against the Wizards in the cave," Pembar said.

"What would you do inside the cave?" Surovov said.

"Find out if my powers are strong enough to stop this bunch. I'll carry my pistol in case I need it."

"How get to cave?" Boss said.

"I'll climb up the hillside and look for a way to reach the cave entrance."

"You good climber?"

Stuart shook his head. "All I've ever done is hike through hilly countryside." The enormity of the undertaking generated doubts about his abilities.

Boss grinned. "We climb to place above cave. I lower you by rope then join you to stop Wizards. This my kind of climb." He flexed his arms to show off his considerable muscles.

Stuart and Boss hiked up the hillside. The Thal stopped to let Stuart catch his breath as they climbed over and around rock outcroppings.

Then they eased their way along a narrow ridge until they stood about 10 meters above the cave entrance. Stuart glanced down, felt his world start to spin and pressed his back against the bluff. It was a long way to the bottom. The shield at the entrance snapped and hissed like a bad-tempered watchdog.

Boss tied the rope around Stuart, and then let it out as he rappelled down the cliff. Halfway to the cave entrance, the shield hissed even louder and Stuart winced at the thought of the imminent itching.

Once he was perched above the entrance, Stuart realized mountain climbers would practice a maneuver like he needed to make to break through the barrier before attempting it. He would have to trust his magic.

He bunched up several loops of rope and waved to Boss before pushing off backward from the cliff face creating an arc to swing him at the cave entrance. Stuart fought down a scream of anguish as his magic shattered the shield.

He landed on his duff and sat motionless listening for the Wizards until the itchiness from passing through the shield dissipated. Remembering Pembar's instructions, he rolled sideway until he reached the wall of the cave. He shut his eyes and used his Wizard sight to untie the knot in the rope. Several blasts of magic from the Wizards ripped past him sending waves of itchiness washing over his body, which pushed him into a murderous rage. He struggled to retain control. The Wizards kept shooting their magic through the tunnel rather than investigating the disappearance of the shield.

To confuse the Wizards, he fired the pistol. The noise of the discharge reverberated through the cave.

Boss scrabbled beside him. "Wait Stuart. They not see me."

Before he could say anything, the Thal crawled toward the Wizards. Keeping the pistol in front of him, Stuart crept after him. He caught glimpses of four figures in the flickering light of a fire in a small chamber ahead.

The Wizards screeched like a flock of angry crows. They must have finally spotted him. Stuart flattened himself against the ground when another wave of blinding light rocketed through the cave. Another bout of itching swept over him, and then he could no longer feel any irritation. By the flashes of light, the Wizards continued to cast powerful charges in his direction.

He aimed the pistol at a Wizard and squeezed the trigger. His target collapsed in a bloody heap against a cave wall.

As Stuart aimed at a second one, he dropped from sight. When a third one disappeared, he feared the Wizards were rendering themselves invisible. Then he saw the first two lay unmoving on the ground while Boss held the third in a crushing headlock. Stuart shot the remaining Wizard before he could help his comrade.

While killing was still repugnant, when it came to The Brotherhood, it really was comparable to eradicating a dangerous virus to save humanity, just as Byron said. They had the blood of millions on their hands from the disasters they had created.

After inspecting the cave, Boss gathered up the rope. "I lower you to bottom of cliff, then drop rope to you. Me climb down fast."

Stuart was still coiling the rope when the Thal reached him. He marveled at the ease with which Boss descended the cliff face. The strength in his arms and hands enabled him to grip outcrops and ledges Stuart could barely see.

Boss picked his way through the broken rocks onto solid ground. While he had set out for the cave in a swagger, now he took each step with care while questioning Stuart.

"Why Brotherhood Wizards different than Omeron and others?" Boss came to a halt and pointed back at the cave. "They not so tough, but do so much bad."

"Byron and the other good Wizards developed their powers to help people," Stuart said. "The Brotherhood pursued magic just to be powerful." He touched the side of his head. "Maybe something went wrong up here." Boss nodded. The rest of the walk back to the others passed in silence.

After Stuart described what happened in the cave to the Wizards, Boss said, "Sad kill, but Thals need learn defend us."

"Like me, you had no choice." Stuart said. "It was kill or be killed." He needed to talk to Judyth about his lack of remorse. Maybe she could explain it.

"Stuart defeat power Wizards aim at him," Boss said. "It make his magic much stronger." He took hold of Stuart's arm and announced to the group, "Great Wizard, very great Wizard."

Omeron said, "We can't leave any trace of magic in that cave." She, Pembar and Wnorom hurled fireballs into it until satisfied it was purged of any evidence of magical occupation.

"If you're ready, Stuart, we can go to the enclaves of the late Wizards," Pembar said. "We know their location thanks to Mendeleev's device. It'll be a couple of days before the magic protecting them wears off and they start to fall apart. That provides us time to retrieve their books and devices."

The first enclave was an elegant looking circular stone and log structure with a hefty chimney in the middle. "No way save?" Boss said. "Make good Thal home like Bahorn."

The Wizards shrugged and shook their heads. "We've never attempted to change magic guarding an enclave," Wnorom said. "We could try."

Boss took hold of Omeron's left hand. "You draw out Wizard magic and I replace." Wnorom and Pembar stepped beside them taking their other hands. The four faced the structure in silence.

Stuart whispered to Surovov. "Can you feel the power swirling around the Wizards and Boss? If we could make it into a light show, it'd be fantastic."

As the Wizards extracted the old magic and the Thal shored up the enclave with a new power, too many colors blended together for Stuart or Surovov to even attempt to describe them.

Abruptly, the Wizards bent forward, putting their hands on their knees and breathing deeply. "That was one of the most tiring bits of magic I've ever done," Omeron said.

Meanwhile, Boss danced around in joyful celebration, and then shouting thank you numerous times, dashed into the enclave.

"It looks the same," Surovov said, "but in the satellite image, the energy pattern around it is completely different. I guess that marks it as a Thal residence now."

Stuart and Surovov waited until the Wizards gained the energy to walk to it. "Next time, we'll remove the magic differently," Omeron said.

The interior of the enclave was modestly furnished in simple wooden chairs and tables. Woodcuttings adorned the walls. "We'll take any books and magical objects we find and send them to my enclave," she said. "Anything practical will be left for the new occupants. We'll share what we learn from the books collected from all the enclaves with the Thals if they wish."

As the Wizards and Mages looked through the enclave, Boss scurried outside and whistled loudly. Thals swarmed out of the surrounding woods and in no time, their excited chirping silenced any conversation.

UNWRAPPING MAGIC

Even though Stuart had attended many boisterous family gatherings, the excitement of the newly-arrived Thals startled him. They stood around the entrance to the enclave, whistling and chirping loudly and pointing at what would become home for some of them.

They quieted when Omeron, Pembar and Wnorom joined them. "They follow several days see if Wizards do good," Boss said. Pointing at Stuart, he chirped away rapidly. The other Thals joined him in chanting a phrase in Wizardese that included Stuart's name.

Through the racket, Pembar said, "They're thanking us and praising Stuart the Great Protector."

Stuart raised his hands and the crowd quieted. "Boss, make sure the Thals understand these Wizards are their friends. I couldn't have helped you without their assistance and Surovov's."

Boss shook Stuart's hand, and then moved onto Surovov and the three Wizards, shaking theirs.

"Go easy," Wnorom called out as the other Thals lined up to follow him. "Human hands are not nearly as strong as Thal ones."

When the introductions finished, Omeron ordered everyone to step away from the enclave. She summoned books, scrolls, tins, jars full of oddly colored liquids and devices Stuart could not identify. They hovered in the air until she organized them into an orderly collection and wrapped them in a magic tarp. Boss instructed two Thals to take the package to Omeron's residence. He sent others to deal with the bundles at Wnorom's and Bahorn's.

As he watched the couriers disappear into the Otherworld, Stuart noticed flocks of birds gathered in the surrounding trees. Squirrels, rabbits and other wildlife peeked at them. He marveled at the array of animals and wondered if they were drawn by the sensation of Omeron's magic at work. Perhaps it was like that elsewhere, and in all the excitement, he did not notice.

"Boss, I leave it to you to decide who lives here and in the other enclaves," Omeron said. "We've many matters to deal with to clean up after the bad Wizards in this area."

At the next enclave, Stuart found out what Omeron meant by stripping away magic differently. Although the Wizards stood behind them ready to assist, it was Surovov, Boss and he who switched the power holding the structure together.

Magic was wrapped like a myriad of scarves around and through the enclave. Stuart fastened his thoughts to one scarf and was amazed how it pulled away when he tugged it. Once free, he let it drift off like a balloon.

"Look at all the colors," Surovov called. "It's a rainbow in flight."

After removing a few more magical layers, Stuart felt more comfortable with the process and removed several at a time. Surovov copied him. Whenever a gap opened in the building's protection, Boss applied magical covering like it was insulating foam. Stuart was so absorbed in the task he did not realize they were finished until Boss tugged his arm to get his attention.

By the end of the day, he and Surovov had taken turns removing Wizard magic from the other enclaves while Boss coated them with Thal protection. Although the buildings looked the same afterward, it was like they had received new siding. Boss assigned Thals to move into them.

As she wove a traveling wrap around all the magical possessions from the last enclave, Omeron said, "My invitation to Wnorom to stay with me I extend to Pembar because it'll take many months to examine everything we've gathered. We must encourage the Mages to visit my enclave so we can learn from each other."

Stuart stared at the Wizards and Thals. "We're getting ahead of ourselves. We're not finished with The Brotherhood. They're still causing disasters." A surge of anger swept through Stuart causing the others to look at him in astonishment. He raised clenched fists in the air. "We need to keep after them until they're finished."

At first, Stuart felt embarrassed by his behavior because he was indulging in the same drama he faulted the Wizards for. While he needed to keep his anger under control, it would be a useful weapon as long as the safety was on.

Surovov stepped up to him. "Battle not over. However, Wizard friends here need rest. They do much. Thals too. We all need think of future. World badly wounded. We need to cure the infection and heal it. Russian Mages go home. You've plenty of Wizards and Mages in Europe, but if need our aid, just call."

Stuart shook his friend's hand. "You're right. We all need some rest. I'll find out where we'll attack next." He looked at Boss. "How will I stay in contact with you?"

Boss smiled. "We find you anywhere. You want us, just think we come."

"Even when they live with us, the Thals mostly keep to themselves," Omeron said. "We'll visit their enclaves from time to time. That could be Wnorom's responsibility. There should not be problems unless they're discovered by humans."

Boss winked at Stuart. "Maybe we make sure Wizards behave." He bowed to Omeron. "Young Thals still welcome your enclave for learning?"

"Always. It should be even more entertaining and rewarding than in the past."

"Stuart, come here," Surovov called out. He had set up his laptop on a bench and spread out the solar panel to recharge its battery. After sending a report about the successful makeover of the enclaves, he downloaded updates from the farm and other Mage groups.

"These two girls are really interested in how the computer operates. They remember everything I tell them and if knew English or Russian, would be able send message. They noticed the energy pattern over the enclave had changed after Boss applied his protection."

Both girls glanced at the two men before returning their attention to the laptop. They had long black hair and delicate facial features. In human years, they were teenagers. By Thal standards, they were adults.

"Perhaps they can bridge Wizard magic and technology," Surovov said.

"Their existence as a species is one of the greatest discoveries of all time except they were already here." Stuart paused. "Learning of their existence could be important for the future of the world."

"We can't tell anyone," Surovov said. "Must protect like members of Realm."

"Maybe we should make them members," Stuart said.

One of the Thal girls burst out in giggles.

"Incredible," Surovov said as he looked at the screen. It showed a satellite feed with a high magnification view of the group of Wizards, Mages and Thals. "They did that without touching screen!" He knelt for a closer look. "The girls manipulate technology like you, Stuart. Send thoughts into computer to find satellite image. Probably don't even understand the technology."

Stuart stared at the grinning girls as Pembar described their accomplishment to the Thals. His thoughts drifted to the possibilities of learning through osmosis and telepathy. *Could these girls emulate me even without my education? Something else about Thals I need to find out more about.*

"Boss, what the two girls did is a big deal. I name them Rose and Bella after my grandmothers."

"Like names," Boss said.

After the group set out for Bahorn's enclave to check on Judyth and the other Mages, Rose and Bella caught up to Stuart and took hold of his hands. "When we rest, I'll give you a tour of the world using the computer."

"First, teach words," Rose pleaded.

He decided to expand their vocabulary and sentence structure first. Before long, Rose and Bella knew about mountains, hills, creeks, rocks, stones and dirt. Next came discussions about wildlife, clothes, continents and countries. By the time they reached Bahorn's, they spoke in simple sentences using pronouns. He did not repeat any instructions.

Judyth rushed to greet them. The Mages and Thals trooped out behind her. As she got closer, Stuart realized she was crying. He had never seen her so upset and when he reached her, she threw her arms around him.

He held her tightly as she spat out her anger between sobs. "The bastards are still creating disasters all over the world. This morning they hit the Pacific Region of North America by undermining all the fault lines. Everything in the coastal region from Mexico to Canada is rubble. Millions are dead and the damage; well wait until you see the video, it's just unbelievable."

While none of Stuart's relatives lived on the West Coast, several friends did. Then it hit him. "What about Harold and the kids?"

"Harold was in Chicago on business and Marconi was at the farm. Their kids were at their home near San Francisco with his parents. She can't communicate with them yet. Thals are attempting to reach their home through the Otherworld."

Thinking of the chaos made Stuart's blood boil with ideas for attacking The Brotherhood. Once again, his anger wanted release, and Stuart needed to control it.

Judyth let go of Stuart to wipe her tears on her sleeves.

"We can leave for Omeron's right away. Not only was the surgery on Bahorn successful, it enabled Pathfinder and Farseeker's healing to actually improve his condition. He'll remain in his enclave. He now wishes the Thal clan would've moved in before. The sound of many contented voices makes his life a lot better."

"All Wizards should learn that," Pembar said. "Some young Thals want to go to the farm to learn more about your world and technology."

"Us too," Rose and Bella chimed in.

"As long as The Realm is okay with it, it's fine by me," Stuart said.

"We'll find a way to communicate with Thal enclaves so they know what's happening with us and Wizards." Surovov said. "Thal magic not interfere with radios and phones."

After handshakes and hugs all around, a Thal led the Russian Mages into the Otherworld.

"I need to return to Tallinn to catch a plane home," Stuart said.

"Why don't you come back through the Otherworld with us and the Thals," Judyth said.

"Having checked my scientific gear into Europe on a temporary basis, I need to remove it or face a lot of questions the next time I come back."

While the Wizards and Mages reached Zagajnik, they found the Thals preparing supper. Judyth took Stuart and the Wizards out of earshot of the others. "Although the Thals speak Wizardese, they don't read or write it. That's why they didn't object to Omeron taking all the magic books from the enclaves. There's no written version of their language either. Their history is all in their heads. We should compile it."

"Sounds like a project that would keep Bethune busy for a bit," Stuart said.

"As well, they don't catch human illnesses," she said. "None of them contracted the colds the Russians had although I would've expected them to because from living in isolation they shouldn't have any immunity to our afflictions."

"In addition to that, you should study the organization of their clans," Pembar said. "They move from group to group quite often. Everyone, not just the parents, is responsible for raising their young and looking after the elderly. The old lady you rescued was Grandmother to Boss's group although we don't know if she was directly related to any of them."

After a side trip to retrieve the van, Stuart spent a day at Omeron's enclave updating himself with events elsewhere and examining all the magical gear the Thals had delivered before heading to Tallinn with Baltic. Most of that drive in the now roomy vehicle passed in contemplation of the measures Merstreem and his thugs were employing to block The Realm from entering their remaining enclaves. If the Mages could eliminate them, the world would return to something like normal. Which would mean he and Judyth could establish a life together.

They arrived in the city in the late afternoon and as he needed to wake before dawn for his flight, Baltic dropped Stuart off at the airport hotel. "I need a really good night's sleep and time to catch up on my business before I return home."

He checked in and settled on the bed with his phone. An e-mail from Harold included a note sent to Stuart's clients. "Stuart is on a specialized security retraining and refresher course that will undoubtedly benefit your business and he'll contact you upon his return." Even with all that had happened with The Realm, Harold managed to make it sound like business as usual. However there was nothing about the status of his children in California.

Harold had organized Stuart's phone messages and prepared a list of clients who needed his attention. Stuart went through the rest of his email and messages, sending apologies for his delayed response to many customers. He saved the schedule and made notes beside each entry. It would be a long week making up for his absence as well as bracing for the showdown with The Brotherhood.

It was almost midnight Sunday night when he got out of the taxi in front of his apartment. While it seemed like he had been away for months, it was only three weeks.

Although exhausted from his adventures and the time changes, Stuart headed out early the next morning. The magic would have to help him cope while he became used to living in several realities at the same time.

His first call was at BTS Designs' new location. Its owner was anxious to show Stuart the manufacturing equipment that replaced his old machines. "While they do a lot more, we'll still need your help because they're much more complicated. By the way, tell your uncle some of the old ones did go to a museum."

Stuart's smile was not just because the owner remembered Byron. The new manufacturing equipment would let him test his abilities. He sent his thoughts into the control panel. Although it was not as exhilarating as stripping magic from an enclave, he roamed unimpeded through the machine. He did it without touching any part, and no longer needed to use circuits or mechanical linkages to move about.

"So what do you think?" While the owner's question brought Stuart back to reality, he tracked his presence in the machine. He walked around, opening access panels to peer inside. The equipment was well made and highly automated. "Its design should reduce the amount of maintenance while being easier for your employees to operate and program."

He examined the control panel. An operator explained the purpose of the dials and gauges. "We mostly control it through the computer keyboard."

Stuart's other stops were more demanding even with his improved diagnostic technique. He was relieved when he backed into his garage just before 7 p.m.

As he opened his apartment door, he thought about the news and the TV came on. He muted it when he saw Judyth and Byron sitting at his table. *With all I can do now, why didn't I detect their presence?*

Byron barely resembled the bedraggled old man from the tavern. He wore a modern suit and well-polished shoes. A few extra pounds made him appear much healthier. He had abandoned his perpetual frown for a ready smile although he still talked like a refined English butler.

"I put him on medicine to lower his blood pressure and make his heart beat more regularly," Judyth said. "He gained weight thanks to Digger's cooking."

Stuart blurted out, "How did you know I was thinking about his health?" Then he remembered Judyth's ability to understand people's thoughts. "You'll have to use your magic to block me when you wish to keep your thoughts private," she said.

"You'll know I'm doing it." Stuart said. "So a lot of good it'll do me to try to hide things from you."

"She understands people's need for privacy," Byron said. "Now the reason for our visit. We're at a standoff with Merstreem and his bunch. Charlemagne's Mages can't penetrate the shields of magical power surrounding the remaining enclaves. One is in the Jura Mountains between France and Switzerland while the other is in the Pyrenees in Spain. We're moving Wizards and Mages into place around those enclaves to prevent them from escaping."

Stuart nodded. "So I must break through their shields and finish the Wizards off before they do something with their powers that is detected by security services or the military. We need to prevent a major military assault on the enclaves that'll give away the Wizards and us."

"When everything is ready, Boss will collect you to head our assault on the last two enclaves," Byron said.

"What's the big deal with their shields?"

"The Brotherhood specialized in particular aspects of magical power. This is one area where they outshine us completely."

"So we can't draw the magic out of their defenses as we did from the enclaves in the Urals?"

Byron shook his head. "They'd replace it just as fast we pulled it away."

"So we need to break down their protection. I sure wish I could do it without all the itching. It's so bloody maddening."

"Every time you've tackled a magical barrier, the itchiness

diminished faster and your own power grew," Judyth said.

Stuart nodded. "The itching triggers my anger and I fear I'll lose control and who knows what I might unleash if that happens. I want to defeat The Brotherhood, not become like them."

Judyth and Byron fell silent so Stuart told them about Surovov. "He can disappear. He's way ahead of me in terms of blending Wizard working with the natural elements and Mage working with technology magic. I'm sure his abilities are even stronger after our adventures in the Urals. I can see inside machines and computers much better and it's become far easier to tap into Wizard magic than before I went to Europe."

Stuart summoned a beer from the fridge "I have an idea about how The Realm could make better use of Harold."

PITCHED BATTLE

Boss was waiting at his apartment when Stuart returned home Thursday evening. After a quick supper and sleep, they entered the Otherworld in the middle of the night and reached the site of the second last Brotherhood enclave in the Jura Mountains shortly after sunrise.

To his surprise, Stuart now could see through a Wizard hiding spell. He pointed at a towering pile of rocks, soil and tree roots. "The enclave is hidden just above that. I can't tell whether the debris in front of it is a natural slide or created by magic."

"Good hiding spot," Boss said with a disdainful grunt. With them were two other Thals and several Mages.

Charlemagne, the leader of the European Mages, studied his GPS for the umpteenth time. "I can't see it."

"The hiding spell makes you see only what Wizards want you to," Stuart said. "The enclave is just below the barren ridge. The mountain goats are like cheap special effects that show any passersby what they'd expect to be there. If you looked long enough, you'd see them graze in the same places over and over. The terrain between here and the enclave is set up to discourage ordinary hikers from trespassing. There's enough magic among us that the Wizards should know a lot of us are nearby unless they still don't recognize the power of Thals and Mages."

"Probably think they better than everyone else," Boss said.

"If they did detect our magic, I'd expect them to attack us unless they're like that bunch in the cave who thought they were safe hiding behind their magic," Stuart said.

"Most Wizards have cut them off," Charlemagne said. He closed his fingers like a pair of scissors. "Stuart should collapse the enclave on these evil men. Even better would be to make a Thal residence out of it."

Stuart summoned his touchstone, and then started stripping away the force that surrounded the enclave.

"See what you do," Boss chimed in. "I take next layer."

With their experience in Russia, Stuart and Boss removed enough magic that within a few minutes, everyone could soon see a rectangular stone wall, about two meters high, and the tile roof of the structure inside it.

"How the devil did they manage to build it here?" Charlemagne said. "They must've moved it from somewhere else."

Boss let out a disgusted grunt. "Probably force Thals transport it."

Stuart motioned for his friends to stand back. A spark in the air in front of him mushroomed into a fireball about a meter in diameter. Satisfied it was big enough, he sent it hurtling at the enclave. Before it hit the wall, it exploded with a flash of light and a resounding boom.

"The enclave is still well shielded." Stuart paced back and forth pondering how to overcome the protection. The shield resembled a chain link fence except that instead of strands of interconnected wire, streaks of red, yellow and silver energy shot in every direction creating patterns far more complex and stronger than what he had encountered in the Urals. This enclave would require a completely different approach to overcome its powerful barriers.

Charlemagne stopped in front of him. "You're an interesting fellow. You absorb magical power readily while the rest of us gain it a little bit at a time. What do you want to do now?"

"We need the site under constant surveillance on the ground and from satellites to know if anyone enters or departs. From here, I can see the patterns in the shield's defenses. When I'm up close, I'll look for a weak spot or a way to drain the power. If we get through, we'll subdue the Wizards in the enclave. I'll probably need backup because this much magic could completely disorient me."

"Subdue!" Charlemagne said. "I thought we intended to destroy them." The Mages murmured in agreement.

"We need to protect any Thals and Halves as well as the building," Stuart said. "I will deal with the Wizards while Boss will look after the others. Iywwan will take charge of any magic material after she arrives."

Boss led the way up the hillside toward the enclave while Charlemagne stationed additional Mages around it. The rough ground made for a slow climb going sideways as often as forward. Stuart frequently grabbed a boulder or tree for support. When they reached the wall, he waited until his breathing returned to normal.

He waved at Boss to indicate his readiness, and then projected his magic into the wall. He fought down the itching and tapped into the energy flow of the shield as if surfing its patterns. He let the magic in it build up inside him.

When he felt in control, he imagined a giant fire hydrant on the downhill side of the wall. Then he opened the outlet to drain the energy by spilling it down the mountainside. It danced with great flashes of light over the craggy surface until it dissipated.

The Wizards must have felt their shield weakening because a giant ball of brilliant yellow light raced through it knocking Stuart backward. It swirled around him blurring his sight. He recalled Judyth's observation that conquering Wizard magic nurtured his abilities. With a grim smile, he placed his feet wide apart and opened himself to the shimmering light.

It rocked him and he could no longer see through its brilliance as the new power mixed with what he already possessed. He forced himself to stand still so he did not trip on the uneven terrain. The energy continued to rattle through him.

His confidence mounting, he decided to surf the energy back to its source. He traced its many rainbow strands to four Wizards standing in a circle feeding their power into a glowing giant crystal ball at the center of the enclave's main hall.

Concluding the crystal ball served as conduit for their magic, Stuart braced himself as he connected to all the links emanating from it. He wanted to boost the outflow of energy from the ball. It sluiced through him and out the hydrant before roaring down the mountainside like water through a breached dam.

While he could hardly stand, he risked a glance over his shoulder. Mini rainbows danced everywhere. *I hope they're getting this on video.*

When the light show dimmed, he saw the crystal ball had lost most of its brilliance. The Wizards slumped forward pouring the last of their strength into it. No longer content to empty the ball, Stuart decided it was time to deal with them as well.

He seized the little power they still possessed causing the Wizards to lose their balance. One fell backward while another collapsed onto the ball and was absorbed into it. Stuart could not discern any changes to the composition of the energy emanating from the ball.

Boss stepped beside him. "Wizards don't want capture. Fear punish."

The two Wizards still standing seized the legs of their fallen comrade and pulled him on top of the ball. The body vanished, and then they grasped the ball and disappeared into it. Within minutes, the remnants of the shield fizzled away.

With magic no longer bombarding him, Stuart finished absorbing what swirled inside him. He felt like he had been spun around repeatedly. Completely disoriented, he staggered like a drunk struggling to keep his balance.

Boss yelled at the Thals and they raced around the enclave wall until they found a gate. Gradually, the roaring in Stuart's ears subsided and he heard the Thals calling to each other as they advanced toward the enclave.

Stuart drank in a world beyond his imagination and which photographs would never do justice. He could see the details of distant peaks. No longer were they just grey outlines. Animals moved about above the tree line.

The breeze caressed him with a greeting from the natural world celebrating the defeat of the malevolent Wizards. Wind rushed through trees and over boulders and rock formations to join the reveille. Mountains groaned as the moon swung into view exerting its tug on the Earth. Startled by the commotion Stuart had created, birds called to each other for reassurance.

The world was alive in ways he could never have imagined. "What a gift," he whispered. When the Thals reached the entrance to the enclave, Stuart's magic unlocked the door and they followed Boss inside. Mages arrived and joined in the search of the structure.

"The stairs are at the back," Stuart called out. Mages and Thals pounded down the stairs and within minutes, shouts of joy rang through the building. "There are a couple of Halves and a dozen Thals in the basement."

While Stuart waited for them to return, his magic delved into every nook and cranny of the enclave locating magic material and summoning it into a pile beside him. Omeron would be impressed with his thoroughness. He wrapped all the goods in a glowing grey tarp.

The Thals and Mages did not need his help to explore the enclave so Stuart remained outside, opening up again to the world. To Wizards, it was a living, breathing organism. How could The Brotherhood have created the disasters on top of the harm being inflicted by climate change? Maybe killing millions of people did not bother them. However, the suffering they had caused the planet should have been intolerable. Here it creaked and groaned with the usual stresses. He could only imagine its screams during an earthquake, tsunami or wild fire.

Magic could not repair the damage that The Brotherhood would continue to inflict until Merstreem and his remaining followers in Spain were eliminated.

His thoughts were interrupted by a familiar voice. "Welcome, nephew. You're one of us now." Byron was in the far-away Loire Valley inspecting a stockpile of magical items with Omeron and Pembar. "We'll have much to discuss when next we meet. Thank you for proving me right."

No sooner had Byron finished his accolades then a nasty cackle assaulted Stuart. "We do not fear you, boy." Merstreem's image floated in the air in front of him. "Your soft hearted friends and their freaks won't defeat us."

The enclave door flew open and someone ran toward him. "Stuart, close yourself off," screamed Anastasia, who was there in her role as an intermediary among the Mages, Wizards and Thals. "Don't listen that bastard."

When she drew close, he put a finger to his lips. She stepped back, her eyes fixed on him.

"Do you know what this is?" Shiny particles swirled around Stuart, unlike anything he encountered since meeting Byron.

As they faded, a raspy voice, which sounded like an ancient hinge moving for the first time in eons, spoke. "I'll be waiting for you."

"Whatever that was, it curious about you, like Thals are," Anastasia said.

Stuart looked about. "I need to find out who it is."

The other Mages and Thals spilled into the night and stopped as soon as they saw Stuart. "So that's what an aura looks like," Audubon said. "You shine like a rainbow all by yourself."

"Him much brighter than others," Boss said. The Thal scratched his head, and then summoned the Thals from the enclave to introduce them.

When Stuart pointed at the tarp-covered goods, Boss spoke to two Thals who disappeared into the Otherworld, the pile bobbing behind them like a devoted puppy. Then he brought forward two boys and a girl. "I send to farm for Harold and Bethune teach. Rest live here. Is enclave okay?"

"I've marked where it needs some reinforcing," Stuart said. "Charlemagne has engineers who can help you."

Charlemagne nodded. "We'll get on it right away. We'll set up a communications system for the Mages and Thals that Wizards could tap into. In time, we need to arrange for Mages to visit Thal residences."

"Wnorom will be doing that as well," Stuart said.

Boss brought the Halves, who appeared to be in their early 30s, to Stuart. "This is a real wizard," Charlemagne said to them in French. "The four Wizards in there weren't safe from his power and you won't be either if you ever anger us."

"You've nothing to fear," a short, dark haired woman said. "Carlo and I have a good life and we'd expose what we do if we talked about Wizards. And who would believe us?" She gave Stuart a curt nod and took her companion's arm. "We want to return to Lyon."

"The only way to send you home now is through the Otherworld if it'll accept you," Charlemagne said. "It's scary, but the trip won't take long. A Thal will guide you and someone will visit you later."

After they successfully disappeared, Boss led the other Thals to the enclave to take possession of it.

"Interesting the Halves have enough magic power to enter the Otherworld," Stuart said.

"Their power probably not strong enough for them to enter it or travel there on their own," Anastasia said. "They need to follow a

Thal, Mage and Wizard."

"Maybe some of them could learn."

"What are the old Wizard powers like?" Audubon said.

"Beyond unbelievable. I can see beyond our solar system and so much else that I couldn't before. The world sounds like a symphony orchestra. Maybe this inspired the great composers. My abilities and my Wizard sight have become so much stronger. At the same time, I'm responsible for protecting the planet and not just from the crazed Wizards of The Brotherhood.

"I'll need to be careful using my magic. Otherwise people will think I'm crazy when I describe what I can see. I'll try all the different powers when I've time although I'd like to know now what they'll enable me to do." He raised his arms while he stretched his power to the last holdout enclave. It radiated chaos and a beacon of light. "Tell the Mages guarding the other place to be ready for anything. The Wizards there are in a panic."

"Can we delay assaulting it?" Audubon said.

"No. As tired as I am, it's too risky for the world to wait even a day. We'll get Boss and his posse to take us there right away."

While stopping Merstreem remained essential, finding the source of the raspy voice now seemed far more important.

THE SANCTUARY

Stuart followed the Mages and Thals out of the Otherworld within sight of a weathered grey wooden cottage nestled deep in an Alpine forest. A thick rock wall surrounded the two storey stone building, which had green windows and doors. A pathway meandered from a wooden gate in the wall through the trees to a fast moving brook.

"Look deserted," Boss said.

"This is a wildlife preserve so you wouldn't expect to find a cottage here," Charlemagne said. "We couldn't find its exact location until Surovov arrived."

Stuart waved to the Mages on stake-out before dispatching his thoughts to scout the enclave. Magic that felt far older than any Wizard handiwork he had already encountered held the rocks in the wall together tighter than concrete.

"The magic is set up to keep animals and unwanted visitors away," the Russian said.

Suppressing a yawn, Stuart headed toward the wall moving from tree to tree. "I probably shouldn't bother attempting to hide my approach, but why take chances." The Thals and Surovov copied his every move. Charlemagne and other Mages followed at a distance. "The scouts reported that no one has entered or left the enclave in days."

When he reached the wall, Stuart expected the magic in it to react to his presence. Not even his nose was itchy.

"Same as last time?" Boss said. "You remove magic and we get Wizards."

Stuart shook his head. "This place is completely different."

"You full of doubt," Boss said.

"It's too easy. It's the last Brotherhood stronghold and it's defended by five strong Wizards including Merstreem. Yet their magic barely registers inside the enclave. There's a lot more to this place than meets the eye."

Boss placed his hands on the ground and searched with his magic. This time, Stuart could feel the power emanating from him.

Boss peered at Stuart. "You right. Tunnel from underneath building into mountain but it empty. Nothing inside." Surovov nodded in agreement.

Feeling even more puzzled, Stuart placed his hands on the wall, admiring the careful placement of the rocks. "A power resides in them." He tested different ones. "The wall is full of magic yet it doesn't respond to mine. Perhaps it doesn't recognize it. I need to attract this magic."

"Me try." Boss put his hands on the wall. "Feel magic too. Very old. Know nothing like it." He stepped back but kept staring at the wall as Surovov tested it.

Stuart touched the rocks in the wall again. "I want to connect with it. I gained a lot from the shield at the last place." He sent his thoughts into the wall as he would a machine. They roamed through many shades of grey broken by colorful streaks of minerals and chunks of quartz. His magic had projected about a quarter of the way around the wall when he sensed something shadowing it.

He had made the right move by revealing himself to whatever power resided in the wall, letting it see the new kid on the block. As his projection advanced through the stones, he wondered if the power in the wall could combine with all the Wizard magic he had gained during the last few weeks. *If it does, the challenge would be to turn out like Byron and not Merstreem.*

A rock vibrated as his presence passed. *Finally some actual acknowledgement.* He moved ahead a half meter. Another rock shook. He projected thoughts of extracting magic from the enclaves and employing his magic to repair machines. More rocks jiggled and a hum sounded in the wake of his thoughts, like birds following Audubon.

Hearing movement, he glanced over his shoulder. The Thals

stood close by; perhaps they feared the magic might try to pull him into the wall. His projection paused when it encountered a large boulder. He directed his thoughts into it. The rocks around it stilled. The magic hovered nearby.

Then glittering particles swarmed around him before vanishing.

"Go inside mountain?" Boss said.

"Inside me." Stuart tapped his chest. "They're meeting the power I absorbed from the previous enclaves. It might be a reunion." The magics mingled within him although the celebration seemed tentative so far. He remembered the last time he absorbed traditional magic. "I better sit down in case this becomes rambunctious."

He lay back against the wall and gave his senses free rein. A Wizard-created hurricane stirred in the Caribbean. He dispersed it. Let the weather office figure that one out. Soaring over Latin America, he brought rain to a drought stricken region. A thousand kilometers away, he unleashed a torrential deluge to drown a gathering of warlords and drug barons. *Let's see Byron top that!*

Although he could spend hours combing the world for good deeds to perform, his mind snapped back to dealing with the Wizards in the enclave. He would explore his new abilities later.

"Just stone wall now." Boss had placed his hands on several stones. "Magic all gone."

As Surovov touched the rocks, Stuart shifted his position so he could stare at the wall while contemplating how many centuries the magic might have lain dormant in the stones.

Boss patted him on the back. "Maybe waiting you free it."

The Thals' ability to read his mind was certainly stronger. Perhaps the magic in the stones had affected everyone accompanying him. Stuart peered at Boss. "It would've been hard work placing all these rocks by hand. It could've been constructed by your ancestors."

"Wonder that too. Can't tell."

Stuart shifted to his knees to examine the cottage. "It appears well made and in good shape, not held together by magic." Shutters covered the windows. He stood, took a step toward it and stopped. He teetered and struggled to keep his balance. "It'll take me a while to reach the cottage. You guys go ahead." He made the door open for them.

With Surovov at his side, Stuart took another step. While the world still appeared blurry, he pressed forward. With every step, his seeing and walking improved. When he reached the cottage, he noted the covers on the furniture and a coat of dust everywhere. "It's supposed to look like no one's been here for a while."

A Thal found the door to the basement. "Can you see well enough to move about in this darkness?" Stuart said. When Boss shook his head, Stuart took out his flashlight and showed him how it worked puzzled the Thals lacked a power similar to Wizard vision. The Thals followed Boss down the stairs to the basement. Stuart searched the enclave with his thoughts until the Thals chirped shrilly.

"We find entrance to tunnel," Boss called.

While his surroundings still appeared fuzzy, Stuart's walking was back to normal and using his Wizard vision, he and Surovov caught up with the Thals. They stood in a group frowning at each other and muttering.

"Make no sense." Boss pressed his hand on the wall near the tunnel entrance. "Not far to big opening."

"You check it out." Pulling out his radio, Stuart reported their finding and the need for flashlights for the Thals.

"We'll be along in a few minutes," Audubon replied. "I'll ask the Mages at the farm to examine the mountain to see if they can get a read on your location."

The Thals did not return from their exploration of the tunnel so Stuart and Surovov set out after them. Thal boot prints mingled with many others in the dirt. The air smelled surprisingly fresh and moist. He detected only scattered remnants of magic. The rough finish of the walls suggested they were hewn with hand tools.

Ahead, the tunnel opened into a much larger space. They stepped onto a smooth floor and looked about. They were in a massive cavern. This was the empty mountain Boss had located with his magic.

They walked to the center of it for a better view. While it was tall enough to house an office building, the cavern disappointed Stuart. While obviously shaped by hands, not the forces of nature, it lacked any trace of craftsmanship or elegant design. Boss approached them. "Not see a place like this before. Old tales." His words trailed off when they heard a distant shout. "Thals find new tunnel."

"Tell your pals to stay where they are so we can see if there are any footprints. There has to be a trap or Wizard defense somewhere.

Unless there's another way out and they've already fled."

Boss shouted to his out of sight pals, and then he and Stuart headed off. "I'll wait here for the other Mages, and then we'll follow you," Surovov said.

The Thals chirped as the pair drew near. "Many marks in tunnel, some fresh," Boss said. "More feet than five Wizards."

"Could it be Thals, humans or other Wizards?"

Boss shrugged. "No Thal feet here."

Stuart's radio beeped and he waved for the Thals to proceed.

"Who could have created the cavern and the mountain that covers it and how?" Charlemagne said. "We're making a video to transmit to the farm. We want The Realm to see this. It'd take big time engineering to design this."

"I'm in a tunnel that runs from the far side from where we entered," Stuart said. "For now, stay behind us but close enough that you can help if we run into trouble."

No longer able to hear the Thals, Stuart used his Wizard vision to walk at a normal pace. Marveling at the smoothness of the walls and ceiling, he let his hand run along one stretch. It felt like glass. The magic that created it was different from what he had encountered elsewhere.

He halted when magic tickled him. His power, enhanced by what he had absorbed from the stone wall, swirled in response almost pitching him off his feet. He put his hands on the wall to keep his balance. The other magic tugged again. He advanced one cautious step at a time, even though his combined powers prodded him to move faster. Then the tickling sensation returned and tugged him back in the direction he came from. It puzzled him until he realized it was telling him he had moved past the source of the new magic. It beckoned him to return.

Rather than turn around, he stepped backward. The other magic pulled him along. A couple more paces and it pressed on him, as if desperate for a reunion with whatever was inside him. He inched forward and backward until certain he stood at the apex of the power. He opened himself to it, inviting it to meet his magic.

Shining light slithered from the wall. Stuart's heart raced as it wrapped around him. The Voice told him to relax. The light from the wall caressed him. While it must be delivering a message, he did not comprehend it. He focused on projecting an image of the dull grey wall in front of him to whatever was reaching out to him. In response, an arch opened in the wall revealing a thick fog.

His Wizard vision slowly dissipated the fog, which matched the color of the tunnel walls, revealing another cavern. Although he did not know how to measure dimensions with Wizard vision, it appeared about as big as a medium sized warehouse.

"Welcome Stuart." The raspy voice he had heard in the Jura came from a slightly stooped, olive skinned man standing with arms open in greeting. The face did not resemble any Wizard pictures that Byron had shown the Mages.

Stuart stepped into the chamber and glanced about. Rows of packed shelves lined both walls. Stacks of wooden chests filled the middle with all sorts of small boxes, spheres and bottles perched on top of them. As he peered about, he noticed he stood on a tiled floor.

"Charlemagne, if you still have radio contact with the others, we need the Wizards down here."

"We're in the tunnel now. Did you find Merstreem?"

"Not yet. I'm in a cavern off the tunnel. It's full of magic that feels like it's been here forever."

If Charlemagne replied, Stuart could not hear him over joyful singing that filled the chamber and tunnel. It erupted from everywhere, sounding like a choir of hundreds. Although the words meant nothing to him, the voices sang in celebration.

Stuart looked at the man. His eyes beamed and a smile stretched across his heavily-lined face as tears trickled down his checks. Finally the choir fell silent. Hopefully the Thals and Mages heard the singing. He tried the radio again.

"I can hardly hear you." Charlemagne's said.

In the background, Anastasia shouted. "What was music? Want to hear more."

Stuart hoped her Wizard status would enable her to find the chamber. "There's an archway in the tunnel that's hidden by magic. You need to look hard to see it."

"Where in tunnel? See nothing."

Stuart's mind raced through questions. *Did the arch open just for me? If so, why did it remain hidden to everyone else? The Wizards had lived in the mountain for ages, probably walked this tunnel thousands of times. Had they never detected its presence?*

All of a sudden, the old man spoke in Wizardese but Stuart heard his words in English. "It is a welcome sign you need a translation of what I say. That means you are not a member of The Brotherhood and magic has evolved."

The old man took a deep breath. "Magic is adapting to what the world needs, no longer rooted in a brutish, ignorant past. You are new to it. Tell me about yourself."

In the hallway, Anastasia called. "Stuart, where are you?"

"She's part of the change as well."

The wall opened and Anastasia entered. She stood still taking in the chamber's contents. Her hand flew to her mouth.

THE LAST STAND

Anastasia finally regained her composure. She looked at the ancient figure in the chamber and softly said, "The Guardian." The man nodded and smiled broadly. A smile lit up her face and her eyes swept over the room. "The Sanctuary. Stuart, many Wizards searched all their lives for this place."

Before Stuart could point out that whatever it was, the Sanctuary had found him, the Guardian said, "Welcome Anastasia de la Montagne. This is what you wished for." The singing resumed.

When it ended, Stuart recounted his unexpected introduction to the world of magic. The Guardian nodded when Stuart mentioned Byron and listened impassively as he related the deaths of the Wizards who attempted to kill him. The Guardian's expression brightened as Stuart explained the aid he received from Pembar, Omeron, Wnorom and Iywwan.

"While it's sad that we came to this, there was no other way to stop The Brotherhood," the Guardian said "They parted company with reason a long time ago."

Finally, an image of what looked like a younger Byron appeared in the air and the Guardian called him by a name Stuart did not recognize. The Guardian listened attentively as Stuart described the last few weeks and became quite animated as he related how Judyth healed Bahorn. "I can see what happened as you recount it." He clapped as Stuart explained the role of Thals in overcoming the Brotherhood.

"They're taking over empty Wizard enclaves and protecting them with their magic. Unlike Wizards, they can use modern technology."

Stuart continued on with his story naming the Wizards who supported the Mages and Thals. "The Brotherhood ones in the tunnel are the last we need to deal with."

"Merstreem and his gang are being aided by Halves."

How old could the Guardian be?

"Centuries ago, we realized that as science displaced magic, some Wizards, angry at their loss of importance, would be tempted to use their powers for personal gain rather than the betterment of the people they were responsible for," the Guardian said. "We gathered books of knowledge and magical objects here to keep them from malicious hands."

"Who is the we you refer to?"

"We were known as The Realm and in time we were proved correct in our decision to hide as much of the ancient magic as we could. I agreed to serve as the Guardian of the Sanctuary on the understanding that if I felt I was losing my power, I would destroy its contents rather than let them fall into the hands of The Brotherhood."

In the distance, gunshots sounded followed by the pounding of feet through the tunnel.

"Your friends need help now," the Guardian said. "I'll withdraw the barrier to let you aid them. Meanwhile, there is much for Anastasia and I to discuss."

Stuart readily agreed and the room plunged into darkness while the wall reopened. He switched to Wizard sight and stepped into the hallway just as Mages rushed by carrying someone.

"The Halves back there have guns," Charlemagne said. "A Thal was hit too."

Stuart jogged in the direction the Mages came from, his Wizard vision scouting ahead of him. The Thals gathered around a figure on the ground trying to stop his bleeding. "Boss, get him out of here," Stuart barked. The Thals picked up their wounded pal and headed for the main chamber.

Stuart stayed close to the tunnel wall as he eased around a corner. The Wizards and Halves huddled together in a dimly lit cavern about 50 meters away. Stuart needed to end their reign of terror now. It came down to him and Merstreem.

The Halves reloaded their handguns while the Wizards screamed at them to shoot Stuart. The Halves looked puzzled and pointed their weapons aimlessly around not knowing where to fire.

Stuart sent the thoughts he used to repair machines into the guns to jam the firing mechanisms. Try as they might, the Halves could not pull the triggers.

"Feeble brained fools," a Wizard yelled sending the Halves flying into the sides of the cave. The Wizard kept screaming. Stuart had found Merstreem. The friendly face Stuart saw floating in the farmhouse kitchen stared at him with eyes that shone with hate.

A swirling ball of yellow, white and red grew in the cavern. Fearing what might happen if it became any larger, Stuart fired a shot of his magic into it. The resulting explosion blew through the tunnel bowling him over.

As he scrambled to his feet, the Wizards groaned and rolled about. The explosion should have killed them. It was powerful enough to make the mountain shudder sending showers of rock and gravel crashing into the tunnel. Knowing the mountain over his head was not hollow, Stuart covered his head with both arms while wondering how magic could protect him if it collapsed.

A light swept through the tunnel into the rock above and below him sealing the cracks created by the explosion. When the mountain quieted, Stuart crept toward the cavern. The crumpled forms of the Halves remained on the ground, their last moments marked by dark smears on the walls.

Blackened and disheveled from the explosion, the Wizards staggered to their feet. His companions watched Merstreem waving his arms like an orchestra conductor as he created another ball of energy by chanting an eerie incantation over and over again. It was the first time that Stuart was happy not to understand Wizardese.

"Wizards owe each other an opportunity to parlay," Stuart called. "We want you to stop destroying our world."

Merstreem did not cease his arm waving or even look at Stuart, and the other Wizards laughed dismissively. "We want to preserve the world," Merstreem said in a heavy accent. "It has too many people and they foul the air, the land and the water. The Dissidents can't stop us and neither can you."

Stuart surprised himself with the vehemence of his reply. "Our magic is a product of our world, not some relic of the past. And we have the Guardian on our side. Your time is up."

The Wizards glanced among themselves. "Impossible," Merstreem snapped. "The Guardian is just a myth. The weak Wizards have fooled you just as they delude themselves. We'll not waste time talking with a group of children." Merstreem waved his hand as if batting away flies.

The Guardian's voice tickled Stuart's mind. "They're the deluded ones if they believe I don't exist. Stay where you are." A breeze swept through the tunnel. While it did not touch him, the wind grew stronger until it howled like a gale. It drove sand, gravel and stones into the cavern where the Wizards struggled to stay on their feet. Covering their faces with their hands did no good as the gale sandblasted their bodies to bloody pulps. One by one they collapsed and the dirt steadily covered them until they were buried under a meter of it. The wind stopped as abruptly as it started.

"I should've done that a long time ago," the Guardian said. "I needed your willingness to face them to make me act."

"Now you know the evil that magic can create if not kept in check." Byron's voice startled Stuart as the Wizard appeared beside him. "It'll tempt you often enough in the future. You need to learn to shield yourself from that side of it. I came as quickly as I could when I realized you were confronting Merstreem. Whose voice did I hear as I arrived?"

"The Guardian. Anastasia knew all about him."

Byron stared at him wide-eyed and mouth hanging open.

"The introductions can wait." The Guardian's voice filled the tunnel. "Before I could stop them, Merstreem and others set in motion a giant earthquake that will destroy a great swath of northern Spain and southeastern France and bury us in here unless we stop it."

Byron put his arm on Stuart's shoulder and said, "Follow us." Two white clouds formed in the tunnel and slipped into the ground. Thoroughly confused but knowing to stay with the two Wizards, Stuart projected his sense after the clouds.

He lost track of how far they traveled through endless layers of strata. The white clouds stopped moving and puffed up. "We're creating a pad to absorb the shock from the quake." Byron's voice buzzed in his mind. "We can't stop it, but we can reduce the amount of damage it will cause."

As he did not know how to make his sense into a super cushion, he sent his thoughts scurrying through the rock around him. While he found nothing to adjust as he did with machines, he stretched himself as far as he could and waited.

Around him, the Earth creaked and groaned. Stuart could not tell if this was natural geological upheaval or the earthquake. Loud booms like artillery rounds pounded his ear drums. As he waited, he thought back to his first meeting with Byron and worked his way to the present day. His already strange life would only become weirder although the Mages would help him adjust to it. All his contemplation about the future however depended on whether they could minimize the effects of the earthquake.

Time drifted, the world moaned and Stuart thought of a soft bed and a long sleep. All of a sudden someone was prodding his shoulder.

"The earthquake passed as a widespread tremor," Byron said.

Stuart opened his eyes. He sat in the tunnel, Byron standing beside him. The pile of dirt and gravel covering Merstreem and his thugs lay undisturbed.

"You've gained control over your magic." Byron shook Stuart's hand. "It'll now be your servant."

"I'd rather it be my companion."

"That'd create a formidable combination. You're already the most powerful person in the world."

"But if it's my servant, I'd be the most dangerous, far more than Merstreem ever was. Magic as my companion would keep me in check. As will Judyth."

Byron rocked back and forth on his heels. Whatever he was thinking, he kept to himself.

"I need to show you the Guardian's Sanctuary."

Byron's eyes widened. "It was lost to us for centuries and you find it."

Stuart led him to the Sanctuary where Anastasia and the Guardian remained in an animated discussion.

The Guardian spoke to Byron in an apologetic manner before shifting his attention to Stuart. "Anastasia explained a great deal about recent events. The magic probably arranged for the Mages to take this enclave last to protect the Sanctuary from the desperation of The Brotherhood.

"We need to find a worthy Guardian to replace me. Someone who appreciates what the Sanctuary contains. I need to see what the world is like these days."

"I hope you're not leaving right away," Stuart said. "We require an explanation of the Sanctuary's contents. I certainly need to talk with you. The Mages understand little of Wizard magic."

"I could run a school." The Guardian beamed.

"Think of it as a graduate school," Stuart said. "A masters of magic. You'll find students among the Mages. My friend Harold could teach science and technology to the Wizards and Thals."

"You better get some sleep, Stuart, for once the rest of the Wizards arrive, we must spend a lot of time together," the Guardian said.

"I'll send Surovov down here; he should learn all about the Sanctuary as well."

Stuart walked through the tunnel and found the Russian busy examining the massive artificial cavern. He explained that Byron and Anastasia were waiting for him in the Sanctuary. Then he headed for the excited voices in the enclave. When he reached the main room, Thals and Mages broke into cheers.

After he told them about the Sanctuary, Charlemagne said, "The European Mages were on their way here by road when the word went out that the final showdown was in the works. The North Americans will be here soon; they're coming with several Thals through the Otherworld."

"Boss also sent Thals to retrieve Omeron, Iywwan and the other Wizards," Diviner said. "They're going to search the tunnels for clues to the origin of the Thals. Mages will assist them."

Stuart nodded and went outside to wait for his pals. His exuberance was short lived when he realized Judyth was not among them.

"They brought the wounded Mage and Thal to the farm so she remained behind to tend to them," Audubon said. "She figured it'd be a good chance to learn a lot more about them. They can also show the Thals how our medicine works."

Stuart finally found a quiet spot and fell into a deep sleep. It was just over three weeks since the Friday night when he met Judyth and Byron. During that time, his whole life changed. So had the world, but few people would ever know it.

It was close to noon when Byron shook him awake. "We went to the Sanctuary to talk with the Guardian, but it wouldn't open to us. Obviously we need you to connect with it."

After getting his first food in a day, Stuart led the group to the enclave.

"The tunnels and the great cavern are not Wizard built," Omeron said as they walked along. "The construction is too solid and practical and lacks the grandiose features that we love to include in our works."

Stuart felt the tingle of the Guardian's magic and slowed his pace until it reached its peak. He pressed his hand on the wall and the archway appeared. Light flooded from it into the hallway. Omeron peered into the room, and then stepped forward. "All these years I feared the Sanctuary was lost forever. Now it's revealed to us."

The Guardian welcomed them with open arms. Iywwan stood beside Omeron, head bowed. "We are blessed."

"Will all the Wizards here now receive mention in the Book of Time?" Stuart said. "We couldn't have succeeded without their help and the Thals."

While no one responded, he could feel their excitement swirling around him as they drank in the Sanctuary's contents. The air smelled fresh as if someone had opened windows in a room that had been closed for far too long.

The Guardian's hair was collected in a ponytail. He wore a bright white robe that offset his olive complexion.

Stuart performed the introductions. The Guardian skipped any pleasantries. "The time of The Brotherhood is spent, none too soon. After centuries of commendable conduct, it ended in shame." His voice was devoid of emotion. "It's to our good fortune The Brotherhood can no longer stain the reputation of Wizards and magic."

Wnorom spoke up. "We lacked the strength to deal with them and were unable to convince our colleagues the leaders had taken the wrong road."

"I too should have done more," the Guardian said.

"We'll form a Parliament to bring together Mages, Wizards and Thals so we can benefit from each other's knowledge." Stuart made a sweeping gesture with his arms to indicate the contents of the Sanctuary. "There's much we can all learn. While it'd be best if you'd remain in charge of the Sanctuary, these Wizards have the knowledge to assist you. They can read the books and understand the significance of the objects here. That's not something we Mages or the Thals can do."

Boss stepped beside Stuart. "He right."

The Guardian peered at Stuart as if seeing something about him for the first time. His look conveyed the kind of curiosity he would expect of a Mage.

"You are wise for one so young," the Guardian said before inclining his head to Byron. "Thank you for finding this young man."

Byron bowed in return. "The magic led me to him and made him realize his potential."

Stuart waited for the other Wizards to say something. Instead, they glanced about. He knew their silence usually indicated there was an issue they wanted to discuss but did not know how to broach it.

Boss approached the Guardian. "Wizards afraid of prophesy."

"Not you? How do you even know about it?"

"We listen and remember. Prophesy seem obvious."

The Wizards glanced at each other while the Guardian addressed Stuart. "The Book of Time predicts a transformation of magic and the rise of an Ultimate Wizard. It provides no details on what powers this person would possess. Your ability to combine our magic with the power of science seems to fulfill that promise. The Brotherhood is finished. While the changes must have implications beyond that, I cannot foresee what all could be possible."

So all along the Wizards were sizing me up to determine if I might be the Ultimate Wizard. Stuart shrugged. "Actually the Thals are learning how to use technology and Surovov can perform Wizard magic better than I can. Perhaps the transformation of magic is meant to include the involvement of the three groups combining science with elemental powers. Maybe it should be ultimate magic."

"That may be the case now or at some point in the future," the Guardian said. "That would be a worthy topic for the Parliament to discuss."

"I didn't notice anything special about the Russian," Omeron said. Pembar wore a smug smile.

"The Brotherhood could be replaced by the College of Ancients," Stuart said.

The Guardian roared with laughter. "The Realm, the Interregnum, which you would not know about, the Brotherhood and now a College?"

"You missed the second Realm," Stuart said. "This'll take a while."

THE OTHERWORLD DISCOVERY

Stuart felt increasingly uncomfortable with everyone in the Sanctuary staring at him.

The Guardian stepped beside him. "Stuart should be the one to take over as Guardian of the Sanctuary. However, he wishes to pursue life on his own terms. With magic as his companion, I charge him with ongoing responsibility for the Sanctuary. No decision should be made about its contents without his approval.

"Wnorom, you lack an enclave and possess a high degree of curiosity. Would you share the administration of the Sanctuary with me? It should be a pleasant enough post with Thals upstairs instead of those vexatious Wizards to whom I refused to reveal my presence."

Wnorom nodded a vigorous yes and rubbed his palms together. "It would be an honor and I look forward with great anticipation to all you can teach me. If you're in no rush to depart, will you permit me to spend time at Omeron's? She has assembled a most interesting collection of books and there are many I've yet to examine."

"While you conduct that examination, I'll prepare the Sanctuary for others to view," the Guardian said.

"With Wnorom and the Thals here, I'll always know what's happening with the Sanctuary and that won't interfere with my other duties," Stuart said.

The Guardian nodded. "The Thals will have complete access to the Sanctuary. Maybe that will help us learn more about their origin."

"Mages ask many questions about that." Boss beamed. "We like know too."

The Guardian smiled. "I've not been out of here in eons. I'm most anxious to see what science has accomplished and how the Mages work with it."

"Charlemagne wants this enclave and the one in the Jura to become retreats for all magical beings," Byron said. "That'd enable Wizards to better appreciate the abilities of the Mages and Thals. Maybe other Mages can learn to harness elemental power."

The Guardian looked about the room wistfully. "It sounds like after centuries of keeping it hidden, the Sanctuary will become a most interesting location. Hopefully, many Mages will come here."

"We should split the magical resources between here and the enclave in the Jura Mountains," Omeron said. "That way we won't lose everything should one of them be destroyed."

Wnorom stroked his chin in contemplation. "Guardian, you could even travel the Otherworld to Omeron's enclave to examine her collection. The Thals are excellent guides and her residence is most pleasant."

When he hesitated, Omeron said, "If it'd help you make a decision, I invite you to visit me at the time of your choosing. In fact, in the future it'd be good for Wizards to spell the Guardian and Wnorom as custodians of the Sanctuary so they don't feel trapped here."

The Guardian nodded. "I also wish to see this farm across the ocean to witness the magic of the Mages."

"You'd always be welcome," Stuart said. "However, you don't have to travel that far. There are many Mages in Europe who'd want to demonstrate their abilities for you. When you're at Omeron's, the ones from the Urals could come to meet you as well."

"Thals too." Boss said.

"I wish to hear Byron's story about flying across the ocean in an airplane," the Guardian said.

"While I don't want to break up this Wizardly telling of tales, I do need to return home," Stuart said. "You folks could carry on without me for a long time." The Wizards laughed.

"Before I leave, I wonder what we should do with the Halves. Would it be worth trying to enhance their magic?' No one responded so Stuart continued. "Maybe the best test of their magical potential would be whether they can enter the Otherworld and travel through it on their own instead of needing to be led by a Thal or Wizard."

"Iywwan and I'll look into this," Omeron said. "Before you leave I wish to impress on my fellow Wizards that I've observed among the Mages many bonds that could in time produce youngsters. It'll be a most exciting time to see what comes of children whose parents are both magical."

Stuart described Marconi's husband.

"Are their children magical?"

"The Mages gained their powers after they reached puberty," Stuart said. "Marconi's kids are young so we'll have to wait a while. Thal children also don't possess any magical ability until age six or seven."

"We used to talk about the golden age of Wizards in the past," Pembar said. "Maybe we're on the verge of a new one. There's little doubt the world needs us."

Realizing that if he did not leave soon, he might be trapped into hours more of conversation, Stuart bowed in farewell. He could still hear the Wizards talking when he entered the great cavern.

It was illuminated with lights set up by the Mages so Stuart shut down his Wizard sight. When he reached the main floor of the enclave, he explained to the Thals and Mages what the Wizards had decided. He picked up his bag and headed for the door. "They won't need me for some time."

"Wait," Boss called. The Thal had followed him from the Sanctuary. "You no condition travel Otherworld alone." Stuart did not argue when Boss attached a safety line to him and led him away from the enclave.

Stuart replayed the events of the last three weeks as he tagged along behind Boss. Before he knew it, they came out of the Otherworld beside the garage of his apartment building. Stuart dug a key out of the bottom of his bag. Thanking Boss, he said, "Are you going straight back, or do you want anything?"

"Stay here tonight, go farm tomorrow. Check Thals and tell Judyth you return."

"Charlemagne will have already informed them," Stuart said, opening his apartment door. Welcome back was scrawled in capital letters on a piece of paper on the kitchen table along with incalculable numbers of X's and O's from Judyth.

"Like beer," Boss said.

Stuart opened the fridge door to find it was well stocked.

"Everything's under control, good night."

While he wanted more sleep, one glance at the clock radio the next morning told him he was behind schedule. Boss had already left. The shower felt wonderful. He backed out of the garage and headed down the street thinking about how he would explain his absence during the last few weeks to his customers.

His first client welcomed him warmly. "Your associate explained your security training was extended and that it'd make the world safer for all of us," said the usually gruff manager of Another Dimension Propulsion. Pumping Stuart's hand, he said, "He probably shouldn't have told me that much, but I explained about my navy service. We need more brave young people like you."

Stuart received the same reception everywhere that day. Harold knew a few tricks from his security work. While all the praise should have cheered him up, Stuart's head throbbed by the end of the day. While he rarely suffered headaches, this one was so intense he stopped to buy painkillers.

While he took two pills at the pharmacy, the aching persisted. Judyth rushed out of the house when he reached the farm. Her embrace made him feel better. She stepped back while he explained about the ache.

"This may sound silly, but I think I'm suffering magic withdrawal. I only used my abilities on machines a few times today." He winced to demonstrate his discomfort. "The ache grew stronger during the day."

"Utilizing one's magic all the time must create a sense of euphoria that stimulates the brain," Judyth said. "It needs release when you're not using it. It's like an addiction. I'll examine you over although just looking at you, I doubt I'll find anything wrong."

Stuart put his arms around Judyth and kissed her. "I'm glad you're my doctor and I think you're the only medicine I need." They entered the kitchen and she pointed to a chair. After checking him over, she declared he was fine.

Bethune made his rendition of a throat clearing sound. "Pardon my intrusion. With you two at the farm along with Marconi and Ears, I need to show you something. It might be very significant although I am not sure of its implication."

"I'll find the other two," Judyth said.

"Stuart, would you put four chairs in front of the large screen

TV," Bethune said. Judyth returned with Marconi and Ears and they all sat.

"The first phase of my mapping of the coasts of the Otherworld using Ears' drones is complete," Bethune said. An immense land mass appeared on the left hand screen. "It'll take a few more weeks to complete the high level over-flight of the Otherworld. It appears to be on a planet that is the same size as Earth."

Ears leaned forward. "Zoom in." The mass grew larger revealing features such as lakes, plains and mountain ranges near the coasts. "You're sure this is the Otherworld?"

"Does it look familiar to you?"

"Pangaea. I can't believe it."

The screen split in two. On the right was Bethune's depiction of the Otherworld and on the left was a map of modern Earth. As they sat, the continents displayed on the left screen drifted until they were joined together in a virtual duplicate of the Otherworld.

"Pangaea comes from the Greek for entire Earth," Bethune said. Its voice rose and fell with excitement. "A German scientist named Alfred Wegener developed the theory of continental drift and postulated that all the continents were once joined in what he called Urkontinent. It formed about 300 million years ago and lasted for at least 100 million years."

Lines appeared on the map of the Otherworld. "They outline the continents and national boundaries of modern Earth," Bethune said.

"Even if the Otherworld is only 200 million years old, its existence suggests the magic could've existed on Earth for a long time before anyone could manipulate it," Stuart said. "Perhaps the Mages could work with Byron on figuring out how we have Earth in its current configuration and the Otherworld in the image of Pangaea."

"Whatever force created this parallel dimension to Earth might have set in motion the development of magic," Ears said. "It's all beyond anything I could even imagine. There are several Mages who want to investigate this. I'd like to know why we travel much faster in the Otherworld than we do in our dimension. That must be connected to the magic."

Ears paced around the den several times. "Now that we know where it is and what it might be, we need to understand why the Otherworld fortunately goes undetected by modern technology. Once Byron led us to it, I could find it at any time with my sensor technology. Also how do we move between that dimension and this world so quickly?"

"The highly scientific explanation is that it's a matter of knowing it's there and wanting to travel to it," Stuart said.

"We could recruit the Thals to help us explore the Otherworld to determine what creatures live there," Ears said. "We might discover a connection between them and the wildlife of modern Earth. Think of what we might learn although I don't know what we'd do with the information."

"I deployed the drones to map the Otherworld," Bethune said. "Now I will have them prepare a climate map of it so we know what conditions to expect and search for any forms of life there. Now there is another matter."

With that a picture of a large cloth covered in strange markings appeared on the screen. "This is the shawl worn by the Grandmother of Boss's group." The image on the screen changed. "This is the other side of it. Some of the markings are the same as on the front side but many are different. "You need to examine it for a while to notice the differences. Now do you remember this?"

The front of a shirt appeared, and then the back. "That's the one Byron wore when he put on his Wizard show and tell," Judyth said.

"Are the markings the same?" Ears said.

"Some are; many aren't."

"You wouldn't spend time studying them without a good reason," Judyth said.

"I think the markings are part of what once was the Thal printed language or the language of a group of hominids they associated with but that we know nothing about. Farseeker and Pathfinder have all the Thal groups looking for any items that have markings on them. If they find anything that might be helpful, they'll show it to the Mages who can send images of it to me. I'm studying how other ancient languages have been deciphered.

"The European Mages have the Guardian's permission to examine all the items in the Sanctuary in case there is something that could assist in deciphering the marking. They will inspect every nook and cranny looking for more examples of any kind of printed language that is new to us. Same with all the enclaves. I will keep you posted."

ROMANCE AND TECHNOMAGE

A week passed, and then a month, without any further natural disasters on Earth. Countries struggled to restore their economies. Millions of people needed to be relocated and supplied with food and shelter. Deadly disease outbreaks and starvation loomed in many regions.

Working through Zagajnik International, the official name for Magic Inc., Mages and Wizards brought the sun or rain to regions needing a change in the weather and defused storms that would compound the global misery caused by the disasters and climate change. They eliminated troublemakers and would be despots just as Byron had terminated the drug dealers and Wizard attackers.

Stuart became the most powerful and least known President and Chief Executive Officer in the world. Surovov was Executive Vice President for Eurasia. Harold was Chief Operating Officer and Director of Training for the Mages and Thals. Marconi was Senior Vice President for Communications, Security and Restoration. While the Wizards declined any permanent role, they were ready to serve as special advisors on particular projects.

Harold and Marconi's two children along with his parents survived the West Coast earthquake mainly because the couple had reinforced their home and provided it with a solar power system. The Thals regularly took the couple back for visits through the Otherworld.

The demand for the services of Watson's Big Machine Restoration Company, now a subsidiary of Zagajnik, grew so fast in Western Canada and United States that Stuart spent three weeks a month away from home helping companies resume operations with a mix of old and new equipment.

At first, he called in Surovov for assistance as the Russian had become equally adept at manipulating machines. However as the demands on the European and Russian Mages grew, Thals were frequently recruited to work unseen on jobs around the world. The pay meant nothing to them compared to the opportunity to explore machines and technology.

Judyth split her time between the Greater Toronto Regional Hospital and working in treatment centers for injured West Coast residents, who were moved inland because the earthquake destroyed most of the hospitals and other facilities from northern Mexico to Alaska. Prince Rupert in British Columbia was the only functioning sea port on the coast. Few airports were even in partial operation.

Stuart scheduled his visits with Judyth for when she worked in a facility that he could reach. In late December, they ate supper at a restaurant in Las Vegas near the shuttered casinos and luxury hotels that now housed refugees from the Pacific Coast. The next day they would return to Toronto for Christmas and New Year's celebrations.

After grousing about the limited menu, Stuart said, "Harold mainly deals with the Mages, Wizards and Thals so I don't hear much from them although I can see their handiwork in the news all the time."

"As leading scientists, a lot of Mages are involved in the investigation of the natural disasters," Judyth said. "Even if we're covering up the Brotherhood's role, it's a perfect opportunity to educate the public about the consequences of climate change."

"We don't get as much time together as we'd hoped." Stuart reached across the table to hold her hand.

"I don't resent your preoccupation with your job and magical duties," she said. "You're talking to another workaholic. While it hasn't been anything like the romance I once hoped for, the last few months were the best time ever. I want to love and admire a man who I count on as my best friend. Even with our magical differences, we're a lot alike, Stuart."

"You mean we deserve each other."

She laughed. "That's one way to put it. Who else could tolerate us?"

They had agreed earlier to meet each other's parents over the holidays.

When they reached her hotel room, Judyth turned the television to the magic channel, which required a special converter that Marconi developed to receive the broadcasts. They cuddled together on the bed.

Stuart felt completely at peace, all the magic and broken machines forgotten for a few special moments. He inhaled Judyth's scent and savored the sheer contentment of holding her close.

Judyth giggled. "Through all this, Byron became an Internet junkie. He asks Bethune to search for information on topics that interest him. It checked out references to magic in movies, books and TV programs. A sci-fi TV show that really got Byron's attention was *Babylon 5* from the 1990s. Its storyline included Technomages who used technology to create the appearance of magic.

"He's convinced you could be a Technomage because of the way you manipulate technology. He's especially intrigued about how the creators of the show came so close to describing reality. When he actually wanted to talk with them, we convinced him they'd likely died or would simply dismiss him as a nut. Or they'd take him seriously and the world would learn about Mages and Wizards."

"Which we don't want," Stuart said.

Judyth nodded. "We did find him some novels about them and videos of the TV shows. They didn't come by their magical powers the way Wizards, Thals, Mages or even you did. They used implants that enabled them to perform feats of magic such as shielding themselves, hurling firebombs, creating holograms and rendering themselves invisible. For appearances they usually wore dark hooded cloaks, often marked with magic symbols."

"He still talks about them?"

"He's still intrigued by the concept. To him, the Mages are an evolution from Wizards. You're the oddball because you can do both."

"As can Rose, Bella and Surovov," he said. "Anastasia is pretty close."

She nodded her head in agreement. "The Guardian and the Wizards are speculating about what magic might do in the future. The modern Realm is a step in its evolution."

★ ★ ★

After meeting each other's parents, Stuart and Judyth announced their engagement with a February wedding. "I think we can ensure good weather for it," he said.

"That'll be the easy part," Judyth said. "Imagine a guest list by the time we combine The Realm and our families and friends. That's a lot of magic in one place. Let's just hope everyone is on their best behavior. I really think if we invite Thals or Wizards, it'll just make things too complicated to explain."

"They could be there and no one has to know." Stuart grinned at the thought.

"You would. And I'd know too because you'd block your thoughts so I didn't find out."

The wedding was held in a hall that had a balcony, which Stuart had closed off. Wizards and Thals sat up there invisible to the other guests. Judyth's Dad approached Stuart during the reception. "I ordered food and drink for 100 people and I'm afraid we'll run out."

"We'll be okay because everyone is having such a good time they won't notice," Stuart said. He had arranged with the caterers to bring extra food and drinks.

In the spring, Stuart and Judyth moved into their new home, a sprawling five bedroom structure on a large tree lined lot. Byron provided the financing and Harold arranged the transaction so no one could trace it back to the Wizard. He recommended the home because it could accommodate visitors and with all the trees, their comings and goings would not be noticed.

"Of course, no one would see its magical security barrier," Harold said. "Unless invited, anyone approaching the property would be overtaken with a notion they needed to be somewhere else."

"That will make it tough to get deliveries," Stuart said.

"Bethune will know who to allow to come to the house."

A jumbo garden shed attached to the garage was a gateway to the Otherworld and guests could enter the house through an enclosed passageway. "The shed is a lot more spacious on the inside than you'd expect just looking at it," Stuart said.

While their home was larger than Judyth wanted, Stuart obtained a talking domestic robot he named Jeeves to keep it clean. Jeeves assisted Bethune with anyone who needed to come to the house.

Wizards rarely visited because they remained uneasy about traveling through the Otherworld. Stuart and Judyth lost track of how many Thals arrived, but houseguests did not come much quieter or neater.

"Watching them experiment with the stove, laundry machines and the robot is better than any TV comedy," she told Stuart. "They treat Jeeves like another magical creature. It learns from the Thals and asks them for demonstrations of magic."

After settling in, they went to Europe for their honeymoon. Despite the inconveniences, they decided to fly rather than travel through the Otherworld. "Our parents will want to see us off at the airport," Judyth said.

The first stop was in Poland where Viking and Surovov greeted them at the airport in Warsaw. The stone in her engagement ring came from the gardens of Omeron's enclave Zagajnik.

After a visit to the enclave, where Stuart named nearly 100 Thals, he and Judyth went with Boss via the Otherworld to the enclave in the Pyrenees. "It hardly looks like the drab old cottage we saw the night we arrived to deal with Merstreem," Stuart said. "It's been repainted and the grounds cleaned up. Even the stone wall looks improved."

Wnorom and the Guardian, dressed in grey slacks and a sweater, welcomed them. "I like your new look. Getting out and about agrees with you."

"So does having people to talk to every day," the Guardian said. "I now use the name Giardino after a man who defended the possibility of magic although it cost him his life."

He patted his stomach. "The main reason for my healthy appearance is the Thals are always feeding us and won't leave me or Wnorom alone for long in the Sanctuary. Their questions never end. They and some Mages are examining the Sanctuary more thoroughly than I ever did."

Like Boss, the other male Thals opted for brush cuts while the females generally went with shoulder length hair. They all dressed casually in pants and T-shirts with jackets when needed.

The day was full of surprises. Many Thals had learned English during the winter to the level that it sounded like their mother tongue. They also wanted to show Stuart their new mechanical and computer abilities.

"Charlemagne and other Mages are coming tomorrow along with Pembar and Omeron," Wnorom said. He had adopted a rumpled university professor style. "There's much to discuss about the contents of the Sanctuary chamber. A lot of its magic went unused for centuries."

"When we first met, you acted like a jaded old grump," Stuart said. "Now you're like a happy school kid."

"With all I've learned from Giardino and coping with the exuberance of the Thals, life is quite enjoyable," Wnorom said. "There's much in the Sanctuary that is part of the myths and lore of magic. And I've held it in my hands. We also found material for Bethune's work on a Thal language.

"Examining what we recovered from the enclaves and the contents of the Sanctuary, we've discovered a lot of Wizard magic that was unknown to us. We're teaching it to the Thals as well. Giardino and I go upstairs for supper every night and watch the news on TV with them."

"Stuart and I came for some relaxation," Judyth said. "I hope you won't take all his time."

"We'll try not to," Boss said. "Many Thals want him to give them a name."

Stuart spent the next morning naming Thals. Afterward Ampere explained Mages and Thals had explored nine tunnels leading from the cavern for many kilometers to outlets in the Otherworld or wooded groves in the Pyrenees where people could slip away. "By the undisturbed gravel and dirt on the floors of the tunnels, it doesn't look like the Wizards ever found the tunnels and exits.

"The tunnels and the cavern predate the enclave and Giardino and Wnorom are looking for information about the origin of their features. The Mages are studying whether they are natural formations or how they could've been created."

Charlemagne stepped forward. "Giardino agrees with the hypothesis that the Thals are Neanderthal offshoots who either learned to connect to magic or were selected by it as the most suitable of the early hominids to bestow it on. The Neanderthals were fading away even before the Homo sapiens arrived. The Thals learned to survive the presence of humans. We think that was because the Thals used their magic to hide from us until the Wizards made contact with them through magic. None of which explains how Thals, Wizards and Mages came into their powers. Always more questions."

In the late afternoon, Mages, Wizards and Thals gathered on the lawn behind the cottage.

"Now it's time to right a final wrong," Stuart said. "Boss, can you find me a large blanket?" When the Thal returned, Stuart called Dog. She sat beside him and wagged her tail furiously as he patted her head.

"Boss, put the blanket over Dog."

Conversations ended as the Thal spread the light blue cover over the animal. Shaking his head, Boss looked at Stuart. "That no dog."

"Very good. Let's find out who she is."

Together, they pulled away the strands of magic wrapped around Dog. Her hair fell out and the face turned slowly to that of a middle-aged human female. As the front paws transformed into hands, the figure pulled the blanket about her and got hesitantly to her feet. Boss put up his hands to steady her. While she tried to speak, her vocal chords would not cooperate. Tears streamed down her face.

"How the hell did you know Dog was not a dog?" Pembar looked red-faced between Stuart and the others.

"I'd wondered about Dog from when we first met and I saw glimpses of an aura around her. When she put her head on my leg so I would pat her, she supplied me with ideas. She did the same thing with you, Omeron and Wnorom."

"Why did you not release her before?" Giardino said.

"At first, I thought my idea was madness. Surely the Wizards would've seen she wasn't a dog. During the last few months, I thought about all the events of last summer and Dog never made sense. I became convinced after seeing her today."

Omeron went over and put her arm around the woman. In Wizardese, she said, "When we're finished here, we'll take you for a bath and find some proper clothes."

"This woman suffered the same fate that might have befallen me if I hadn't escaped," Anastasia said. "It'll be my duty to discover who she is and who did this to her. I'll help her regain her voice."

"Restoring Dog to her proper life is the least we could do after all the aid she gave us," Stuart said. "While the choice is hers, I think she'd like to stay with Pembar."

The woman nodded her head. Pembar walked over and wrapped his arms around her.

"Did the Voice ever suggest there was anything unusual about Dog?" Byron said. When Stuart shook his head, the Wizard said, "Magic wanted to see if you could figure out what Dog really was. Just like it brought Judyth and you together. It expects much of you and the other Mages in terms of learning our magic and enabling the Thals to achieve their potential."

"But I still can't make myself invisible," Stuart said.

"While deducing what Dog really was should be proof enough as none of the Wizards noticed the woman's captivity, I have a final test for Stuart to erase any doubts that he is the Ultimate Wizard," Giardino said. "Summon the Book of Time and request the latest information on Byron."

While he was uncertain what to do, the Voice said, *Say to yourself I wish to read the Book of Time. It will appear in front of you.*

As soon as Stuart made the request, what looked like a thick book with a well-worn leather cover floated in front of him. "What is written in your pages about the Wizard Byron?" Squiggly lines appeared in front of him.

"In Wizardese, it says Byron stood against the Brotherhood at great personal risk and foreseeing the wisdom of combining magic and science searched for the Ultimate Wizard," Giardino said. "Finding him, Byron led the way in ending Merstreem's corruption of magic. His conduct should be an inspiration for all those with magical power. His name will stand in the Book of Time for truth and honor."

"Nicely played, Uncle," Stuart said to Byron who stood beside Judyth, tears streaming down his face. She pulled him close in a one-arm hug. Before Stuart could reach him, Wizards and Thals, led by Omeron and Iywwan, had gathered around them adding their congratulations.

Once the celebration ended, Ampere stepped in front of the gathering. "If we need money for future endeavours, we could bring gold and valuable minerals from the Otherworld to our dimension to sell. We need to manage it without upsetting the markets. I've thought about how we could do this since my first visit to the Otherworld with Diviner."

"We could probably arrange this through Zagajnik International," Charlemagne said. "Might be a good project for Quake and Seismic."

Giardino called the gathering to order. "In the ancient days, an assembly of Wizards was a major event and its conclusion was eagerly awaited by kings and emperors because we could tell the rulers what lay ahead in the coming years. It seems that our gathering would cause alarm if today's leaders knew we existed."

"Haven't you seen the news during the last few days?" Judyth said.

"We've been preoccupied getting ready for this gathering," Charlemagne said.

"The fact that the disasters stopped so suddenly has many governments convinced they were deliberate. They want to punish whoever's responsible. The leading suspect is Europe because it suffered so little compared to the rest of the world. More than a third of the global population is dead and another billion may starve to death because there's no infrastructure to deliver food to them. The U.N. is trying to contain all the recriminations by setting up scientific panels to investigate what happened. Many Mages are already involved.

"Wizards and Thals can hide from prying eyes," she said. "We Mages will have to be especially careful."

Giardino stepped forward. "The late Wizards were right in determining we could no longer let humanity continue to blunder along unaware or unwilling to acknowledge the harm to our world. But The Brotherhood didn't have the right solution."

After a pause, he said, "We need to combine the old magic and the powers of the Mages to make major changes. While it's late, there's still time."

Iywwan called for everyone's attention. "There's something Judyth really wants to discuss with us all."

"Stuart needs assistance in coping with his powers," Judyth said. "While he seems relaxed, that's because now he's surrounded by people he trusts. However, it's much harder in the outside world where he must be constantly vigilant not to reveal his abilities or try to solve every problem. He could easily take over the world in a way The Brotherhood could only have dreamed of.

"He has nightmares regularly about what might happen if he lost his temper or someone provoked him. The disasters The Brotherhood caused would pale in comparison. He feels like a time bomb."

"The strains of magic that Merstreem accumulated eventually unbalanced him," Giardino said. "We need to protect Stuart from that. At the same time, we must discover how his magic combines with ours and what it enables him to do."

"He wants a regular life," Judyth said. "Raise our family, run Zagajnik and his repair company, which now employs several Mages, and learn more about combining magic and science."

"After all Stuart has done for us, we'll do all we can to help him cope with the burdens of his magic," Pembar said.

Boss took Judyth's hand. "We Thals will make it our duty to help Stuart. He freed us and we won't let magic take him prisoner."

THE END

ACKNOWLEDGEMENTS

I am indebted to my stalwart band of beta readers who carefully went through earlier versions of Ultimate Wizard and pointed out typos, missing words and errors in the story line and the science side of my story. Anne Marchand, Felicity Harrison, Katherine Williams, Christine Cram, Ken Byars, Steven Nelson and Ron Hodgson gave many ideas for improving Ultimate Wizard. It's very reassuring when beta readers get into the story the way they did. Any lingering faux pas rest on me.

ABOUT THE AUTHOR

Alex Binkley is a freelance journalist who, after several decades reporting on the Canadian Parliament and government, became inspired to write science fiction and fantasy stories. He starts off with a 'what if scenario' and explores where it might lead. The optimistic tone in his stories reflects his hope for the future.

For more information on his books, *Humanity's Saving Grace* and *A Biot's Odyssey* as well as short stories, see his web site **www.alexbinkley.com**.

He has more speculative fiction books in preparation including *By Intelligent Design* and *Consciousness Rising* as well as fantasy story entitled *The Circle*.